SOMEPLACE North, SOMEPLACE Wild

MOUNTAIN RANCH ADVENTURES—BOOK ONE

ENDORSEMENTS

Someplace North, Someplace Wild stirs the soul—strenuous adventure, exasperating mystery, loving romance, vigorous conflict. Here is a crafted account of fighting the good fight physically, mentally, and spiritually. Writing like an evangelical Louis L'Amour, Gary Brumbelow has an uncanny ability—by engaging our senses and implanting us into the middle of the story—to lead us to evaluate our own lives.
—**Stu Weber**, Pastor/Author

I'm impressed with Gary's debut novel and proud of him. His story has all the twists and turns you want in a yarn that just might keep you up all night. Enjoy and be looking for more from him!
—**Jerry Jenkins**, author of the *Left Behind* series

Someplace North, Someplace Wild is a raw tale of courage, resilience, and the pursuit of one's dreams against all odds. Gary Brumbelow delves into complex relationships, unfulfilled expectations, and the transformation of letting go of the past to embrace the promise of a new beginning.
—**Britney Ta**, Founder and Owner of Fish4Ever Aquatics, Social Media champion with eight-million followers

Gary Brumbelow

We admire those who brave strenuous and risky outdoor adventures. In *Someplace North, Someplace Wild*, Gary Brumbelow tells a story about challenges with elements, geography, and people set in the high mountain grassland of British Columbia. Hard work, romance, crime, and biblical values shared by some of the characters in the story kept me reading and reflecting. Fasten your seatbelt—you are in for a ride with this book! I hope for a sequel, perhaps cast in a rugged region of Alaska.

—Loren Leman, P.E., former Alaska legislator and Lieutenant Governor

SOMEPLACE North, SOMEPLACE Wild

MOUNTAIN RANCH ADVENTURES—BOOK ONE

Gary Brumbelow

A Christian Company
ElkLakePublishingInc.com

COPYRIGHT NOTICE

Cover and Interior Design: Kelly Artieri, Faithe Thomas, Deb Haggerty

Editor(s): Marcie Bridges, Cristel Phelps, Deb Haggerty

PUBLISHED BY: Elk Lake Publishing, Inc., 35 Dogwood Drive, Plymouth, MA 02360, 2024

Library Cataloging Data

Names: Brumbelow, Gary (Gary Brumbelow)

Someplace North, Someplace Wild / Gary Brumbelow

414p. 23cm × 15cm (9in × 6 in.)

ISBN-13: 9798891342163 (paperback) | 9798891341999 (trade paperback) | 9798891342002 (e-book)

Key Words: Christian Contemporary Western & Frontier; Christian Mystery & Suspense; Christian Cowboy Lifestyle Fiction Westerns Murder; Western Fiction God Jesus Bible Prairie Suspense; Romance Faith Suspenseful Redemption Frontier; Church Murder Investigation Detective Cowboy; Gospel Crime Thriller Inspirational Ranch

Library of Congress Control Number: 2024939498 Fiction

DEDICATION

To Valerie—
Beloved bride and fellow pilgrim for fifty years. You were the first to say, "You should write a novel." And stayed beside me through the journey.

You gave me so many plot ideas, read so many drafts, honed so much of the copy. And refused to be called co-author.

"Many daughters have done nobly, but you excel them all." Proverbs 31:29

ACKNOWLEDGMENTS

Thanks to:

Darrow Miller—your model and encouragement are rare gifts to me, brother.

Robert Dunkle and his staff at the Clackamas County Jail for the gracious and educational tour of your lockup.

Constable Justin Thiessen—you gave me an inside view of RCMP work, much needed for this story.

Ken Baker, for carving out the time to help me understand the legal nuances needed for this story.

Brian Smith—your excellent editing on my first five chapters got me in the door.

Jill Horsman, for sharing your actual experience teaching in a First Nations school in B.C.

Jim Seymour, for the briefing of detective work given early in this writing process.

Thomas Moore—my literary friend whose friendship and encouragement have proven so valuable.

Tom Bingham, for sharing your grandpa's stories about life in the Kootenai Mountains. You'll see a couple of them in these pages.

Jerry Jenkins: This book was birthed in your coaching class, brother. And thanks for the wonderful endorsement.

Gary Brumbelow

Hancock House Publishers, for permission to use two stories from *Mountain Ranch at the End of the Road: Horses, Cows, Guns* and *Grizzlies in the Canadian Wilderness.*

Herman Shaw, for permission to put your actual testimony of coming to faith in Christ into the mouth of Willie Joe.

Julie Johnson, fellow author and Jesus lover. You read a very early draft and cheered me on!

Deb, Cristel, Marci, and the rest of the team at Elk Lake Publishing. The first time I read on your webpage, "More than anything else, we want to point people to Jesus Christ," I knew you were the publisher for me. So glad you agreed!

Let the rivers clap their hands,
let the mountains sing together for joy.
Psalm 98:8

CHAPTER 1

THEY LIE IN WAIT FOR MY LIFE

Northern Idaho, Tuesday, October 13, 1987

After three months of intense planning, the murder seemed almost anticlimactic. Too easy.

Waiting for a miscellaneous stranger to motor off around the bend and out of sight, Frank Johnson opened his driver's door. He reached in to steer and muscled the Datsun into motion. Its front wheels dropped over the shoulder's edge. With one mighty sweep, he slammed the door and shoved. The little car rolled into the lake and stopped, its rear protruding above the water like a giant feeding duck.

Perfect. The poor sucker's fingerprints remained intact on the trunk. And Joan would be dead in ten minutes.

He checked his watch. 11:32 a.m.

Bye-bye, Joan.

With Joan, nothing was ever good enough. Ninety days after the marriage, the luster was gone. The original charm had mutated to deep dissatisfaction and moved toward disgust.

A divorce was against her religion. He didn't dare walk out since he worked for her old man. He'd accrued a small mountain of debt trying to please her and couldn't jeopardize his job.

If only he could have back the three years he'd squandered trying to please her.

Bubbles rose to the surface and burst. 11:33 a.m.

Mind you, she fooled her family and friends. She could put on a real show at any gathering, going out of her way to touch him and kiss him. Public was the only kind of affection he ever got.

They all believed the marriage was happy. But, like some wag had said, "Beauty is only skin deep, ugly goes to the bone."

And it did get ugly. She'd never loved him, and his own heart had petrified.

Now it was over. No more coming home to hell. No more shame. The inconceivable had become the actual.

11:34.

On top of everything else, she couldn't conceive. That was his fault too.

"I should've married Brad. You're a pathetic excuse for a man. Can't even get me pregnant." She'd dated Bradford Reynolds in high school. Now he had his own commercial construction business and five kids.

Frank made decent money, but never enough—she outspent King Solomon.

But no more. No more buying jewelry he couldn't afford or flowers she ignored. No more cooking, cleaning, and coddling a spoiled woman who vegetated all day watching TV.

No more coming home every night to clutter, magazines strewn everywhere, dirty clothes mounded, sink piled with dishes.

11:35.

No more wading through her mess to reach the closet. He'd long since moved to the couch to escape the bedtime drama.

Whenever he closed his eyes and pictured Joan, nothing pleasant arose to his inner sight—no small joys, no mutual pleasures, no tender moments. Only two hearts blackened by cross words and dark looks. For far too long.

11:36.

How does anybody stay married he wondered. Do people tolerate each other for decades? More than a few friends lived in pathetic relationships. He had witnessed their wretchedness, he knew people who woke to misery every day.

Like him. But no more. A new future lay before him. The nightmare named Joan was fading fast. Five minutes to go.

He waded to the window to watch.

CHAPTER 2

I Must Go On My Way

Northern Idaho, Tuesday afternoon

Ten thousand diamonds danced in the sun on Bishop Lake as I drove the narrow shoreline road nestled in the thick Idaho forest. I could almost smell my long-held dream of a life in the Canadian wilderness, far from the boring high plains of West Texas.

Dad had given me a pocket tape recorder to journal about my trip. With one hand on the wheel, I punched the record button and spoke.

"Dad, you and I both know so many people satisfied to ranch by ATV on the dusty panhandle flatlands, fifteen minutes from the nearest Walmart. Not for me. I want adventure. Give me the raw contest of man against mountain in a wild land of cold and snow."

I hit the pause button and pictured riders on horseback pushing cows through remote grass valleys surrounded by snow-capped peaks. High mountain meadows somewhere in British Columbia called, and I must go. My four years of disciplined university studies were peanuts in exchange for adventure in the north.

I touched record again.

"I'm almost there. Just four hundred miles to my dream job—manager at the Double Bar Ranch in Cache Creek, British Columbia. That'll be the first step to having my own spread."

Only eight more hours. Good thing. I had four days to start a job or kiss a quarter million dollars goodbye.

Go, Cody, Go. No time to lose.

Twelve winding miles farther, the road left the lake and slipped into a pocket of civilization, a tiny logging settlement whittled from the woods. A vintage country store boasted a single gas pump. I parked and stepped out into the fresh pine fragrance from the timber mill across the road.

A pay phone clung to the outside wall. This might be my last opportunity before the border to call home. Mom would be hungry for a scrap of news like Oliver Twist on a London street.

But I dreaded the conversation. When I had first announced my intention to pursue this career, she'd expressed shock and dismay, launching a one-woman crusade to change my mind. She was the best mom, but she couldn't understand why I wanted to leave. She feared I would suffer, maybe die, far from the nest. I loved her, but I would not abandon my dream.

"I love West Texas, Mom. I love you and Dad. But I must do this. It's as simple as that." I went to bed, leaving her crying on the couch.

Now, two days later, I wondered if she was crying still.

I picked up the phone and dialed. She answered on the second ring.

"Hi, Mom."

"Cody. So glad you called. Are you there yet?"

"No, I'm at—"

"Wait, let me get Dad. Bob, Cody's on the phone." She paused, "It's so good to hear your voice, Cody. Where are you calling from?"

"I'm at a little—"

"Hello, Son. How goes the trip?"

"Hi, Dad. It's going well, except I drove thirty miles out of my way to see Bishop Lake. Be sure and tell your neighbor Mike. I hope he's happy."

"What do you mean?"

"When he insisted on installing that fancy new oil filter on my truck the other day, he made me promise to visit his favorite north woods lake in exchange. And I have my doubts about that filter."

"You may be right. He saw a bulletin about it yesterday. Apparently, the weld sometimes fails, and you lose your oil. Better replace it when you get there."

"That's great. Another thank you to Mike."

Dad changed the subject. "How far will you go today?"

"I'm about an hour from the border. Need to travel as far north as possible tonight."

"Okay. No problems so far?"

"No, nothing really. I stopped to help a stranded driver a ways back. He seemed a little strange, but nothing happened."

"What do you mean?" Mom's voice registered concern.

"A guy's car was broke down in the middle of the road. Said his motor had quit and could I give him a push? We got his car off onto the shoulder as far as possible. He figured his distributor cap had come loose. Said it did that sometimes, and he didn't need any more help."

She spoke again. "Jerry called today. He was planning to come for your birthday."

"Oh. Would've been nice to see him." I sighed. "But, as you know, Grandpa's inheritance deadline didn't give me the luxury of sticking around."

"When will you call again?" Mom's voice had a familiar edge.

I clenched my teeth. "Still on the same plan, Mom. Don't expect to hear from me for at least a month once I cross the border." I held my breath.

After a moment, Dad spoke: "Son, everybody knows you can do this. You don't need to prove anything to anyone. We all need help sometimes. Remember when your brother had trouble getting started in Chicago? There's no shame in calling home."

I looked at my boots and shook my head. *Can't you accept I'm not Jerry?*

A scene popped into my mind, a memory that—ever since my departure Sunday—had visited me whenever I closed my eyes. I'm pulling out, Mom and Dad are grieving on the driveway, holding each other vertical.

"I don't need to prove anything to anyone else, just to myself." My toe found a stone to kick. "But don't worry. I'll be fine. And I will call. I promise."

The quiet lasted several uncomfortable seconds before Dad spoke. "Did you find the problem with that dash light? I'd rest better if you could read your gauges in the dark."

"No. But I'm not worried about it. This old truck runs like a scared coyote."

CHAPTER 3

I Was Appointed A Teacher

Wolf Creek, Chilcotin country, British Columbia, Tuesday afternoon

Julie Stewart suppressed a shriek of frustration. She lay down her book, shook her head in disbelief. Even hands against her ears failed to silence the whomp, whomp, whomp from the schoolhouse's back wall.

She'd have to go out, again, and ask Danny to please stop bouncing the basketball against the building.

The boy would exasperate a bassett hound. Why he persisted in this irritating behavior, she could not understand. He was not mean-spirited nor stupid. What was it with him?

She exited the one-room schoolhouse, walked to the back, and stood by the corner of the building. He pretended not to notice her, but she knew subterfuge when she saw it.

"Danny." Whomp, whomp. "Danny." She raised her voice without yelling.

He caught the rebound, held the ball, and looked at her, eyebrows arched.

"Do you know what I'm about to ask you?"

His wordless answer, hunched shoulders, and a blank look said it all.

"Please stop throwing the ball at the building. If you want to play with the ball, please use it on the court." She pointed beyond him to the concrete slab.

As always, he shrugged and turned away.

She returned to her desk, sat, and looked around. Within these four walls, she taught eleven children, grades one through six. This one-room school on the reserve, a far-flung First Nations village of twenty-five households, comprised her professional domain.

"I belong here. I love what happens here."

Her heart warmed every time a student lit up with a new insight. But two months into her first job after graduation from university, she was questioning her judgment. Out loud.

"Have I made the biggest mistake of my life?"

On the gravel road ten meters from the schoolhouse, a loaded logging truck lumbered by. The driver was bound for the mill in the nearest trading center, a small town two hours away. Older students boarded there for high school. That arrangement was a key factor in Julie's decision to apply. She wasn't ready to manage a cluster of prepubescent hormones but liked the idea of teaching multiple younger classes in one room.

"They didn't tell me about Danny when I signed on. Was that by intention or neglect?"

Every day, she woke up with Danny on her brain. Every night, she lay her troubled head on the pillow, second-guessing her actions, or inaction, in her effort to educate that boy. A school day seemed like one continual battle of wills—Danny's versus hers—relieved only by the occasional delightful discovery by another student.

But she was managing, partly by acquiring the skill of self-reflection.

"I'm down but not out," she told herself. "He's thirteen, I'm twenty-two. He's tough, I'm tougher." She reached for her book. "Besides, I signed a contract. I must find a way through."

With a sigh, she returned to *Great Expectations*. Two paragraphs in—whomp, whomp, whomp.

Julie peered at the clock. Three more minutes of recess. She expelled a lungful of air and decided to persevere rather than correct Danny this late in the period. But she needed a change of scenery.

Outside, Julie stood on the stoop and held the clapper of her brass handbell for a moment, listening to children playing in the beauty. The little valley stretched out from the schoolhouse along Wolf Creek. From this tiny village westward, four hundred kilometers of wilderness rose higher and higher to the Coast Mountains before dropping into the Pacific Ocean.

Ten summers ago, her family had rented a cabin somewhere out here. She and her sister had spent a week climbing the slopes, exploring the woods, wading the streams. The rustic charm had invaded her heart, and she'd secretly vowed to return someday.

Julie closed her eyes and whispered, "I love this place. I was born to teach. And I'm going to learn how to reach Danny."

She called to mind her visit with Danny's mom last week. She'd walked to their house at the other end of the village and knocked.

"Come in." The female voice from inside suggested no emotion, neither welcome nor displeasure. Julie hesitated, then pushed the door ajar.

"Did someone say come in?"

"I did." A woman was tending the fire in her woodstove. She turned to Julie and the briefest glimpse of surprise showed on her face. "Oh, sorry." She stood and stepped toward the door. "I thought it was my neighbor. She's the only one in the village who knocks." She bit her lips to suppress a smile while gathering her long, black hair behind her head.

"Oh. Well, I'm new. I have lots to learn about how things are done." She stuck out her hand. "I'm Julie Stewart. The new teacher."

The woman placed her hand in Julie's without gripping. "Everybody knows that."

"I suppose so."

"Come in." The woman stepped back and threw out a welcoming arm. Julie stepped into a spacious area that combined living room, dining space, and kitchen. The pleasing fragrance of wood smoke and moosehide leather filled the log home. She felt like she'd stepped into another era.

"I love your house." She scanned the interior in a half second. "Is Danny here?"

"No, he's at his cousin's. Why? What did he do? He's always getting in trouble."

"No." Julie groped for words. "I didn't come because of anything he's done." She clasped fingers together in front of her. "I mean, I'll admit he can be a challenge, but I didn't come to tell you anything. I came to listen."

"I don't understand. Listen to what?"

"Are you Danny's mother?"

"Yes."

"And your name is—?"

"Dorene."

"Okay, Dorene. Good to meet you." Julie stroked her forearms held against her tummy. "Do you have a moment? I would be grateful for anything you could tell me about Danny."

Dorene's narrative had explained much and armed her with helpful information. Now to apply all she'd learned to the situation. Progress would require patience, resolve, and prayer. Much prayer.

She joggled the bell. "Time for class, everyone. Let's come back in."

CHAPTER 4

MY DAYS ARE SWIFTER THAN A WEAVER'S SHUTTLE

Northern Washington, Tuesday afternoon

Two frustrating hours later, I was still fifty miles from Canada, crouched on a narrow shoulder at a low point between hills, changing a flat tire. I groaned, putting all my weight on the lug wrench. The cussed nut refused to move.

Semis, seeking momentum for the climb, roared past ten feet from my back, their draft rocking my pickup. After retrieving my cap twice, I stuck it in the truck and attacked the lug nut again. Every hour counted now, and this one was disappearing like Cinderella down the stairs. I did not want to overnight in my truck at a closed border crossing.

The nut finally yielded, at the cost of knuckles shredded by the pavement. I wrapped my hand with a hanky to staunch the bleeding, finished the job, climbed behind the wheel, and motored up the hill.

Cresting the ridge, I reached for my recorder. Time to give Dad an idea of what's happening.

"Just changed a flat on a narrow shoulder with semis whizzing past me. I've had my share of problems on this trip. But I reckon a person doesn't set out on an epic journey for comfort and ease.

"At least it's not raining. Or dark. My motor's running fine, and I've got plenty of gas. Now that I've finally changed that confounded wheel, I'm guessing the worst is behind me."

I could not deny this adventure was my own doing. That was the whole point. Hadn't I just told the folks I need to do this myself?

I hit the record button again. "If I'd taken your advice to buy hubcaps, I would not have wasted an hour fighting lug bolts encrusted with grime. I'd be in Canada right now."

I mentally flogged myself and drove on.

Canada or bust.

Bishop Lake, Idaho, Tuesday afternoon

Idaho State Police Sergeant Greg Barlow and Officer Doug Willis stood on a narrow lakeside road and watched a tow truck winch a car from the water.

"Great way to spend my fifteenth anniversary." Willis sighed and shook his head.

"Congratulations," Barlow said with a smirk. "Get used to it. In my experience, criminals rarely show consideration for our schedules. If you're worried about that, you might prefer a job at the library."

Barlow clenched his teeth, recalled nasty wrangling with three successive wives before he'd abandoned marriage entirely. Police work and matrimony didn't mix well. Willis had better adjust his expectations, and soon. The workload emerging from the water right in front of them—plus three aggravated assaults and an armed robbery case on his desk back in Coeur d'Alene—left little energy for empathy.

Nearby, a camera operator captured video of a young female reporter standing before the lake.

"Police say they were directed to this spot on East Shore Road where Coeur d'Alene resident Frank Johnson's 1975 Datsun was mostly submerged in Bishop Lake with his wife's body inside. Johnson told investigators his car was pushed into the lake by an angry driver who had been unable to pass on the narrow road. Police are looking for a suspect described as a white male in his mid-twenties. He may be driving a 1972 red Ford pickup truck with Texas license plates MPG-06H. The truck was last reported heading south from the scene about 11:45 a.m. Anyone with information about this matter is asked to call 800-555-1212. Susan Collins, KTVB news."

The newscast generated five tips to Barlow's office in the Coeur d'Alene ISP headquarters, four useless, one closer to the bull's eye. The attendant at a convenience gas station in Hardin, five miles south of the scene, said a man fitting the description and driving a red Ford pickup stopped a little before noon and filled his tank.

But the guy paid with cash, and said nothing more than "Hello" and "Thanks."

Barlow was drumming fingers on his desk and praying for a break when Willis, at his workstation against the opposite wall, hung up the phone and turned around.

"Okay, I just talked to Texas State Police. We're looking for Cody Brandon. Vehicle registered in Dalhart, Texas. But he was immigrating to Canada."

"Really? How did you learn that?"

"Chatty county clerk."

"So, we need to contact the RCMP."

CHAPTER 5

THE BURDEN IS TOO HEAVY FOR ME

Wolf Creek, Tuesday afternoon

The school day ended. In her one-room teacherage thirty meters from the schoolhouse, Julie put the tea kettle on the stove and called her sister, Jessie.

"Oh, Julie, so good you called. Missed you so much yesterday. It was good to talk but not like having you here, eh?"

"I know, me too. Couldn't squeeze it in on the same week we have a professional development day."

"I don't understand how they could schedule an official event on Thanksgiving week. Who does that? I don't get it."

"Rumor has it someone in the district office is a recent immigrant from the States and he didn't know Thanksgiving is in October here in Canada."

"Wow. And no one else caught that?"

"Right. But they're giving us two extra days at Christmas so that will be nice."

"Oh, good. So, how was your day?"

"Let's talk about your day. We can talk about mine later."

"Okay, Big Sister, I know that tone of voice. What's going on? Are you okay?"

"I'm okay. Better than okay, in fact." She stood at the window and admired the view, the dry-grass slopes falling from the timbered hills above to the enormous Fraser Valley below, punctuated by benchlands of alfalfa. "How could I be unhappy here?" She watched a hawk cross the sky, then returned her attention to her sister. "And the quiet, the slow pace." She sighed. "Of course, there are moments—days even—when I miss the bustle. But those are the exception."

"Your world is so isolated."

"Yeah, but I like it."

"Did you call just to tell me how wonderful everything is?"

"Hold on a second. My kettle is whistling." She cradled the phone on her shoulder and poured boiling water over a tea bag. "Remember Nathan?" The face of their fourteen-year-old cousin appeared in her mind. He spent six months living with them after his dad abandoned his family, and Nathan's mother, Dad's sister, couldn't handle him.

"Oh my goodness, how could anyone forget? He drove us all batty. Until Dad figured out how to deal with him."

Julie spooned sugar into her tea. "Poor kid, he had so many strikes against him. But we paid for it." She smiled. "Dad put up that basketball hoop for him."

"Yes, and he threw the ball against the garage a million times in a row. Said it helped him calm down. Ha. It sure didn't make me calm."

"Me neither." She paused. "I think I have his reincarnation in my classroom."

"Uh-oh. Sounds like trouble."

"If you only knew. He reminds me of Nathan. But now, no Dad to fall back on. It's my problem."

"So how do you solve a problem like—what's his name?"

"Danny. He's Nathan on steroids. A year behind in school. Heart issues. Lives with considerable family baggage. Should be in boarding school with his friends. But he struggles to keep up with students two years younger."

"That's rough."

"For him and me, both.

"Yikes."

"Yes. Lots of coping behaviors."

"Like bouncing a basketball against the wall."

"Exactly. At the end of the day, I'm a wet dish rag."

"I don't doubt it."

"I hate to whine. At first, I was so confident I could change him. Boy, was I wrong." She set down her cup and lay on her stomach across the bed, knees bent, feet in the air. "Change of subject. What's new with you?"

"Hmm. Well, I think I've told you about our young adults' group at church, right?"

"Yes. You started having monthly outings?"

"We did. And I like the group fellowship more than just a couple of friends getting together."

"My sis, the social butterfly."

"Should I be like you? Choose one friend out of the universe?"

"Sure. Be like me. Why not?"

"But you left, and now you're friendless."

"Yes, that's hard. But it will change. We'll see what happens."

"What about Paul?"

"I'm good with the Paul thing. We're just friends now."

"Woman does not live by friends alone."

"Stop quoting the Bible at me. Even if it is true." She wrapped the long, coiled phone cord around her fingers. "I have a social life."

"Really?"

"Sure. Bible study every Sunday evening at the ranch. There's no church nearby, people drive for miles."

"Wait. THE ranch? Aren't there dozens of ranches?"

"No. Here, the typical ranch is three-hundred thousand acres. One operation controls the area for miles around."

"Wow. That's different all right. Good luck finding a guy who's not a hayseed."

"My sister, the modern-day Cupid." Julie sat up and drained the last of her cup. "I need to hang up. Got to finish getting ready for this trip."

"You're not going alone, are you?"

"No. I'm riding with two other teachers from nearby reserves. They're picking me up in an hour."

"Do you know them?"

"We've met briefly, but never got acquainted."

"Anyone interesting?"

"Everyone's interesting. You just have to know how to ask questions."

"You know what I mean, silly."

"Well, now that you press the matter, it is curious. Most reserve teachers are women, but these two are both male."

"Oh, that could be very interesting."

"Or not. Don't let your imagination run away with you. I'm rolling my eyes, in case you didn't notice."

"Well, sounds fun to me. And Kelowna is how far?"

"Five hours. We should be there before ten. The sessions start tomorrow at eight."

CHAPTER 6

Cross Over to Enter The Land

US–Canada border, Tuesday late afternoon

At ten minutes till five, I nosed the truck against the curb at the border office and went inside to stand at a bare counter. Two uniformed agents scowled at a computer screen. One attacked a stubborn keyboard with two index fingers. He sported long hair and a beard. His name tag read "T. Hague."

"This is the third time it's done this," he said, expelling a weary sigh and dropping into a chair to add eight more fingers to his efforts. He growled an obscenity, pushed back from the desk, and threw out his arms, palms up. "What are we supposed to do? Something's wrong with the system."

His companion looked up. "How can I help you?"

"Don't you need to see my papers?"

"You coming into the US?" His tone and puzzled frown intimidated me.

"No, sir. Going to Canada."

"Well, you don't need permission to leave. You need to talk to the Canadians." He gestured north with his head and turned back to his colleague. "Try it again."

Two hundred feet farther, the sign for the Canada Border Agency pointed to a drive-up booth extending from a single-story brick building. An agent behind the glass waved me forward. The sun-shafted forest beyond her drew my gaze. Tufts of tall, dry grass and huckleberry bushes, a few orange leaves stubbornly clinging to their branches, poked up at the feet of evergreen trees wrapped in rust-colored bark. The scene resembled the last fifty miles of countryside I'd just traveled, but to my awed eyes, everything seemed exotic. I hummed *La Bamba* and cranked down the window.

"Good afternoon. Your name?" The young officer's countenance said, *No nonsense, please. I'm all business.*

"Cody Brandon."

"Where have you come from?"

"Dalhart, Texas."

"And where are you going?"

"Cache Creek, BC."

"How long will you be in Canada?"

"Well, I hope to immigrate. But for now, about six months."

She went stiff, eyebrows arched. "You plan to be in the country for six months?"

"Yes. Is that a problem?" My fingers gripped the wheel. Had I stumbled at the starting gate?

"What's the purpose of your trip?"

"I'll be working on a ranch."

"Please park your vehicle over there, bring your papers, and come in that door." Her set jaw forbade questions. There was the door. I could only obey and hope for the best.

Inside, another stark countertop, another pair of grim-featured government agents. Who would have guessed duty at a slow international border crossing could be so bleak?

For an uneasy hour they grilled me and sent me to the tiny lobby, apprehensive and alone.

I found a pay phone and grasped the receiver like a climber gripping a rock. I needed a friend, and I knew who to call.

Rod Castle, fellow Texas A&M student, lived with his mom in Winnipeg. He had crossed the border many times. But even more, his loyalty had endured over long stretches of separation. We were last together at graduation in May.

Rod had also landed a job in BC. He might be on the road already.

The phone rang, I prayed, he picked up.

"This is Rod."

"Hey, bro, I'm so glad I caught you. I'm stuck at the border. They asked me a zillion questions."

"What's the problem?"

"I didn't realize what a big deal the work permit was."

"You're kidding. You didn't get your paperwork together?"

"I thought I did. Mostly. Not all of it, apparently." I pulled off my Aggie cap and scratched my scalp.

"How you ever got elected senior class president is beyond me. You may be the most spontaneous grad in the history of A&M, brother."

I thought he might be right. "I've missed a detail here and there. But this time, I'm scared."

"What's happening?"

"They're talking, calling the brass. Who knows? They told me to list everything I'm bringing in."

"Have much stuff?"

I looked at my notes, scribbled earlier as a looming agent drummed meaty fingers on the counter. "Guitar, saddle, three guns, chain saw, sleeping bag, tent, chaps, ammo, rope, books, tools, gas cans, and clothes. And my truck."

"You still driving that same heap you had at A&M?"

"You think I'm going to replace that faithful beast?"

"How many miles on that thing?"

"What difference does that make right now? I didn't call about that."

"Well, whatever. I'll pray for you, bro." He paused. "Pray for me too. I'm leaving early in the morning. Start my new vet job in Kamloops Friday."

"It'll be great having you just an hour away from Cache Creek."

"We'll be neighbors."

When Rod had learned about my job offer, he shifted his employment search to be closer to me. Rod was to me a nearby mountain, distant enough to admire, close enough to enjoy, and always present, standing in silent strength even when hidden in the predawn dark, waiting for the sunrise.

We hung up, and I paced for ninety minutes, until the male agent summoned me.

"Mr. Brandon, we could have turned you away. That was my recommendation." His eyebrows reminded me of a porcupine. "But fate has smiled on you. You're approved."

He shoved paper at me. "Sign right here, and you're free to go."

I scribbled, muttered a meek thanks and headed for the door.

"Next time, do your homework."

I cleared the empty parking lot, praising Providence. I was in Canada. Nothing could stop me now. A steady overnight pace should have me rolling into the Double Bar Ranch before the deadline, despite the delay.

SOMEPLACE NORTH, SOMEPLACE WILD

Frank Johnson doodled at a table across from Sergeant Greg Barlow in the bowels of the Coeur d'Alene ISP office.

"Thank you for coming in, Mr. Johnson. We'll most likely need to talk again, but that's all for now."

Frank grunted, and Barlow continued. "Can we drop you off at home?"

"No. I want to be alone."

Frank exited the building, head cocked, smiling on the inside. The interview had gone as he expected. Nobody in the room had a clue about his true feelings. His drama experience and his weeks of prep had served him well.

But he had to keep up the pretense, and that would take effort.

At home, he went to the bedroom and opened a drawer to pull out a single page. He found a pencil, sat at the kitchen table, and read the few lines he'd written so far.

Joan was the dearest to my heart,
Of all the girls I've known.
And when we finally had to part,
It cut me to the bone.

"Not bad," he congratulated himself aloud. He grinned and chewed the eraser, bits of it falling on the table.

CHAPTER 7

TROUBLE AND DISTRESS HAVE COME UPON ME

Southeastern BC, Tuesday evening

Seventy loping miles into Canada, my cramped muscles requiring relief, I scooted to the middle of the worn bench seat, put my lazy left foot on the gas pedal and stretched my overworked right leg to loiter on the passenger-side floor. After three days on the road, my grooming was crumbling around the margins like a day-old muffin, leaving a mop for hair, scuffed boots, rumpled jeans, wrinkled flannel shirt. Only my neatly trimmed beard had escaped the ravages of travel.

But never mind appearances. The hobo look disguised a summa cum laude Ag Business graduate. I was more than qualified for the promised ranch manager job in Cache Creek. This assignment was just the beginning. I would raise cattle in Canada's mountain-meadow wilderness.

I moved back to the driver's side, pressed a knee against the wheel to steer, tugged a fleece over my sleepy head, and downshifted for a steep climb. My V8 motor strained and roared but we reached the top, the ridge rolled under us, and we dropped into a long, roller-coaster plunge. Over the right shoulder, far below, a river foamed white over rocks.

At the bottom, the roadway leveled, trailing the river back and forth, seeking the gentlest path through the canyon. Sudden mountains rose, now on the left, now the right.

I picked up my recorder and talked to Dad again.

"I'm in the mountains here. The road twists around the hills and over the high ridges. I'm not seeing any animal life. The woods are dark and kind of gloomy. But I'm sure wild creatures great and small are watching me all the time."

The black-on-white trunks of slender alder and birch poked through a heavy brown carpet of untended, natural compost. Silence settled over the vast northwestern wild as the sun drew down to kiss the earth goodnight.

With the dark came the cold, the first taste of the northern climate I had eagerly looked forward to. Nine months of winter and three of late fall suited me just right. I intended to live and die in such country.

A heavy blanket of woods thick as the hair on a Siberian husky swaddled the scenery—in places crowding the highway. Signs warned drivers to pay attention. The narrow slip of clearing between forest and road would offer little notice if a woodland creature decided to cross.

I fished a snack bag out of my pack, thanking Rod for teaching me how to stay alert on a night drive. On a twenty-hour trip to Winnipeg last year, he'd introduced me to the invigorating effect of sunflower seeds.

"Pop one in your mouth and work the kernel out of the shell with your tongue and teeth. Surprising how it fights off drowsiness."

He was right, and now twelve months later and a thousand miles to the west, I nibbled in silent salute to a true friend.

SOMEPLACE NORTH, SOMEPLACE WILD

An hour later, I spit one last husk into the overflowing cup. By now, even the sunflower magic had faded. I nodded. Must not sleep. Must stay—

A streak of brown fur jolted me wide awake. An enormous boulder of a bear broke from the woods and raced across the highway a hundred feet ahead, running hard downhill and disappearing into the timber. In three seconds, it felt like my pulse had jumped fifty points.

Had I just seen a grizzly? At that fast clip, I couldn't be sure. But even the possibility I had spotted *ursus horribilis*, just two hours into Canada, thrilled me. Nothing said wilderness more loudly.

Two years before, I had spent a satisfying hour at the bear pit in the Denver Zoo and wondered what it would be like to encounter one in its native habitat.

My musing collapsed at the sudden, violent hammering of the Ford's engine, shuddering as if shaken by an invisible giant. *What's happening?* Another vicious snap and the motor quit. *Cut the ignition. Get off the highway.*

Blue smoke bellowed between the hood and fenders, steamed through heater vents into the cabin. My gut turned to wax as the truck rolled onto the narrow shoulder. I scrambled out and lifted the hood, wincing. Nasty smoke billowed out, its heavy burnt smell flooding my nostrils. Scorching oil smeared the pavement.

I'd blown a rod, the motor was dead, the truck was junk.

A heavy shroud of dread settled over me. I stood alone beside a dark, silent road on the edge of the world.

CHAPTER 8

He Has Made Me Walk In Darkness

Wolf Creek, Tuesday evening

Vehicle headlights pierced the window of Julie's teacherage as she finished stuffing her backpack. At the last minute, she'd decided to add to her food cache. *Who knows if these guys will think of bringing anything? I don't want to eat in front of them.*

She bundled in warm outer gear, stepped out, and locked the door. A faded blue sedan sat puffing exhaust, a young man behind the wheel, another in the front passenger seat. She climbed into the back, happy to have it to herself.

"Hi, guys. How are things with you?"

"Fine," William answered from the passenger seat. "Dominic and I were talking about this conference. Never been to one—hope it's worth it."

"Me, too," Julie said. "This will be my first, also. How about you, Dominic?"

"My third," Dominic spoke as he turned out of the village onto the main road. "The first one was mostly a bust, but last year we had some good presentations."

"Like, for example?" Julie said.

"How to keep your top students engaged while you're working with the herd. Writing lesson plans that connect with students across six grades."

"How about classroom management?" She talked about her problems dealing with Danny. They spent two hours discussing their respective "Danny" problems. William articulated the consensus, "Julie, you have it the worst. I feel sorry for you."

"Thanks for the sentiment. I appreciate that," she said. *Here's an opportunity to sow a seed.* "To tell you the truth, I could not endure without God's help."

After a brief silence, William spoke again. "I enjoy the remoteness of Gang Ranch, but I'm not planning to stay. I don't see a future here. More like a year of living dangerously."

"Not everyone is cut out for village teaching," Dominic said.

The three grew silent as the dark deepened. The steady hum of the motor lulled Julie to restful sleep.

Southeastern BC, Tuesday night

Some people consider their vehicle a friend. They pat the dash and say "Hang in there" climbing uphill. They get cross when it fails them and tear up at trade-in time.

Not me. This truck had failed me at the worst moment and left me in anguish, not affection. I morphed to a disembodied witness, hovering overhead, watching a worried driver peer under the hood at the smoking hulk of metal, no longer purring, now cooling and clicking, loud against the hushed, murky woods, wrapped in the thick stink of hot oil and antifreeze.

SOMEPLACE NORTH, SOMEPLACE WILD

A half-moon low in the west lit the highway where it folded over three ridges rising in series for several miles, its entire visible length unbroken by a single pair of hopeful headlights. For a frozen moment, I stood rooted to the tarmac, without hope and seemingly without God in the world.

An owl screeched nearby, and I jumped, striking an innocent shin against the front bumper, the pain clearing my fogged brain. I leaned my forehead against trembling hands on the raised hood. "Lord, I'm in a fix. Can't think what to do. Please give me wisdom."

As if from the heavens came a silent whisper: *Civilization lies somewhere ahead. Find a town, buy another truck.*

Sweet answer to prayer.

"Thank you, Lord. Now, please bring help. I need a ride. I want to trust you, Lord. Please help me."

I massaged my neck, until, wonder of wonders, clarity arose like a summer sunrise. Getting to town was job two. Job one was securing the truck and contents—a saddle worth seven hundred dollars, a fine guitar, new chain saw, tools, and books—virtually all my earthly goods awaiting plunder. How was I supposed to protect my stuff way out here? Any thief could happen along, smash a window, and help himself.

I kneaded my temples but the gray matter within, paralyzed with fatigue, declined to answer. And no wonder, when you consider the day I'd had—oversleeping this morning, pulling out late, helping a stranded driver ...

Hold on. I stepped to the edge and looked down the slope falling from the narrow shoulder. Head-high bushes grew about fifty feet down, within reach of a tow-truck cable. The downhill grade of the road might allow me to coax the front wheels across the lip where gravity could take over. The thick shrubbery would stop the truck—who cared about scratches on an old pickup? The only question, could it be done?

I crammed a rucksack with provisions for a couple of days, leaned my rifle against the backpack, and moved my few remaining treasures from the bed into the cab. Praying, and steering with one hand, I heaved against the door frame. Nothing. Again. Ever so reluctantly, the F-150 at last yielded, its right front wheel, then the left, dropping over the rim of the pavement. The vehicle gave way, picked up speed, and plowed into bushes that partly closed behind it—four tons of steel, rubber, and glass now undetectable from above.

Across the roadway, I sliced a length of bark from three trees at the fringe of the woods, exposing the moist, white flesh to mark the location for my return. With a mental note to memorize the first mile marker I came to, I shouldered my pack and walked north into the unknown. The moon had set, the heavens blazed, Polaris hung straight ahead.

My Double Bar deadline lay shattered like fine China splintered against granite. How would Mr. Harper react to my delayed arrival? I walked and fretted and prayed.

"Nobody ever did anything that mattered without plenty of trouble." Grandpa had said that many times. As a kid it didn't mean much to me but now, I got it. Seemed like I went from one scrape to another. Would my troubles get me somewhere that mattered? What if all this agony led to nothing?

I couldn't let that happen. As much as was in me I had to succeed.

CHAPTER 9

Do Not Be Afraid, Do Not Be Discouraged

SE BC, Tuesday late night

I'd always enjoyed a long, vigorous walk. Not this time. After three days of travel at a mile a minute, I'd been reduced to a sloth's pace. Gone were the comfort and security of an enclosed, heated cab, the companionship of a radio, and twin light beams pushing back the dark. I felt naked on a solitary, nighttime march through a winter wood, wondering where that bear was now. The vast, dark terrain ripped my courage to tatters, like a faded flag left too long in the prairie wind.

I tried to scan the dark timber flanking both sides of the roadway, alert to any motion, my rifle locked and loaded, my nerves taut. I held to the center line with a light step, trying to avoid discovery by any wild thing. But one can tiptoe only so long. Finally, I gave in to my complaining calf muscles and let my boot heels thunder against the asphalt, a deafening racket in the silence.

In two hours of brisk striding, not one vehicle appeared. Needing rest, I sat against a Ponderosa pine, enjoyed its vivid scent, and closed my eyes.

Gary Brumbelow

A growling sound snapped me awake, in terror, until the soundwaves clarified in my muddled head. A truck was grinding up the hill toward me. In a scurry, I fished a Maglite from the pack at my feet and darted to the road in time to alert the driver of an approaching eighteen-wheeler of my predicament by pointing the flashlight beam at my face while waving like a sailor stranded on an uninhabited island. When the trucker slowed and braked, I muttered a quick prayer of thanksgiving and dashed fifty yards to meet my rescuer.

Not sure how close to approach the cab, I stopped near the front of the trailer and leaned my rifle against the big duals. The tractor's twin exhaust stacks rumbled, exhaling the unmistakable fragrance of diesel. After a moment, the classic stereotype of the North American truck driver emerged. In order of appearance—a pair of snakeskin cowboy boots followed by creased Wranglers, a fleece-lined denim jacket and black western hat framing a wide smile and affable bearing.

"Hey, young feller, looks like you need a lift." He said and stuck a hand back inside the cab to withdraw a short, blunt club. I tried to say thanks, but the words jammed in my throat as I looked at the weapon.

"Uh, yeah," was all I could muster. My hand moved slowly toward the hidden rifle.

He saw my alarm and glanced at the weapon in his fist. "Oh, not to worry." His relaxed grin set me at ease. "This is just my tire thumper. Decided since I was stopping anyway to make sure I don't have no flats." He laid the baton on the running board and stepped toward me, hand out. "Howdy, name's Barnett. Sam Barnett." We shook and I breathed again.

"Good to meet you. I'm Cody Brandon."

"You had the right idea to shine your flashlight on your face. Told me all I needed." Barnett picked up his club and cocked his head toward the pulsating cab. "Go around and climb in. Just want to whack the trailer tires. Won't take a minute." He moved toward the back, whistling a familiar tune I couldn't place.

In a whisk, I grabbed my rifle and rounded the front of the gleaming Kenworth tractor, deep red in the black night, its chrome grille even with my head, to swing open the passenger door. Randy Travis's voice spilled out, pledging to love someone forever and ever, amen. I hefted my backpack inside, secured the rifle beside the seat, hauled up and sat on superb leather the color of pale silver, perched high above the landscape like an eagle in its aerie. Gauges green and red glowed in the dimness.

I closed my eyes, reveled in the comfort, and listened to the giant vehicle grumble low in the night.

The driver's door opened, and he climbed in, tire thumper in hand, the pleasing fragrance of Old Spice wafting from his clean-shaven face.

"Well, all them tires got air. So, we're good to go." He lay the club beside his seat and slipped the tractor into first gear. The massive rig responded to the driver's touch, easing onto the road, then slowly accelerating like a miniature, rubber-tired locomotive, drawing eighty thousand reluctant pounds to regain the highway.

Barnett lovingly coaxed the tractor through eighteen gears to reach cruising speed again, and I recognized the trouble he'd taken to stop for a young stranger.

"I sure appreciate the lift, Mr. Barnett. It's a big deal to get a loaded semi rolling again. No one could have blamed you for going on by."

"None of this mister business. Just Sam. And you're welcome. Not inclined to pass up someone on foot way out here in the middle of nowhere."

"That's a good description of it, I'll say. I broke down and hiked for two hours. Was starting to think nobody else drove this route at night."

"It's a lonely road, for sure. Where's your rig?"

I described my now-abandoned pickup, talked about the noise, the stink, oil, and antifreeze spattered everywhere. Did not admit to my sick, hollow helplessness, or loss of courage.

"You blew a rod, sounds like."

"That's what I figured. And I'm pretty sure I know what happened."

"Oh? What's that."

"So, my dad's neighbor back in Texas, he's into the latest car stuff. Subscribes to JC Whitney, you know, that kind of guy."

"Gotcha. You just described a couple of friends."

I nodded. "Well, anyway, he found a fancy new oil filter that has a nut welded on the bottom, so you can take it off easy. He insisted on installing it, said it was the cat's pajamas and wanted me to have it, figured I would be so happy." I shook my head at the memory, trying but failing to forgive Mike, whose act of "generosity" had caused such disaster.

"I needed an oil change, so I said OK. Big mistake. My dad told me on the phone today they're saying the weld can break, and you lose all your oil."

When Barnett said nothing, I realized I'd set up the obvious question *Weren't you watching your gauges?* and that would expose my foolish decision to drive in the dark without dash lights. As he opened his mouth, I recovered just in time. "Can you believe that? Have you heard about this filter?"

"No, I guess not." Barnett's left hand stroked his chin, his right on the wheel. "Sounds like another newfangled, bad idea." Then, "How far back didja break down?"

"Six or eight miles, I reckon, judging by how long I walked before you came along."

Barnett's eyebrows scrunched. "Don't remember seeing a vehicle."

A flush of hot blood rose to my face, invisible to Sam in the dark. For the first time, I saw what I had done through the ethical lens of a professional driver. I had dumped several thousand pounds of contaminated litter in a pristine ditch.

Nothing but the truth would serve, so I plunged ahead. When the tale was told, I tensed for the deserved rebuke. Several strained seconds passed before Barnett responded with a cocked eyebrow and a glance in my direction. "You're telling me you got that rig off the road by yourself?"

How sweet is mercy, how welcome its arrival.

"Yes, sir, that's right. Thankfully, I was on a downhill grade." Time to change the subject. "You drive this route regularly?"

"Run between Kamloops and Spokane couple or three times a week. Usually on 97, but sometimes I take this road for a change of scenery."

"How long have you driven truck?"

"Ten years."

"See much wildlife on this road?"

"For sure. Lots of game in a wilderness like this."

"A bear ran across the highway earlier. Happened so fast I couldn't be sure, but wondered if it was a grizzly."

"There's plenty of 'em in these mountains."

"The Rockies?"

"Kootenays. Wild country. My grandpa was a prospector. He searched for precious minerals in these parts. Dad spent much time with him as a kid and told me bear stories from their time out here."

"Like?"

Barnett grinned. "My grandpa feared nothing. He got tired of grizzlies stealing the bacon at night, so he started putting it under his pillow. Must've been a sound sleeper." He looked at me and winked. "Woke up one morning, and the bacon was gone."

My jaw fell like a dropped shoe. I had read of many mighty deeds by brave men. But this tale formed a whole new hero class. I looked at my rescuer with new eyes: Trucker Sam, grandson of Barnett the Fearless.

"Another time, they were getting ready for bed, and Grandpa heard a horse around the fire, sent Dad over to shoo it away from the cooking gear. In the dark, my old man stepped up and was ready to slap the critter with the frying pan when he realized it wasn't a horse." He threw a glance at me, my mouth still agape. "Yessir, grizzlies in these mountains big enough to resemble a small mare in the night."

As Sam's stories fell away, my imagination filled the dark mountains with fierce beasts and daring men. Would my courage hold in the face of a deadly danger? Or would it fail? Aspiring to rugged adventure and actually living it are different things. I hoped my performance would match my ambitions.

The big rig floated through black, rolling hills, an immense wilderness. In the cab, Willie Nelson begged his girl to give him one more chance cause, after all, she was always on his mind. The tune was fun, but I didn't relate to the lyrics. Always on my mind was the adventure ahead, ranching in the high country on the frontier.

Willie grew quiet, and I found my voice. "Speaking of grandparents, my grandpa and grandma used to drive truck."

"Sure enough?"

"Sure enough. First, grandpa drove, and she rode along. Then she trained and started driving too."

"Where was that?"

"We come from west Texas. They hauled cattle east and brought steel and such back."

"Good for them. Trucking is hard on a marriage. Takes the right couple." He reached to adjust the heater setting. "Better than ranching, for sure."

"What do you mean?"

"I grew up on a ranch in the interior of BC. It was hard, brutal work. When my dad passed away, my brother and I tried, but couldn't make a go of it."

I grimaced and scratched my cheek, uneasiness creeping over me. "What was the problem? What happened?"

"You name it. Nasty weather, cattle diseases, predators, unpredictable markets, leaky fences, never a moment of rest, never enough money to cover the payments. Frankly, I don't understand how my folks made it work. Somehow they didn't need as much money I reckon. But after fifteen years, we finally sold out and walked away. Smartest thing I ever did. Shoulda done it years earlier."

Sam's sad report of a failed ranching career rocked me. After years of planning, weeks of anticipation, days of preparation, and hours of driving, doubt rose in my chest, my confidence crumbling like a sandcastle in the surf. A hard lump grew in my throat.

Gary Brumbelow

I leaned against my window and listened to Kenny Rogers reminisce about a seasoned gambler's advice, knowing when to hold 'em and when to fold 'em. I sensed the entertainer wasn't talking about a card game.

Barnett glanced my way. "Said you come from Texas?"

"Yes, sir. Dalhart. Little town in the panhandle."

"So, what brings you to BC?"

CHAPTER 10

THEIR FEET RUN TO EVIL

Coeur d'Alene, Wednesday, October 14, 6 a.m.

Greg Barlow parked at Carl's Café downtown Coeur d'Alene, went in, and took a stool at the counter. He liked to watch the griddle through the opening where the cook set the food. The breakfast aroma was best here too.

Millie, the early-shift waitress, appeared and poured coffee. "You're early."

"Woke up too late to go back to sleep and too early for work." Barlow enjoyed the attention of the thirty-eight-year-old single mom, found it a salve to his lonely psyche. "How are you, Millie?"

"Well, I'm sleeping okay. Don't suffer from insomnia, that's for sure."

"Count your blessings."

"Don't tell me, let me guess. Somethin' big going down at the ISP."

"You're a mind reader, young lady."

"Not gonna tell me all about it?" She set down the pot and propped her hands on the counter. "You know I can keep a secret."

Barlow nodded. "Mm-hm, I know how that works. You can keep a secret—it's your friends that can't keep a secret."

"Well, I'll be. You musta been listening to my phone calls."

"You got it, kiddo. We've bugged every suspicious actor in town." He grinned. "But if you'll hustle back out here with ham and eggs, I'll put in a good word for you with the county attorney when your name comes up."

She laughed and went to the kitchen.

Notwithstanding three failed marriages, he still found charm in an attractive female. But he refused to date again. Relationships always got complicated, and he didn't need more grief. Or any more kids. One from each marriage was quite enough to keep him busy with concerts, ball games, and high school plays. All that on top of work. And retirement was ten years away at least.

He ate slowly and tried not to think about Millie.

Later, at his desk, Barlow reviewed the leads chart on the wall before him before lifting the phone. That RCMP liaison in Calgary told him he'd call back but he'd probably forgotten.

"Barlow, Idaho State Police," he said to the constable on the phone. "I wondered what you can tell me about the Brandon matter."

"Nothing. No report of such a person at either border crossing from Idaho into Alberta."

Barlow's next call was to the RCMP liaison officer in Vancouver.

"Yes, Officer Barlow, we've got a call in to HQ to talk to the Washington border crossings. There's thirteen. It will take a day or two to get back to you."

"Look, I know you guys are busy but any chance that could happen sooner? I need to find this guy."

"We're doing what we can. I'll get back to you as soon as I have anything."

He hung up and turned his swivel chair to his partner, Doug Willis, against the opposite wall. "We're stuck right now with the Canada boys. Can't do anything about it."

"What about Johnson?"

"Yes, we need to talk to him again, for sure." He picked up the phone once more.

Frank Johnson popped open a beer can and changed the channel again. Nothing to watch, the usual drivel of talk shows and soaps, but he plowed ahead in a desperate hope driven by a boredom big as Bishop Lake. The phone jangled four times before he answered.

"Mr. Johnson, this is Sergeant Barlow at the Idaho State Police. I'm sorry to bother you, but I really need your help on this case. We need to go over the sequence again. Can you to come into the station, say, in about thirty minutes?"

"Look, I already told you everything."

"I'm sure you did. But we need to be thorough. And time is critical if we're going to find the man who did this."

"Okay, okay." Johnson paused. "I'll be there later. About three o'clock."

Johnson dropped on the sofa and stared at the ceiling. The preparation phase was over. He wished he had a couple more weeks for planning and surveillance, but that luxury would not be his. Had to make his move now.

CHAPTER 11

I Will Arise and Go

Kelowna BC, Wednesday, October 14, 6:30 a.m.

By the time we rolled into Kelowna, two hours of listening to his failed-ranching narrative had eroded the keen edge of affection for Mr. Barnett. He meant no offense and had no idea I was hurting. I had ducked his question about my motives for coming to BC with a vague reference to adventure and tried to change the subject. But he pressed on with his sorry saga, tramping on the fragile psyche of a young adult as a heedless steer might crush a seedling into mud.

He stopped at a light, I said thanks with all the sincerity I could muster, climbed out, and watched him pull away. Now, besides tired and hungry, I felt disheartened. The car dealerships would not open till eight o'clock at the earliest. I found refuge for the second time in six hours from another savior, a fifty-something woman in jeans and a flannel shirt unlocking the door of the Hometown Café.

"Come in, young man. You look hungry, and you've found the right place. I'm Sally. You won't find a better cup of coffee or breakfast plate for a hundred kilometers around and that's my guarantee. Fact is, my little café made the top fifty small-town eating places in the *Restaurants Canada* magazine, and I've got the clipping to prove it. Have a seat, wherever you want. Coffee?"

"Thanks." Her warm smile, a bright, cheerful interior, the prospect of coffee, and the wonderful smell of bacon spitting on the grill spoke comfort. Sally's good-natured if mildly bothersome babble seemed small payment for such a gift. I found a booth. She poured coffee before I sat and laid her simple menu on the Formica.

"Don't remember seein' you before. Must be passin' through. Tourist season's dried up, but we always have a few travelers later in the fall. I see you're a hunter. Get those every fall. Reminds me of my son, another outdoorsman. Works up north, Alberta oil patch. Four weeks on and two off. Left day before yesterday so won't see him now for a while. But he likes his job. I'm just thankful he's working." Her friendly chatter was interrupted by the jangle of the front door. "Another customer. Have a look at the menu, I'll be right back."

Ten minutes later, Sally unloaded a huge plate, pancakes stacked beside a six-egg omelet, bacon, and coffee. After another quarter hour, I felt much better, armed now to revisit Barnett's cheerless story, especially with reference to my own future. Why had it rattled me like that? But on the other hand, when your first encounter with a failed Canadian rancher reveals such pathetic defeat, how could I be confident of success? Maybe the Barnett Cattle Company was the norm. In fact, it fed two families for fifteen years. It could be the gold standard.

I nursed three cups of coffee before a new thought took shape, one that led steadily up out of the gloom into broad sunlight. I should have asked him some simple questions.

SOMEPLACE NORTH, SOMEPLACE WILD

How many cows did you run? How much ground? What was the quality of the pasture? What was your feeding program? What was your debt load? What interest rate? How did you market? What's your weather cycle? How often did you require a vet? How did you maintain your fences? How did you get along with your neighbors?

I'd responded at gut level to a friendly driver who seemed to know his subject. What's wrong with me? We studied all that. In university, we read case studies like Barnett's experience. We examined the causes and solutions. I learned from the best in the industry. In my fatigue, I had lost sight of my training.

The threat of Barnett's story faded. I chalked up the last twelve hours to character growth and moved on. I *would* buy a spread in the wilderness of BC. I *would* conquer the challenges. Nothing had changed, and it was past time to take up my journey again. I rose from Sally's table restored, expectant and resolute.

At the checkout, I paid my bill. Chatty Sally was too busy to gab. I said a simple thanks and turned toward the door, where I witnessed something unexpected and unforgettable.

Three customers walked in, two guys and a young woman, all about my age. The girl glowed with a stunning, luminescent beauty. Was I dreaming? Everything about the last two days—a thousand miles of travel, trouble at the border, hitchhiking all night, the dread of missing the deadline in Cache Creek—all that hard reality dissolved, replaced in an instant by this perfect image of feminine charm walking toward me.

Our eyes met and held briefly before she blushed and looked away. I stood, unable to speak, as the three passed me to sit at a booth, a faint whisk of enchanting perfume trailing behind her. My heart pounded. A strange magic, unknown in twenty-two years, whirled in my chest.

The moment lingered, a brief mist of wonder that soon disappeared. The real world returned. I recovered my stride toward the exit and spotted something on the floor, a woman's glove. *Yes.* I snatched it and whirled.

"Excuse me, miss. Did you drop this?"

She turned. Her eyes danced from my face to the glove and back.

"Oh, yes, I did." In two steps, she stood before me and reached out.

In the handoff, our fingers brushed. Our eyes met again. Time stood still, that unfamiliar but wonderful feeling flooded my chest. My heart stopped as everything else fell away, only her and me in the universe.

"Thank you. These gloves were a gift from a very special person. I would regret having lost one."

"You're welcome. My pleasure." *Think, Cody.* "I'm glad I could prevent that grief." The only phrase I could extract from my muddled brain— "Do you come here much?"— would have been lame beyond description.

Her companions reached a booth. One sat, the other stepped to her, touched her elbow. "Everything okay, Julie?"

"I ... I guess I better go. Thanks again."

"Sure. Hope you have a nice day."

She smiled and turned around. I somehow found the door and walked away, dazed and laden with regret that words had failed me at the most crucial juncture.

Two realities slammed my heart, one cruel—I could never hope to see her again, and one wistful—I would never forget her radiant beauty.

CHAPTER 12

THEY MADE A CONSPIRACY AGAINST HIM

Coeur d'Alene, Wednesday 11:00 a.m.

Johnson took a corner booth facing the door at the No Place Bar, a Ma and Pa joint in midtown Coeur d' Alene where Ma served while Pa cooked and complained to Ma about chest pains.

County attorney Marc Malone entered at his usual time, with his usual strut, and sat at his usual spot. The waitress passed seated customers to fawn over him, pour his coffee, and flirt while taking his order. She left, and Frank slipped, uninvited, into the county attorney's booth.

"I'm sorry, do I know you?" Malone dripped condescension.

"We've never met. But I have something you want."

"I doubt that."

Frank pushed a large manila envelope across the table. Malone lifted an eyebrow, glanced around the room, moved the envelope to his lap and looked down. A moment later he closed his eyes and inhaled through his teeth.

Frank had been lucky. Very lucky. Six weeks earlier, he'd stood on a stool in the men's room at a Spokane truck stop drawing graffiti when the door opened. He ducked and crouched. The guy was on a cellular phone. Must be somebody important.

"Look, Mary, I told you I'd be late. What do you want me to do? Tell the judge to take a hike? ... What? ... I don't have to listen to this." The phone beeped once, the urinal flushed, and then dial tones in quick succession.

"Debbie, I had to get my wife off my back. I'll be there in five." The sink faucet splashed, footsteps to the door, and silence.

The voice had sounded vaguely familiar. On an impulse, Frank followed, eyebrows raised, every nerve alert. In the car, he stayed well back as the guy drove to an apartment building on North Indian Trail Road, parked and went to a door. A young woman met him with a kiss and the door closed.

Three days later, Frank was in the kitchen when he heard the same restroom voice coming from the TV. He stepped into the den to see a suit talking about a criminal case. The graphic read, *Kootenai County Attorney Marc Malone,* and Frank whooped. He had stumbled on a huge prize.

That was six weeks ago. He applied planning and patience, and used a quality telephoto lens to snap a clear photograph of the Kootenai County Attorney kissing a woman who was not his wife. He figured he might have use for such a photo someday, and now that day had arrived.

Malone stared at Frank, his eyebrows narrowed.

"You're Frank Johnson."

Frank nodded.

"What do you want?" Malone growled, jaw clenched, hate in his eyes.

"I want you to get your investigators off my back."

"I don't have any investigators. I'm the County Attorney."

"I know who you are. And I know what you're going to do. You're going to turn things in my favor."

The waitress approached with Malone's order and their faces went flat. "Anything for you?" she said to Frank. He shook his head and she walked away.

Malone flashed a glance around. "Are you crazy?"

"No. It's very simple. I did not kill my wife, and your guys have evidence to that effect. You don't need to make up anything. Maybe they're lazy, what do I know about law enforcement? Who am I to tell you how to do your job? You figure it out."

Malone steepled his fingers against his forehead and closed his eyes again.

"Starting now," Frank said. "They called today and wanted me to come in again, but you know what, I really don't like their coffee. I've told them everything, and I don't want to talk to them again. See that I don't have to, or your little affair will be front page news." He slid to the end of the bench.

"Hold on." Malone was pleading now, his brow wrinkled, emotion choking his voice as he whispered. "You've got my attention. But I have no authority in the investigation," he whined like a five-year-old deprived of his toy. "I'm a prosecutor. I can't stop the police from doing anything. You must understand, I can hinder the prosecution, I might thwart it, but I can't get the police off your tail."

Frank pushed back and ran fingers through his hair. This was not going like he'd expected. He took a deep breath and exhaled noisily.

"Okay. I'll talk to these guys again. But you're going to see that I walk. If I go down, you're coming along. You got that?"

Malone grimaced.

"Good." Frank slid off the bench and walked out.

After three wretched years trying to live with Joan, Frank had spent three pleasant months preparing for her murder. Surprising, really, how therapeutic the planning had been, and heaven knew he needed therapy. He'd felt himself slowly souring in their miserable marriage, loathed what he was becoming—his old man, the miserable circuit-riding bachelor, running from one woman to another and never having a family. Gloom settled over his soul like a December drizzle on a homesick hitchhiker.

He could cite so many ways marriage to Joan was impossible. With money, for example. She was not stupid, except for all things financial. In that dimension, she lived in la-la land.

Three weeks ago, he'd opened the mail and found her credit card bill. "What did you charge at Penny's for $340? You said you would close that account."

"Don't hassle me about that." She stomped off to the bedroom. "I've been wearing the same coat for two years."

"Two years is a long time to wear a coat?"

"Just be quiet. I can't live this way."

"Makes two of us." he'd muttered.

The phone jangled him back to the present. His bowling buddy, Billy, spoke over the other end of the line.

"Hey, Frank, want to hit the lanes this evening?" Billy was the only person in the state who never turned on the radio or watched the news.

"Thanks, but not tonight. Perhaps next week." He grunted a couple of times to Billy's follow-up and got off the phone.

Joan had despised all his friends, but especially Billy. "Maybe Billy should go back to school. Third grade."

Frank sat back, sighed, and pinched his bottom lip. He waffled between conflicting emotions, glad to be rid of her, but worried about the investigation. *Mustn't get careless. I've worked too hard to mess this up now. Can't afford to make a stupid mistake at this juncture.*

CHAPTER 13

THE HOUR IS ALREADY LATE

SE British Columbia, Wednesday, 11:00 a.m.

Four hours later, I pushed south, the direction, of all points on the compass, most to be avoided. The destination I had pursued for three days fell further behind with each mile, but I had no choice; I could not afford to abandon the gear in my deserted truck deep in the ditch. The F-150 itself lay beyond salvaging, but the goods in it had to be retrieved. Hours behind, and seven hundred dollars poorer, I drove a black, sixty-five Chevy half-ton, and, like a conscripted newlywed, dreamed of one direction and headed the opposite.

At the three white blazes on the wood's border, I pulled off. The tow service quote was out of reach; muscle power alone would have to transfer my treasures from the Ford to the Chevrolet.

Forty-five minutes later, all was in order. My fingers touched the ignition key when I remembered another item to fetch. I grabbed a screwdriver from my toolbox and scurried down one last time to remove the license plates from the Ford. Back up at the Chevy, I put the plates behind the seat and headed north.

I didn't need the Texas tags. I wanted them for a keepsake. My aunt had a vehicle tag from every place she and my military uncle had lived displayed above her kitchen cupboards, an often-admired exhibit and conversation starter. Any similar collection in the Cody Brandon home would certainly require a Texas plate. *Rod would call me sentimental.*

In one of those rare encounters with a stranger that launches a lifetime friendship, Rod and I had met the first day of Introduction to Biology, seated in a theater classroom with a hundred other freshmen of varied appearance but largely conformist in culture. The prof droned on in a tone suited to the material about physiochemistry and Darwinian doctrine, while his enthralled students responded fittingly, yawning or nodding, some nearly comatose.

I fought fatigue and put pencil to paper, tried to distill useful notes from the endless lecture when the student on my left bobbed one last time and parted company with consciousness, his elbow sliding across his desk to release a book to gravity, the tome slapping loud against the hard floor just as the professor paused.

The sleeper sat up, surveyed his surroundings, and caught the prof's icy glare. "I—" The bell shrilled, interrupting his feeble attempt at apology and rescuing student, professor, and bystanders from further embarrassment.

I retrieved the offending textbook and returned it to my flustered neighbor, still flushed and uncertain. "This guy can get boring," I said.

"Good grief. Can't believe I fell asleep."

"Too much midnight oil?"

"Up till three finishing a paper for English."

"Oh man, I can't do that scene," I admitted. "After twelve, I'm too tired to care."

"Some people are larks, some are owls."

The disgrace of that moment soon faded from all memory, but the shared experience launched an enduring friendship still growing five years later fed by a mutual passion for baseball. We both received scholarships and lettered our final year—him at catcher, me on the mound.

Rod's Canadian citizenship elevated his status in my eyes. I was a proud American, but his birthland evoked all the northerly magic of Jack London—hoarfrost and deep powder, lofty mountain silence, wolves howling in winter wilderness, campfires under snow-laden boughs.

Later, when Rod and I drove to Winnipeg for Canadian Thanksgiving, I realized southern Manitoba boasted strong soil and flat farms, not forested mountains. From that weekend, my imagination would accommodate only one life—ranching in British Columbia's mountain wilderness.

Five years later, I was closing in on my dream. The hills cloaked in piney woods ranged and rolled to the horizon. But somewhere beyond lay high, grassy meadows and cattle. *Double Bar Ranch, here I come.*

I had pored over the ranch directories in the A&M ag library, looking for a BC operation big enough to require a manager. Seven near Cache Creek fit the bill. I dialed the first, someone listened for fifteen seconds and hung up. The next said he wasn't in the market. Only then did I remember an essential, missing ingredient.

"Lord, forgive me, I should've prayed before I called anyone. I depend on you. I believe you have the right job for me. So please enable me, grant me wisdom. Please give me the words I need."

Four in a row listened but weren't interested. My last pitch struck home.

"You've got the credentials," the owner had said. "What's your background?"

Every rancher had the same exact question. After responding four times, I'd honed my reply.

"Mr. Harper, I won't mislead you. I didn't grow up on a ranch, but spent my free time on friends' ranches, and worked on one for six months after university. You can find guys with more experience, but nobody with more heart. And I understand the cattle business. I'm learning bloodlines and breeding techniques, and I'm a good judge of conformation. I'm able to monitor a cow's health, when to treat and when to call the vet, how to spot calving problems.

"I understand feeding, how to control inputs for the most effective gain. I know when to breed and wean. Have worked all sides of branding. I can build and maintain a solid corral. I know how to select a horse suited to the job, know when it's time to move cows off a pasture, and how to find fence problems before the critters do.

"I'm not familiar with your weather patterns. I'll admit that. But I learn quick. I guarantee you won't be sorry you hired me."

After a few seconds of nerve-wracking silence, Harper responded. "Okay, this might work out. I'll need a manager for at least six months starting late fall. If the walk's as good as the talk, you'll do." He grew silent, and I heard the rustling of paper. "Be here by noon October fourteenth. We'll be loading."

It was noon on the fourteenth of October and the Double Bar was four hours north. Hopefully, the old guy wouldn't check his watch.

CHAPTER 14

WHO IS THAT COMING UP FROM THE WILDERNESS

Winnipeg, Manitoba, Thursday, October 15

No thugs had gone through Rod Castle's room looking for something, appearances to the contrary notwithstanding. Shortly after midnight, he took stock of his packing progress.

Clothes were piled on the bed, books and papers scattered, three half-packed backpacks slumped against the headboard, drawers open, a bag of veterinarian tools on the floor propped against a worn cardboard box full of back issues of Popular Science, a set of banjo strings, dog leash, pocket knife, gun cleaning kit, moccasins, seven boxes of .45 pistol ammo, an unfinished carving project intended to be a seal but better resembling a squash, a Phillips screwdriver, ball cap, and a book of Robert Frost poetry.

At one-thirty a.m. all was packed and ready. Two hours later, he was at the kitchen table savoring his mom's pancakes and coffee. They talked about the weather and his travel plans. Yes, he'd be careful on the road. No, he wouldn't drive straight through the twenty-hour trip. Sure, he'd call her after he got to Kamloops.

Gary Brumbelow

Daylight found him in Saskatchewan wheat country, the V6 in his Ford Ranger humming west on Highway 1. Gently rolling hills on both sides of the freeway prickled with short stubble after the harvest. The skies filled with Canada geese and Sandhill cranes, tens of thousands winging south.

"Just think, Bo," he reached over to scratch his dog's ears, "I'm going to stalk elk in the mountains of British Columbia." The black Lab cocked his head. "But I'm sure there'll be bird hunting too." Bo's tail thumped the floorboard in approval.

Rod's thoughts were suddenly interrupted. He glimpsed something in his rearview mirror. A bright green Mazda RX7 flashed by him, the high pitch of its motor dropping as it passed. Had to be doing 150 kilometers per hour. What was that about? The vehicle shrank and disappeared over the next low ridge.

Who did the guy think he was? He was tempted to nurse the offense but willed himself to let it go. The morning was too fine, his prospects too pleasant to be spoiled by a stranger's rude driving. He was on a mission and couldn't afford to lose his focus.

Calgary, Alberta.

Fourteen hours west of Winnipeg, Rod crossed the Bow River in Calgary and headed for the Rockies. Daylight steadily faded. He loathed missing the rugged topography of those magnificent mountains in the dark. But if he kept driving, he'd make Kamloops by midnight.

In the end, urgency won out over curiosity. He'd be back and forth between British Columbia and Manitoba many times to see his mom.

He changed lanes for a merging vehicle, then looked again—it was a bright green RX7, identical to the car that had flashed by him in Saskatchewan.

"Look at that, Bo." The black lab across the seat whined and thumped his tail. "Could that be the same car we saw yesterday?" Bo sat up. "What are the chances of that?"

The vehicle accelerated, pulling away. Rod just had time to catch a glimpse of long, silky blonde hair. The car on the prairies had passed so quickly he hadn't seen the driver.

"Would a woman drive that fast?" Bo looked out the window without weighing in.

CHAPTER 15

THE ONE WHO CONCEALS HATRED HAS LYING LIPS

Coeur d'Alene, Wednesday 3 p.m.

Johnson parked in front of the ISP headquarters shortly after three, walked in and asked for Barlow. The woman behind the glass told him to sit but he stood to wait. Three minutes later, Barlow led Frank to a room without windows, furnished with one table and two chairs, all bolted to the floor.

"Mr. Johnson, I know this is tough. But I need a few minutes."

"Okay." Frank shrugged and sighed, ever the bereaved husband.

"I need you to go over your story again."

Frank bit his lip, pushed up in his chair and drew on his high school drama training.

"Like I said, the thing started at the campground, almost as soon as we arrived. I parked and put my stuff on a picnic table, and this guy came out of the bathroom claiming that was his table. When I tried to object, he started cussing and screaming. Like he was on something." He presented raised palms. "I'm not a fighter, so I moved to a different table. But the guy kept looking at me. It was creepy. He was definitely off his rocker." He sighed heavily.

"Okay. Carry on."

"So, my wife is diabetic, and she had accidentally overdosed on insulin, got to feeling pretty bad, so I packed up and we left. When I drove out, the guy followed me and got madder and madder because I was driving slowly, attending to Joan in the back seat. I couldn't keep my speed up, and the guy was tailgating me, honking, driving right on my bumper.

"When I finally found a place to pull over, this idiot was in such a rage, instead of passing he stopped and got out, screaming, and kicking the car. I locked the doors and got in the back to comfort Joan. She started having spasms and choking. I was terrified and so focused on trying to help her I didn't realize at first that the car was rolling. He was pushing it toward the water. I barely had time to climb over the seat and get out. The car was already in the water, and I must have bumped the lock before the force of the water closed the door."

Barlow's pressed lips suggested doubt.

"I know, man, it sounds crazy. But I swear to God it's the truth."

"He got mad and pushed your car in the lake."

"That's exactly what happened."

Barlow scratched his jaw. "And you're saying you got out of the car and climbed back up and he was still there?"

"No, he was already gone."

"So how did you get his plate number?"

"I had memorized it when he was following me. I had a bad feeling about him, so I read it backwards in the mirror."

"Why were you on that road?"

"I called in sick, and we went for a drive. We'd never seen Bishop Lake, so we got up early and drove there. Picnicked by the lake and left for home a little before noon."

"You drove two hours to the park and started back at noon?"

"That wasn't the plan, but she accidentally overdosed. I had to get her back."

"Did you talk to anyone else at the park, anyone besides this guy you've told me about?"

"No."

"Did you stop anywhere? Buy anything along the way?"

"What's going on, officer? Are you accusing me of something? I told you how my wife died. Why are you asking me these questions?"

"Sorry, Mr. Johnson. Just a routine interview. We'll sort this out, but it requires some difficult conversation."

"I don't understand why you haven't found this guy. I gave you his description and plate number days ago."

"Yes, and we're looking. He seems to have vanished, but we'll find him. In the meantime, I have a few more questions. We're going to need your help to solve this crime."

Barlow's partner Willis opened the door and beckoned with a nod. Barlow stood. "I'll be right back."

In the next room, Willis spoke. "How's it going in there?"

"Same story as before. Full of holes."

"He reported at the scene that the guy pushed his car, right?"

"Yes, and he said so again."

"You might ask him where that guy placed his hands. Just got the prints off the trunk and they don't match Johnson's."

"Hmm." Barlow turned to the door, then back again. "Any previous crime on Johnson's record?"

"Not much. Couple defacing charges that got dropped. He's something of a graffiti artist in his spare time. Remember the weird art on the back of the bus depot last summer?"

"That was him?"

"Could be. A witness described someone at the scene that sure sounds like him."

CHAPTER 16

THEY ARE CRUEL AND HAVE NO MERCY

Cache Creek, BC, Wednesday afternoon

"Sorry, Mr. Brandon, I can't use you. I need a manager I can count on, someone who knows how to plan and prepares for any reasonable contingency. In my judgment, you should never have started off in the truck you described. But you didn't ask my opinion, so I won't elaborate on it. I hope things turn out better for you someplace else." Harper turned and walked back toward a pen where a couple of hands were pushing bawling steers into a semi.

I was stunned, rooted to the spot. Three minutes ago, I'd stepped out into a beautiful day, the familiar sounds and pungent smells of cattle loading, my dream taking shape, my possibilities bright. Now it was all a horrible mockery.

I couldn't think. I walked to my Chevy in a fog and stood to stare into the distance. A brown butte rose to the south, dry grass flanked by scattered sage brush. Angus cows dotted its slopes. A pickup was crawling along a jeep track, rounding a switchback on its way up the grade. That should be me, checking on the herd, planning the next pasture move, estimating how much hay they'd need for the winter.

But it wasn't me. I was nothing but an unemployed, almost broke outsider from Texas. What did I read last week? "I am a stranger on earth; do not hide your commands from me." That was me. A stranger, friendless, without support, my prospects dashed by a thirty-second monologue from a rigid gatekeeper.

Too proud to try to convince the rancher to give me another chance, it took a minute to realize the old guy was right. I'd arrived four hours late. But it stung when Harper slammed the door in my face.

A gnawing homesickness ate at my heart. I desperately wanted to find a phone. Two loving parents on the line would give me comfort. Dad would give solid advice, Mom would gush empathy, Jerry would make me laugh. I'd feel loved. They'd wire money.

But I resisted the sentiment. I had to make my own way. This whole scheme was my adventure. Was I a man or not? Right now, that was all that mattered.

I closed my eyes and gripped my temples, striving to direct my scattered thoughts into a thread of logic. "When you lose sight of your vision, keep muddling through. Take the next step," a mentor had instructed. So, what was the next thing?

I'd no sooner formed the question than the answer came. That breakfast in Kelowna was all gone. A grilled cheese sandwich would hit the spot.

Highway 97 stretched north from Cache Creek. On the east side of the road, irrigated alfalfa bore witness to the winding Bonaparte River, fields cut six weeks ago and now a faded green awaiting the first snow. Beyond the fields dry, timbered hills rose several hundred feet. My truck tires thumped over the cracks in the pavement.

I had been right about one thing. Lunch was what I'd needed. As I twirled fries in the ketchup and mulled my next step, I remembered occasions when I'd been stuck on a problem. I'd spent time praying, and a solution had come to me.

At the lunch table, immersed in the delightful smell of frying comfort food, I counted my money: $237.55. I needed to find a bank and exchange it for Canadian dollars.

"What's the country like north of here?" I'd asked the stressed, forty-something waitress as I paid my bill.

"Just like this, ranches and cattle. And further north, the Cariboo."

"Caribou? Sure enough? I didn't know they ranged this far south."

"Not that kind of caribou. It's what they call that part of BC. C-a-r-i-b-o-o. Not o-u."

"Where's that?"

"Williams Lake."

I wanted to ask more about that, but she shoved the cash drawer shut and grabbed her coffee pot.

"Sorry, stranger, got customers."

Whatever. I needed a place to sleep. With the Double Bar well behind me.

I drove an hour north, passing homesteads and ranches, unadorned gray barns, plain houses, old pickups. Irrigated hayfields. Here and there ancient irrigation ditches and primitive wooden aqueducts scored the hill faces, gently sloped to bring water from a higher source to the hayfield below, testimony to weeks and years of grueling labor. I ached to make the same investment on land I would call my own.

Gary Brumbelow

North of Clinton, I came to Big Bar Road, a wide, graveled route heading west. Somehow, it beckoned, and I complied. Three miles along, I found a little-used dirt track leading into the dense forest. This would do. A half-mile in, I parked, dug my Bible out of my pack, and sat against a tree.

"Lord, here I am. Please speak to me."

I read and prayed until dark, then heated a can of chili over a small fire. A little before seven o'clock, I rolled out my down bag and crashed, overdue for a long sleep.

CHAPTER 17

You Guide Me with Your Counsel

Big Bar Road, BC, Thursday, October 15

At first light, I stirred and woke. A heavy, hooved animal stomped through water somewhere to my left. I scrambled up to stand behind a tree and peered into the forest, holding my breath. The white bark of leafless birches gleamed bright in the dark pine timber. The sound had come from about forty yards downhill behind a thicket of bushes with red leaves.

There it was again. Three cow elk ran through a creek at the bottom and stepped from behind the bush. One looked in my direction, the other two reached down to feed on the sparse grass.

Another motion caught my eye, the tips of antlers protruded above the sumac, moving toward the cows. A moment later, a huge bull elk walked into view, six points on each side of his magnificent rack. I stood still as stone, my heart hammering. The bull lifted his nose, sniffing, as the cows started off again. The little band, now silent as ghosts, kept moving to the right and slightly in my direction. A few yards further, without warning, they wheeled and ran straight away from me, hooves stamping, breaking sticks. And they were gone.

Ten minutes later, my blood pressure was back to normal. To see the wariest of all North American big game was a fun and unexpected benefit to a random dry camp.

But it changed nothing about my reality. What to do next? Head somewhere, but to what, and which direction? I could not afford to simply wander and hope for some kind of epiphany that might never appear, in fact would almost certainly not appear.

I'd spent three months planning for the Double Bar Ranch. To have that blow up in my face left me feeling like a mismatched fighter pummeled, reeling and ready to collapse.

Maybe if I thought out loud.

"Get it together, Brandon. This will never do. Pull your head together, man, and make a decision. A bad decision is better than no decision."

I opened my Bible at random to Psalm 3 and started reading and stopped at verse two. "O LORD, how many are my foes. Many are rising against me; many are saying of my soul, there is no salvation for him in God." *Yep, that's me right there.*

Another sound broke the silence, something human, someone clearing his throat. I stepped around the tree to another surprise. A hunter looked at me, not twenty yards away, his rifle in one hand, the other stuck in the pocket of a black leather jacket pulled over worn green coveralls. Tennis shoes and a billed cap of heavy red-and-black checkered wool completed the outfit. His face carried no trace of expression. We regarded each other for a long moment.

"You scared off my game."

"I don't think so." I couldn't guess where this was going, but I wasn't feeling wonderful about it. "They never saw me."

"They smelled you."

Of course. That explained the sudden flight. They'd caught my scent and hightailed it.

"Well, I'm sorry. Didn't know anyone would be hunting. Figured the season was over by now."

"For you, yes. Not for me." He spoke with a sort of musical lilt. Another long silence, a squirrel chattered, his *chik* rising, falling away. Silence. Finally, "What are you doing out here?"

I could not read the blank look on that swarthy face. Was he angry, or simply curious?

"I camped here last night." I looked away, then back. "Look, I'm real sorry I spooked your game. What can I say? I'll just get out of here and be on my way." I turned away.

"Where are you going?"

My gut recoiled; my chest unnerved. This pokerfaced stranger had a right to be upset, but how could I have known I was intruding on somebody's hunt? What were the chances I would stumble across anybody here? And what intentions lay behind that inscrutable, bronze countenance? How to get away from this guy?

Then it hit me. Last night I'd spent an hour asking God for direction. And now somebody walks up to me and starts asking questions. *Pay attention, bonehead,* I rebuked myself.

"Uh, well, I ... I'm not real sure. I ... I was praying about that."

A glimmer of response, the tiniest lift of an eyebrow. I pressed on.

"I'm not from around here. Arrived in Canada two days ago. Had a job lined up, but I got there late, and they turned me down. I reckon I'm looking for a job."

"What kind of job?"

"A ranch job." This wasn't likely the perfect moment to mention a college degree. "I came up here from Texas to work on a ranch."

"Texas got no ranches?"

"Oh yes, Texas has plenty of ranches. But no mountains. I've always hankered for mountains."

"If you want to work on a ranch in the mountains, you want Grand Valley."

"Where's that?"

"West. Go to the Gang Ranch and then south. When you get to the end of the road, you're at Grand Valley Ranch."

The hunter turned and walked away.

And I was reminded that God answers prayer.

Coeur d'Alene

Frank Johnson dumped dry cereal in a bowl and opened the fridge. He'd discovered heavy cream was much more satisfying than milk and watched with pleasure as the silky froth drenched the Corn Flakes. He poured till they drowned, sat and ate.

That poor sap from Texas came along at the perfect time. Lucky for me. Laid his hands right on the trunk like I figured.

He laughed. "Good job, Tex. Good for you. More like, good for me, bad for you."

At the sink, he added the bowl to the pile of dirty dishes and watched a squirrel digging in the backyard. He thought about the police interview. *The sergeant, that Barlow guy, might not be as stupid as I figured. I'm not sure he's buying my story. Especially after he left the room and came back. What was he doing? Going to the bathroom? Did he talk to someone? Did he hear something that made him suspicious?*

He stretched and scratched his ribs. *What Barlow thinks really doesn't matter. The county attorney is on my side, now. Not to worry.*

CHAPTER 18

You Are Altogether Beautiful

Chilcotin country, BC, Thursday, a.m.

Why didn't I buy that map at the café? I had never been so far off the pavement. After an hour of navigating a gravel road following that strange conversation in the woods, I was lost. I'd driven along miles of split-rail fence, meadows, and meandering creeks. Nothing for it but keep driving and pray for a road sign.

A little later, I rounded a bend to a splendid, broad vista, the Fraser River basin. The land dropped off to my left in huge steps to the lip of a deep defile where the Fraser ran at the bottom. The hills rose on the other side to even taller timber-crowned heights. Here and there emerald benches of irrigated alfalfa interrupted the gray grasslands. This grand country is what I had envisioned back at A&M. A cow would need seventy-five acres in a country like this, I judged. A ranch would need to be big.

At a fork above the river, I went right. I was pretty sure Grand Valley was the other way, but the sign read "Wolf Creek 9 kilometers" pointing right and I needed gas.

The road switched back and forth to sparse timber at the bottom of the grade, then dropped steeply through thick forest. At the bottom, I came to civilization for the first time since leaving Clinton—a country store with a house and a few outbuildings. And a gas pump.

Finally out of the truck, I stood wide and stretched my arms before filling my tank.

I stepped inside to pay my bill. The proprietor, a smiling, slightly frazzled woman of about fifty, was stocking a shelf with canned beans.

"Welcome, stranger."

"Well, thank you very much, ma'am. Your gas pump was my salvation."

"Well, good. Glad to hear it."

"And it looks like you've got a good stock of general supplies too."

"You bet. Let me show you through the store."

We walked through the aisles filled with basic supplies like buckets, matches and lanterns, pots, pans and dishes, canned food, dry goods, tools, hardware, ammo, rope. I selected some groceries and followed her to the cash register.

"Well, it's good to know about your store. I'll likely be back."

"Good. Live around here?"

"I'm on my way to Grand Valley. Drove in from Clinton. In fact, I'm a little fuzzy on the directions."

"That's easy. Go back over Dog Creek Mountain, cross the river, and turn left. When you get to the end of the road, you're at Grand."

Heading out the door, I looked back to say thanks and collided with someone coming in. We tumbled from the porch onto the pine-needle carpeted ground. I scrambled up and helped her to her feet.

"Sorry, I didn't ..." I shut my mouth. Standing in front of me was the girl from the Hometown Café in Kelowna. "Oh my goodness. I saw you at the café yesterday. In Kelowna."

She shared my shock. "Oh my. Yes. I can't believe it."

"I can't believe I knocked you down. I wasn't paying attention. Are you okay?"

"I'm fine." She smiled, and I had to lean against the steps. "I wasn't looking either. I was watching a chipmunk." She pointed to a clump of tall, dead grass by the corner of the building.

"I'm Cody Brandon."

"Hi, I'm Julie Stewart." She reached to shake my hand, an offer I was happy to accept.

"Glad to meet you."

"You too." She brushed fingers through her hair. "So, when I saw you in Kelowna, you were on your way here?"

I put a hand on my head. "Umm, you could say that. Sort of."

"You weren't following me, though. Right? I mean, I got back last night." Her eyes were stars in the twilight. I tried to breathe.

"No, of course not." *But I would have, believe me, girl, I would have.* She smiled again. In a thousand years I could never get used to that.

"And I see you're an Aggie?" She looked at my cap.

"You know about A&M?"

"I have a very good friend who graduated from there."

"Your boyfriend, maybe? The one who gave you the gloves?"

She laughed and wagged her head. "No, a girlfriend. Her name is Linda Adams."

"Okay. And I take it you're not new around here?"

"I've been here since August. I'm the teacher at the local school."

"Oh. So, you live right here in this little place?"

"You didn't suppose I commuted?"

"Good point." I traced an arc in the dirt with the toe of my boot. "Pretty far from civilization, I reckon."

"That it is. At least for someone who grew up in the Lower Mainland."

"The Lower Mainland?"

She chuckled. "Sorry. I forgot myself. Most of the people in BC live in Vancouver and within a hundred kilometers east. That's the Lower Mainland."

"Now you've educated me. Thanks.

She tilted her head, every move she made charming and full of grace. "So, what brings you to Wolf Creek? We're not exactly on the way to anywhere."

"I'm headed to Grand Valley Ranch."

"Oh. You have a job at Grand Valley?"

"Well, not yet."

Her eyebrows arched, another lovely aspect. "You came up from Texas headed to Grand Valley without a job?" Her countenance and tone were so kind, all offense fled away.

I hesitated, cocked my head, grimaced. "Well, uh, something like that." I paused. "It's a long story."

"I'm sorry. That was impudent of me. None of my business."

"No, it's no problem. No offense." I opened and closed my mouth. "So, this Lower Mainland, that's like, civilization."

"You got it."

"So, a place like this is kinda like frontier even to people from down there?"

"Yes, for sure. Most of my friends consider me a little crazy to be up here."

"Well, most people lack imagination." I saw intrigue in her eyes. "I'm with you. We both left home and came north. We share a sense of adventure." She nodded, lips parted. Who would have anticipated such loveliness on the edge of the wilderness?

"So how do you like teaching?"

"I love teaching." A shadow swept her face and moved on. "But, like any career, it has its ups and downs. But sometimes, I think I was born to teach."

"Good for you. I can relate to that, but in a different career."

"What's that?"

"Ranching."

"Well, you've come to the right country for that."

A truck pulled up to the gas pump. The driver got out, spoke angrily to someone in the cab and slammed the door.

I looked back at her. *Say something.* "I guess I'd better go."

"Me too. School in a half hour."

"I'll likely see you again. I'll be needing supplies."

"Could be." She glanced into the distance. "But Gang Ranch has a store. You could probably get everything you need there. It would be closer." Her smile turned my insides to apple butter.

"Just four miles and fifteen minutes closer. Not enough to worry about. And besides, I don't know anyone there." I pulled the door open. "Anyway, at least I can do something gentlemanly before I go."

She flashed another knockout smile and slipped into the store. Back in my truck, I sat for a moment to process the last few minutes.

I'd escaped girl fever in high school and all through college, as a matter of discipline, I'd pushed off the temptation. Girls were interesting, no question. I'd always figured Texas girls were the prettiest, and I would be far from Texas. Far enough to shield my heart.

So much for that notion.

Climbing up out of Wolf Creek seemed even steeper than the earlier descent. But the effort paid off as the grade fell away on the other side to a splendid view, rugged hills rising higher and higher to one snow-capped peak far to the southwest. The road dropped steadily by hairpin turns to a suspension bridge across the swift, strong Fraser River far below.

Across the river I rattled across a small bridge over Churn Creek. Now the Fraser was on my left, the road hugged the hills to my right. Sage clumped here and there—eagles soared above. A huge mule deer sporting an enormous rack bounded across my path.

The road flanked the river, winding around grassy hills and over ridges, climbing higher and higher. No sign of human activity for forty-five minutes. I topped another ridge and stopped to take in the view.

Ahead, the road dropped into a valley a mile wide and long. At the bottom, straight below me and three hundred yards away, a ranch headquarters nestled. Barn and corrals, outbuildings, a bunkhouse, and six homes, one prominent. Clumps of birch in their papery white bark kept watch here and there, and five black cottonwoods towered over the lonely outpost. The road ended at the barn.

This has to be Grand Valley Ranch.

SOMEPLACE NORTH, SOMEPLACE WILD

I checked my watch. Sixty-one minutes from Wolf Creek. I found it hard to focus, fought a dangerous distraction— the temptation to think about a fox I'd just met.

Pull it together, Brandon. You're here. Find the rancher. You need a job, and you have no idea of your prospects or what you'll do if you get turned down again. Concentrate.

Right now, mental discipline was a matter of survival. With great effort, I filed away the mental picture of Julie Stewart I'd superimposed over the miles of superb scenery. I'd see her again. Right now, I had to get a job—I could not afford to indulge a distraction.

Lord, please go before me. Please give me favor with this owner. I'm trusting in you. Somebody down there was working with a horse in a corral, as good a place to start as any.

CHAPTER 19

YOUR STEADFAST LOVE IN THE MORNING

Grand Valley, BC, Thursday

I set a boot on the bottom rail of the log corral and admired a cowboy swinging a rope at a tall dun horse circling just inside the perimeter. The creature ran wild-eyed, snorting. The roper stood beside the snubbing post in the corral's center, turning with the horse, watching intently. He flicked a wrist, and the loop flew and settled over the horse's head.

The cowboy took two quick wraps around the post, and the horse, in unbroken stride, wound itself to the center where it stopped, quivering with suppressed energy. The man spoke softly, stroking the animal lightly on the neck and withers. He slipped a hackamore over its head and threw a saddle on its back, cinched it, lifted off the rope, jumped on the saddle and hollered "Open the gate."

Only then did I notice another man on the other side. The mare half ran, half bucked through the gate, between two houses and threaded a line of broken-down vehicles and rusty farm equipment. Finally, she broke into a run and the rider let her go, headed uphill. After five minutes, she slowed to a walk, and he turned her back to the corral.

"That was impressive," I said to the rider. "I've never seen anything like it."

The cowboy climbed down and tied the reins to the fence rail, his mount blowing noisily, winded and trembling. "No big deal, done it a hundred times."

"Grow up on a ranch?"

"Yeah. Started breaking horses at eleven. Scared my mom to death once or twice. Broke both legs twice and my back once." He loosened the cinch and removed the saddle. "But I love it. Just gotta learn how to be tougher than a bronc."

Whaddya know, not all the pretty girls and not all the champion bronc busters live in Texas.

I looked past the corral and scanned the headquarters. "Where would I find the boss?"

"Down at the barn." The cowboy gestured with his head.

"Thanks." I took three steps and turned back. "What's his name?"

"Holder. Tom Holder."

A woman stacked firewood beside the back door of the big house. A boy, about nine years old, led a horse from the barn. Down the hill, a hayfield stretched across a flat bench of land from the road to the far edge above the Fraser River. Someone down there crept along on an ATV.

I stepped into the barn and stood till my eyes adjusted to the relative dark as the sweet aroma of cured hay swept over me. A man and boy were loading bales onto an old pickup. The man looked big enough to wrestle a bear. He lifted two bales from the ground at once, one in each hand, and set them on the tailgate. He stood wide and tall and moved with the easy, confident bearing of a leader.

"Mr. Holder?"

"That's me," the giant replied. He stopped working to face me.

I took off my cap and breathed a quick prayer. "My name's Cody Brandon. I was told you might be hiring."

"Could be." Holder looked me up and down, measuring me without a trace of rudeness. "What can you tell me about yourself?"

"Well, I just got into Canada day before yesterday. Drove up from Texas. Had a manager job lined up in Cache Creek but when I got there four hours late the guy turned me away."

"What place?"

"The Double Bar."

Holder nodded. "Chuck Harper."

I nodded. "Yes. Do you know him?"

"Met him. Runs a pretty tight ship." Holder removed his cap and scratched his head. "Why were you late?"

I related the story, careful to include the part about the oil filter. No sense taking the full blame for a disaster that wasn't all my fault.

Mr. Holder tilted his head. "What's your background in ranching? You managed a ranch before?"

"No, sir. But I graduated from Texas A&M last spring with a degree in Agricultural Business."

"Is that so?"

"Yes, sir. I know the cattle industry. To tell you the truth, I want to have my own place someday. But I reckon it'll take time to get there. In the meantime, the more experience I can get, the better."

Holder looked at the floor, lips compressed, brow furrowed. He looked up and shook his head. "I'm sorry, son. I don't have a manager job open. I brought my own man with me when I came up from New Mexico."

I pulled in a breath and steeled my countenance against the sucking feeling in my gut.

"Okay. Thanks anyway." I turned to go, but he wasn't finished.

"But I never turn away anyone willing to work. If you can ride, throw a rope, and fix fence, or run and repair machinery, I can put you to work for a thousand dollars a month and a bunk. You'd be on your own for board. Weekdays eight to five and occasional Saturdays, but we don't work Sundays. Payday at the end of the month."

I paused. That wasn't much money, barely half what I'd been promised at the Double Bar. But out here I could probably live on two hundred dollars. If I saved the rest, in a year I might be able to double my money. Besides, I was almost broke.

"I'll take it." I stepped to Holder and shook his offered hand.

"It's a deal. The bunkhouse is up the hill above the tool shed. Get around and meet the other guys and be ready to work tomorrow morning at eight."

I walked back to my truck. My dream wasn't much closer, but I could relax a little. I was employed—I wouldn't return home in defeat. No doubt there'd be wrinkles, but my major troubles were finally behind me.

Now I had to figure out how to see Julie Stewart again.

CHAPTER 20

THEY SOUGHT HIM BUT DID NOT FIND HIM

Cache Creek, Thursday

The Double Bar Ranch headquarters pressed back against grassy hills rising three hundred feet. A Royal Canadian Mounted Police car idled in the yard, its exhaust swirling like a ghostly dervish.

The Mountie and the rancher, Chuck Harper, stood on the porch looking at a photo.

"Yes, that's the guy all right. Cody Brandon."

"Driving a red seventy-two Ford pickup?"

"No." The rancher shook his head. "He said his Ford broke down, and he had to replace it. Was driving a Chevy. Black. Mid-sixties, I would guess."

The Mountie frowned. "Did he say anything about his plans?"

"Nothing. I said I couldn't use him, and he drove off without saying anything."

"What time was this?"

"Yesterday afternoon."

"Did he say where he'd spent the night?"

"Drove all night. Didn't sleep. Got here late, looking like he hadn't slept for a couple of days. Didn't look like anybody I'd want to trust with responsibility."

"Say anything about what route he took to get here?"

"No, sorry."

"Or where he was headed?"

"Nope."

"Thanks. If he contacts you again, let us know right away."

"I don't expect to hear from him, but sure," he nodded. "Can I ask why you're looking for him?"

"He's a suspect in a homicide in Idaho last week."

"Sure enough? That's quite something. Guess I did the right thing to turn him down." He turned, opened his door, stepped in, and shouted, "Marge, guess what the Mountie just told me." The door closed behind him.

Back in his car, Constable Darrell Seymour drummed fingers on his steering wheel. Six months into his policing career, Seymour loved his job. He would succeed, notwithstanding his father's efforts to apprentice him to take the family printing business. He'd tried that. For two years. No more. Ink-stained fingers and tedious document prep held no allure. He would succeed as a cop. Dad was dubious, but Seymour refused to consider failure. Every day presented new opportunities to prove he could do this.

He pulled out, headed for the nearest cafe. Three stops later, he struck gold.

"That's him." The waitress nodded at the photo. "A little rough around the edges but a decent kid. Why're you looking for him?"

He ignored the question. "Did he say anything to indicate where he was going?"

"Let's see." She looked out the window. "I think he said something about heading north." She cocked her head. "Oh yes, he asked what the country was like up there. When I mentioned Williams Lake, he seemed interested. You might look there."

"Thanks, ma'am."

"No problem. But why're you looking for him?"

"He's a suspect in a homicide down in Idaho."

"Really? Wow. A murderer? Seemed like such a nice kid."

"Didn't say that. Suspect."

From his car, Seymour radioed dispatch who connected him with the Major Crime officer in the Vancouver headquarters.

"Seymour here, Kamloops. About Cody Brandon, the Idaho murder suspect. I just talked to a Mr. Chuck Harper, owner of the Double Bar Ranch in Cache Creek. Brandon was there yesterday, but Harper fired him for showing up late. Said Brandon told him his Ford pickup broke down somewhere, and he was driving a black Chevy, mid-sixties model. A waitress at a local café said he asked about points north. She mentioned Williams Lake. That's all I have for now."

Within minutes, thanks to Seymour's sleuthing, the RCMP national database was up-to-date. The Canada Border Security Agency knew Cody Brandon had not hired on at the job approved by his work permit. He was now in the country illegally.

CHAPTER 21

A FALSE WITNESS BREATHES OUT LIES

Coeur d'Alene, Thursday

Frank Johnson pulled into his back driveway at 522 Randle Street. He killed the engine and sat to relish a pleasure he'd anticipated for many months—arriving home in utter peace.

Joan was gone barely forty-eight hours, the glow of freedom undimmed. Warm contentment enfolded his heart like a mother's embrace. He'd forgotten serenity's touch.

Why did I wait so long? I could have had this months ago. How many miserable homecomings in those years, how many migraine-inducing fights, how many evenings soured by sullen cynicism?

Not even Job could endure such misery indefinitely. And nobody could accuse him of recklessness. How many hours had he sat and considered options? How many times had he reached the same conclusion.

Murder.

Having come to that conviction, all that remained were the details—when, how, where.

Gary Brumbelow

As to when, her parents traveled every fall. Their current vacation, a four-week China tour, put them safely out of reach of a phone call from the law.

The bigger question was how. He owned three guns, but weapons could be traced, and besides, Idaho abounded in rugged topography. Mountain roads, deep canyons—who needed a gun?

But a push off a cliff wouldn't work either—he got dizzy cleaning the roof gutters. Murder by precipice was too squeamish. *I can't take the chance I might chicken out.*

A moment of epiphany surfaced the perfect method. *I don't need a cliff; I only need water.* He would shove the Datsun into a lake.

He studied maps in the evenings and scouted sites on weekends. She was used to him being gone, so he had plenty of time to find the perfect spot.

Two weeks ago, he'd hit the jackpot—Bishop Lake. The road was a single lane for eight miles. At one point, it ran right beside the water for a thousand feet, the steep bank tumbling fifteen feet to gray waves slapping against gravel littered with stinking fish carcasses.

He'd stood where the road emerged in a curve from the silent forest three hundred feet north and spoke aloud to himself.

"I'll overdose Joan on her diabetes med, lay her in the back seat asleep and pretend to have engine trouble." He tapped a toe against the pavement. "I'll stop right here, and flag down the first driver that comes along."

He crossed his arms and scrunched his face in thought. "I'll ask him for a push, get his prints on the car, and send him on his way. Then shove her in the lake."

The plan was so simple. He amazed even himself.

Now, here in his own driveway, in the quiet privacy of his pickup, he nearly wept for joy. And thought about the future.

Eventually, he would date again. He had not lost his taste for female company. But that would need to wait. Had to act like the grieving widower, innocent victim of a heartless crime at the hands of a cruel stranger. For how long, he wasn't sure, but he could be patient. And first, the law had to deliver on job one—get the "killer" behind bars. His new buddy, Marc Malone, would see to that.

Thank you, Eastman Kodak.

He went inside, switched on the TV in the living room, and stepped to the kitchen. He stood at the fridge, surveying his evening meal prospects when he heard the news teaser.

"Next up, new developments in the Johnson murder case."

Five minutes of commercials gave him time to fix dinner—a peanut butter and jelly sandwich fried in oil, a heap of corn chips and a tall glass of cold milk. He brought the comfort food to the couch just in time to see the anchor pop back on.

"Idaho State police have identified the suspect in Joan Johnson's murder. On Tuesday, Mrs. Johnson drowned after the car she was riding in went into Bishop Lake. Her husband, Frank Johnson, who was driving, told police a man following them in a pickup pushed their car into the lake."

Frank spoke to the reporter, "Yes, baby, tell me more."

"Police now have a warrant out for Cody Brandon of Dalhart, Texas. They believe he may have been traveling to Canada. Brandon is a white male in his early twenties with dark hair, a beard and about five feet nine inches tall. An all-points bulletin has been sent to law enforcement agencies throughout Idaho and Washington. The public is encouraged to report any sightings of a red 1972 Ford F-150 pickup with Texas license plates MPG-06H by calling 800-555-1212. Susan Collins reporting for KTVB news."

"Yes." He pumped a fist, spilling the entire glass of milk on the carpet.

"Hello, Cody Brandon. Good to meet you. So happy we ran into each other Tuesday."

Now that his new friend, Malone, had a name to work with, the rest was details.

He sang and danced his way to the kitchen to fetch a towel which he stomped into the wet carpet.

This news deserved a celebration. "Let's get drunk, baby."

CHAPTER 22

To The Pure, All Things Are Pure

Wolf Creek, Thursday evening

Julie stuffed laundry into the small washing machine, turned it on, stepped to the phone, and dialed. She smiled in anticipation. *I hope Jessie's home. For once, I have something she'll want to hear.*

"Hi, this is Jessie."

"Oh, I'm so glad I caught you home."

"Julie. Me too. I was supposed to have ensemble practice, but it got cancelled. What's up?"

"Well, something I think you'll want to hear, if I know my little sister."

"You met someone."

"In fact, I met many people."

"At the professional development day?"

"Yes."

"So, anything special with one of those male teachers?"

"No. Just colleagues and friends."

"Okay. So you went to a conference, met some people, and spent time in a car with a couple of fellow teachers who are just friends. You called to tell me that?"

"You're so funny. My sister, the comedian."

"I'm waiting."

Julie took a deep breath. "Okay, here's the scoop. We got up yesterday morning and went to a café for breakfast. We walked in and I looked up to see a guy looking right at me. Our eyes met, and I noticed he was wearing a Texas Aggie cap."

"Isn't that the school Linda attended?"

"Yes. I wasn't prepared for that, walked right by him without speaking."

"He didn't say anything to you, either?"

"No—"

Jessie jumped in. "Julie, I can't stand it."

"Hold on. I'm not done."

"Okay, keep talking."

"So, nothing was said, not at first. But after we passed, he found my glove I had unknowingly dropped. He asked, 'Is this your glove?' and we talked briefly."

"What else, what else?" Julie could hear Jessie's bouncing bedsprings.

"Not very much. Of course, I thanked him. Told him the gloves were a gift from someone special. He said 'You're welcome. My pleasure. Hope you have a nice day.' That was it."

"Okay. That's good. I guess."

"You know, there was a special moment when he handed me the glove and our fingers touched."

"Oh, wow. You were right, I do want to hear this."

"It was a fun feeling. A little tingly. But I knew I'd never see him again."

"Well, I don't know whether to be happy or disappointed."

"That's how I felt. Like a brief enchantment that passed, never to return."

"Like in a movie."

"But that's not the end of the story."

"What do you mean?"

"We actually met today. He showed up here in Wolf Creek.

"What? He was in Wolf Creek? What are the chances of that? What would bring anyone to Wolf Creek?"

"He was on his way to a big ranch west of here. Stopped at the store. We literally ran into each other at the store."

"Ran into each other? Literally?"

"Yes. We both came to the door without looking and collided. We fell off the step onto the ground." She moved from the bed to sit at the table. "To tell the truth, it was sort of magic."

"Chemistry?"

"I think so. We only talked a few minutes but discovered we have much in common. He seemed really nice. I wouldn't be surprised if I see him again."

"What did you find out about him? What's his name?"

"Cody. He moved up here from Texas. Seemed interested to get to know me. Said he liked my sense of adventure for moving to the frontier." She paused. "I must admit, I found him charming."

"What does he look like?"

"Rugged good looks. Great smile. A little ragged around the edges but that's normal up here. Especially for someone who's been on the road for several days."

"So how would you see him again? Did he ask for your phone number?"

"No, but he said he'd be back to get supplies."

"He has to drive an hour to shop?"

"The scale of things is so different here. The nearest town is another two hours beyond us."

"My sister, the hermit."

Julie ignored the sarcasm. "In fact, someone told me the other day that sometimes people running from the law get hired there. It's that isolated."

"Interesting. You think Cody's on the lam?"

"No way."

CHAPTER 23

IN DUE SEASON WE WILL REAP IF WE DO NOT GIVE UP

Grand Valley, Friday, October 16

In the gray light of morning, I lay on my bunk and watched a spider on the ceiling two feet above me spin her silky thread. I'd read about someone who was inspired to try again after observing a spider start over nine times. *Hmm. That could be me.*

I'd been naïve about what it would take to reach my goal. So many setbacks I hadn't anticipated.

But I wasn't quitting. Dad had said many times, "Never look back, son. Never give up. Never say die."

Time to get up.

I climbed down from the bunk and dressed. Gordon, another cowboy I'd met yesterday, snored in the lower bunk. He'd driven out last night about nine and hadn't returned before I slept.

Burt, the bronc buster, occupied a bunk in the other wing of the cabin. He'd pulled his boots on and stomped out ten minutes ago, waking me in the process.

Both men had the classic cowboy frame developed from days in the saddle. Gordon sported a fine handlebar mustache, but Burt was hairless above his collar. Even his eyebrows were missing.

A third pair of boots stood by the door. I peeked into the other wing of the cabin. A snoring form lay on the lower bunk. In that instant, the sleeper woke and our eyes locked. Embarrassed, I ducked back out of sight, but that was no better. I scratched my head, turned to the stove and was fooling with the coffeepot when I heard the bunk springs crunch.

"No coffee yet?"

The voice sounded familiar. I turned around to introduce himself and my jaw gave way: I was looking at the hunter I'd seen yesterday in the woods.

"I talked to you yesterday."

The hunter nodded.

"You're the one who told me I should come to Grand Valley."

"Yep."

"But you didn't tell me you worked here." It did not occur to me to hide my surprise. *What was going on? Who is this guy?*

The man lifted his shoulders and eyebrows. "Never asked."

"Well, I reckon that's true. I never asked." I bit my lower lip. Yesterday, in the woods, I had been vaguely aware of a culture gap. Now, the same guy stood in the doorway shirtless and hatless, and I could clearly see he was Native.

"I'm Cody Brandon." I stepped up and offered my hand.

"Willie Joe." Willie's lackluster grip seemed aloof. Maybe it wasn't realistic to expect a Canadian to act like a Texan, but I found Willie's manner a little strange. Not rude, just lukewarm. *I'm sure we'll become friends.*

"Looks like coffee will be a little while yet."

"Afraid so. I just got up myself." I set the pot under the tap. "What do you guys usually have for breakfast?"

"Bacon and eggs. Every day. And bannock."

"What's bannock?"

Willie grinned. "Indian bread. Don't you have any Indians in Texas?"

I had to think about that. "We probably do. But I've never met an Indian." I set the pot on the stove and turned on the burner. "Oklahoma has plenty of Indians."

"So I've heard," Willie replied.

"So that's what you were talking about when you said the season was over for me but not for you."

"Yep."

"Hmm. Sorry I messed up your hunt. Hope you get another try."

"Not to worry. Lots of time left." Willie pulled on a shirt. "I was getting hungry anyway. Left you and went for breakfast."

"Hunt around there much?"

"Yep. My sister lives in Clinton. Anytime I can get meat for her family that's good."

Grand Valley, Saturday, October 17

Twenty-four hours after my first bunkhouse breakfast I sat at the table again, another cup of coffee steaming beside me. Yesterday I'd toured the ranch headquarters and gotten better acquainted with the other hands.

Burt, whose horse-breaking skills could land him a job with any cattle outfit in Texas, hailed from a ranching family in southern Alberta, horse country, where kids rode before their second birthday. A mentor had spent four summers teaching Burt how to connect with a horse's soul, or something. Sounds strange, but he knew his stuff. That was beyond dispute.

Gordon grew up not far from Cache Creek, my personal Waterloo. He'd ridden with the famed Douglas Lake Ranch for three years but, like me, restless for a more rugged country, had come northwest and landed this job three years ago. Everything about Gordon said cowboy, from the Sam Elliot mustache to the narrow waist, bowed legs, and worn boots sporting spurs.

Willie's mom was Native, his dad German. He could out-mechanic most pit stop crews. An operation so far from town required someone who could diagnose equipment problems and jury rig till parts arrived. Those were Willie's gifts exactly.

I was especially interested to meet Steve, Holder's ranch manager. Forty years my senior, Steve's spine remained erect, and his long legs and huge stride kept me running to keep up.

I was punching a calculator and scribbling when Willie got up.

"Hey, Willie, how many miles is it to Wolf Creek?"

"Don't know."

"Really? I thought you were from around here."

"I grew up in Wolf Creek." He grinned at my cocked eyebrow. "You're in Canada now, cowboy. We don't got miles. We got kilometers."

"Oh yeah. I forgot. So how many kilometers?"

"Thirty-one."

"Okay, so that's about eighteen miles. But takes about an hour."

"Until the snow comes."

"When does that happen?"

"Anytime now."

"How much?"

"Sometimes a little, sometimes more." He pulled on both boots before speaking again. "And it never melts till April."

In his office in the big house, Grand Valley Ranch owner Tom Holder was also calculating. He lay down his pencil, leaned back in his leather chair, and surveyed the splendid sweep of scenery beyond the window—grass and cattle and hay and ridges falling off into the rugged, commodious Fraser River basin a mile east and five-hundred feet down.

The six-foot five-inch cowman propped his feet on the windowsill and quoted aloud a favorite memory verse. "The boundary lines have fallen for me in pleasant places; surely I have a delightful inheritance."

But he was troubled by a nasty surprise he'd just uncovered. He'd fallen six weeks behind in his monthly profit and loss analysis due to labor problems. In those weeks, the numbers had deteriorated. Worse than he'd expected.

"Things are going to be tight for a while, sweetheart," he said as Carrie walked into the room. "Looks like feeders have bottomed out. That's good. But it'll take six months to recover from that last sale disaster." He sat back and scratched his scalp. "We need to get a good price for those calves."

"Well, we've been praying about that, haven't we?" She stood next to him, stroking his hair.

"Yes. Let's pray again right now." They knelt together and he spoke.

"Father, we're so blessed to be your children. And we know you're always faithful. We've seen your provision many times. And we know you're watching over our family and our ranch and these folks who work for us. Lord, please open your hand. And open our minds. Give us wisdom. For your own sake, break through into our lives."

They stood and watched a horseback rider far out on a ridge toward the river.

"We may have to let a cowboy go," Tom said. "I'd hate to do that. Seems like we finally have a crew we can depend on. And the new guy has potential. I'd hate to lose him, but last in, first out. If anyone has to be laid off, it will be him."

He closed and shelved his ledger book. "We'll give him thirty days; see how he does. And how the market does."

CHAPTER 24

In The Day of Disaster

Grand Valley, Friday, October 23

My first challenging assignment, a week after I arrived, took me nearly to Wolf Creek. A cattle truck en route from Kamloops to Grand to pick up a load of calves couldn't make the sharp turn onto the Fraser River bridge. He was waiting there. Somebody had to drop everything and deliver the critters to him. Steve, the foreman, appointed Gordon and me.

As we loaded sixteen yearlings into the ranch's twenty-five-foot stock trailer, I turned to Gordon.

"So how flexible is Mr. Holder?"

"He's okay. Never unfair. But he's nobody's fool."

"I need something from the Wolf Creek store, just fifteen minutes from the bridge. Since we'll be so close, I wonder how he might feel about me running over there when we're done."

"I don't know. Probably depends on what else he's got going."

Calves loaded, Gordon climbed into the semi and drove out hauling the trailer. I was to follow in the two-ton. I stood for a moment, took a step toward the big house, then stopped. I badly wanted to see Julie, but asking favors one week into the job seemed foolhardy.

Holder walked out and headed for his pickup. I took it as a sign.

"Mr. Holder, can I ask you something?" I removed my hat and swept the hair off my forehead.

"You can call me Tom, Cody. What is it?"

"I need something from Wolf Creek. Um, how would it be if I ran over there after we finish at the bridge? I'd only be a few minutes, could be a half hour. Or an hour. Or so." *Yikes. He's gonna ask, What do you need*? I bit my lip and hoped Holder subscribed to the code of the West—never ask a man about his private affairs.

"It's okay with me, but you need to check with Steve. I'm not sure what he's got in mind for today."

When the manager agreed, and I was in the truck with the windows rolled up, I let out a whoop and sped off in pursuit of Gordon ... and Julie Stewart.

At the Fraser bridge, I pulled off where Gordon waited in the semi and backed the two-ton truck to the ranch trailer. We moved four seven-hundred-pound calves into my truck. Four trips across the bridge to unload into the Kamloops semi, and we were halfway done and headed back to the ranch for the rest of the yearlings.

Ninety minutes later we were back with the final batch. First three loads, all went well. But as I backed up to Gordon's trailer one last time, distracted by mental images of Julie, I came in a little crooked. One corner of my rear bumper touched the trailer, but a gap tapered to the other corner, about four inches at its widest.

"Better try that again," Gordon told me. "I don't have a good feeling about that crevice."

112

SOMEPLACE NORTH, SOMEPLACE WILD

I wasn't listening. The prospect of visiting Wolf Creek had pushed prudence out of my head. I scrambled up and lifted the gate at the back of the truck. The first heifer stepped into the gap and stuck, bellowing like a three-year-old girl with her fingers slammed in the car door.

"Oh no." I yelled and jumped behind the wheel to pull away, but overdid it. The heifer hit the ground and broke a leg, bawling her agony. The other three calves tumbled out, uninjured, smelling water and tasting freedom. They darted down the steep grade toward the river at a run. I grabbed the rope off the seat and pursued in panic.

"Bring hay," I shouted at Gordon over my shoulder. Then the hill dropped off sharply, and I fell. Scrabbling, trying to arrest my slide, I didn't see the heifers at the moment of disaster. But three heavy splashes told me they had been unable to stop. I finally got my footing and stood to see the trio, submerged up to their faces, wild-eyed and bawling as the strong, swift current swept them downstream.

"No." I yelled to the sky. The three heads disappeared around a bend and were gone.

Was this a bad dream? In two minutes, I'd cost Holder four head of cattle. The whole fiasco seemed surreal.

I closed my eyes, my gut hollow again. What a perfect idiot. Now what? I'd probably lost another job. I dropped back in the dirt, shaking my head. An empty, unheeding sky stretched above me.

A moment later the crack of a handgun shattered the silence. Gordon's voice floated down to me. "I put this one out of her misery. Guess I'll head back and bring the loader."

And you'll have a story for the boss, I'm sure.

What made me think I could ever manage a ranch, much less have my own place? I couldn't even back up straight.

Even worse, I couldn't be counted on to be careful. *When will I ever learn?*

I recalled my first fender bender—on my sixteenth birthday. Newly licensed and driving about forty-five, I reached to fetch a paper from the floor when the car slammed to a stop. I sat up rubbing my head. The car's nose shoved against a pole on the median, steam rising from the grille.

That was the beginning of my driving career. The beginning of my ranching career boded no better.

I sat in the dirt while the trucker pulled out with our calves, short four head, and growled up the hill headed for the Kamloops cattle market.

Gordon returned, and we loaded the carcass onto the truck. Time to face the music. All the way back to the ranch, I went over the disaster in my mind. I had regarded myself such an asset for a ranch owner, equipped to succeed in the cattle business, had a fancy paper to prove it, knew more than many ranchers, certainly more than the cowboys. *What a big shot. Now look at me.*

Humiliation and shame stormed through my chest like a desert whirlwind.

At the ranch, I parked at the big house and knocked, fumbling with my hat, and wondering how to slant the story to make myself look less stupid. But Dad's words came to me. "Nobody wants to listen to a whiner. When it's time to admit a mistake, don't mumble and don't grovel. Hold your head up, look the other man in the eye, and speak without hedging."

Mr. Holder opened the door and stood. He was not smiling.

"Well, I understand you had trouble. What can you tell me?"

I swallowed and released the breath I had been holding.
"I suppose Gordon told you what happened."

Holder didn't flinch. "Need to hear it from you."

I looked away. "I didn't get straight when I backed up."
I turned my face back to him. "Didn't figure it was a big
deal. But I was wrong. The first calf stepped into the gap
and bellowed bloody murder. I got behind the wheel to
release her and, in my hurry, pulled away too far. She fell
and broke her leg. The other three fell on top of her, ran
down and slid into the river before I could get there. The
last I saw of them, they were swimming downstream."

The rancher looked up the hill and then turned back
to me. Not one muscle on his countenance moved. Time
stopped—bile rose to my throat.

"What do you have to say for yourself?"

I wiped a hand across my face. "Mr. Holder, nobody
could blame you for firing me. Least of all me. If that's what
you're going to do, I'd just as soon hear it now than have to
wonder." No response.

"But if you can find it in your heart to give me another
chance, I'd be grateful. I've wanted to own a mountain
ranch for a long time. I've worked hard toward that goal. I
turned a corner today when I saw how a careless moment
can cost an operation. If you'll give me another chance, I
think you'll see a sobered hand, more careful." I replaced
my hat and squared my shoulders. "One more thing. I'll
pay you back. You can take it out of my wages, over a year,
if that works."

I counted to twenty-three before Holder spoke. "Everyone
makes mistakes." Twenty-four, twenty-five, twenty-six.
"I never hold an honest mistake against a man." Twenty-
seven, twenty-eight, twenty-nine, thirty. "But the timing

on this one was bad." Thirty-one. "And the consequences costly." Holder massaged his temples.

"You wanted a decision right away, but I need time to pray and think." The rancher sighed. "We'll talk Monday morning. I hope you can live with that."

With a grim smile and slight nod, I turned away.

CHAPTER 25

I GRIEVED FOR MY FRIEND

Kamloops, Friday, October 23

Rod Castle found an apartment sporting a fine view of timbered hills from the bathroom window. The unit's biggest asset was the location, close enough to walk to his new job at the Thompson River Veterinarian Clinic. The job provided twenty-five hours a week with the prospect of full time. He waited tables to make ends meet.

Eight days after arriving in Kamloops, Rod was weaving through the lunch crowd at the Thompson River Inn when he overheard something that nearly pinned him to the floor.

"He came up here from Texas A&M University. Wanted to be a ranch manager. Showed up late. Said his truck broke down." Rod wiped down the empty booth next door to eavesdrop. The speaker, a weathered septuagenarian in boots and cowboy hat, regaled two companions of similar ilk.

"I fired him on the spot, and the next day the RCMP came around looking for him, said he was a suspect in a murder in Idaho. Can you believe that? I almost hired a killer."

Is he talking about Cody? It must be Cody. How many Aggies would show up around here looking for a ranch manager job?

But why would the RCMP be looking for Cody? And what was that about murder?

He resumed his serving but watched the customer. When the man got up to leave, Rod begged his boss for three minutes. "I'll happily skip my break. I know it's crazy, especially on my first day. But I wouldn't ask if it wasn't important. I'll explain later."

He got the nod and hurried out, catching the rancher just as he reached his pickup.

"Excuse me, sir. Sorry to bother you, but I think I overheard you talking about a friend of mine. Did you say something about an A&M grad looking for a ranch manager job?"

"I did. Why?"

"Would that be a man named Cody Brandon, by any chance?"

"Yep. That's him."

"And the RCMP is looking for him?"

"Yeah. Do you know him?"

Rod closed his eyes and stopped breathing.

"He's a friend of mine. We went to university together. I knew he was coming up here. Wanted to work on a ranch. I heard you say, 'Texas A&M,' 'ranch manager.'" He shook his head and looked down, and then up again. "Why is the RCMP looking for him? What was that about a murder? And where is he?"

"Look here, buddy. First off, I have no idea where he is. And anyway, I'm not the one to answer your questions. You'd better talk to the police."

The old guy clammed up, climbed into his truck, and cruised off. Rod stood on the sidewalk, trembling. *What's going on? What am I going to do?*

After his shift, he rushed home and dialed a friend from high school days. Jake would be sound asleep—it was after midnight in Winnipeg—but he had to talk to someone.

"Jake, it's Rod," he replied to a groggy hello. "Sorry to wake you up. Something's wrong with Cody, and you're the only one I could call."

"What's up?" He could picture Jake looking at his clock.

"I just got terrible news. I don't even know where he is, but he's in big trouble."

"What do you mean?"

Rod told him what he'd heard and relayed his brief conversation with the rancher.

"Man, that is bad news. What are you going to do?"

"I don't know what to do. I guess I need to talk to the RCMP. Find out what's happened." He fiddled with the coiled phone cord. "I should try to contact his folks, but I don't even have their number."

"Look, Rod. There's nothing you can do till morning." He paused. "Even if you call the police tonight, they're gonna tell you to come in tomorrow. Detectives don't work the night shift." Jake could think more clearly after a rude awakening from a sound sleep than most people well-rested and coffeed up.

"Makes sense."

"Go to bed. Sleep. And keep me posted."

Rod hung up and knelt at the couch.

"Lord, Cody is in trouble, and I don't know how to find him, don't know what to do. But you know everything; you know what's happened and where he is. Father, please give him whatever he needs right now. And please give me wisdom and direction. Put light on my path. Show me the way I should take."

"Hey, Bo," he said, turning to his faithful black Lab, who was feeling neglected and confused by his master's odd behavior. "Sorry to ignore you, buddy. But Cody's in big trouble."

Coeur d'Alene

Nosy neighbors were Frank Johnson's newest plague. He'd not stepped out his front door for ten days, frustrating the media hovering at the curb. Sadly, the other residents on the street were only too happy to gab about him on camera. He stood well back from the window and watched the live action, then at the five o'clock broadcast, viewed the edited version, and listened to their drivel.

"Don't really know him," the guy two doors down lied to the reporter yesterday. "He pretty much keeps to himself."

You've borrowed my lawnmower three times, but you don't know me. Right.

He had nothing but contempt for TV news reporters. Pathetic, how they pounced on anyone within five-hundred feet of his house and aired their empty talk. People like that were a menace to the community.

CHAPTER 26

SHAME HAS COVERED MY FACE

Grand Valley, Saturday, October 24

Leading my horse, I stepped into the barn and stood for a moment, drawing deeply on the sweet smell of cured hay. Its wholesome, familiar aroma awakened fond memories—jumping from the loft, tunneling in the bale stacks, hayrides at Halloween, evening chores in the twilight. How simple, how carefree those moments, a vivid contrast to this brooding heaviness squeezing me like a gopher snake crushing a mouse.

At the tack corner, I saddled the bay gelding, led him out of the barn, and mounted. Saturdays were generally free, but when Steve asked for a volunteer to check the fence line around the south hayfield, I took it. Alone sounded appealing, and activity much preferred to idleness. I'd fretted here and there all day and needed a distraction.

Besides, I'd never met a horse that judged a man for talking stupid.

"What makes me think I could own a ranch? Sometimes I wonder how I ever managed to graduate from college." The gelding cocked his ears toward my voice. "I'd get to class without my notebook, and Rod would say, 'Brandon, how you can ever beat me at chess?' Or I'd run out of gas dreaming about weekend plans. Mostly, I don't readily slow down and think things through step-by-step."

I dismounted to tighten a sagging strand of barbed wire, then leaned a rigid arm against a post and stared across the river. An early, high-country snow topped the massive hills to the east, their slopes falling to the Fraser, cut by deep creek beds lined with poplar and alder. To the northeast, Wolf Creek Mountain stood between me and Julie Stewart.

"I'd figured to see her again by now. But not like this. I'm a whipped pup since that fiasco at the bridge."

The fence needed little attention. I finished before I was ready to face anyone. But it couldn't be avoided.

Back at the bunkhouse Willie was visible through the kitchen window making supper pancakes. I paused at the door. Nobody had mentioned my debacle. The unspoken code of the West discourages personal questions. You don't probe, don't reference an embarrassing subject.

And nobody was going to shame me. If I wanted to talk about it, hoped to hear reassurance, I'd have to broach it.

I stepped into the cabin, the elephant already there. Willie's gaze locked on his skillet.

"How was the fence?"

"Couple of loose spots. But not bad." I started a pot of coffee. "Anyway, it's fixed now."

Willie looked up from the stove, glanced out the window. "Looks like we could get snow."

I sat at the table. "Willie, you know Mr. Holder. What do you think he'll decide?"

"Who can say? Holder can be hard to read."

"I'm going crazy not knowing what to expect."

"Anyone would." Willie set the plate of hotcakes on the table. "What's the Lord saying to you?"

I turned from the window to face Willie. "Are you a Christian?"

"You've been here a week and never noticed me reading my Bible?"

"Well, come to think of it, I did wonder what you were doing in your bunk sometimes."

"Let's eat." We sat, and Willie prayed. "Lord, thank you for this food. Please give Cody peace. Help him be strong."

"So how long have you been a believer?" I slid pancakes onto my plate.

"Twelve years." Willie sliced a perfect tab off the butter cube. "In 1975, I was out of work and drawing unemployment. I had a little money coming in, but I was spending it on beer.

"One night I was sitting in a bar, drinking, and thinking of my rotten life. I was sick of it. Somehow, I found the strength to get up and walk out. It was about five blocks to my apartment, so I had plenty of time to think on the way." He stood and fetched the coffeepot.

"It had rained that night and froze on the ground. The last five-hundred feet was a steep hill, coated with ice. I tried to climb it but kept falling. That's when I came to the end of myself. I was on my knees and cupped my hands over my face against the ice and started crying. 'God help me.' I wept and wept. That was the turning point of my life." He refilled our cups, put the pot back on the stove, and sat.

"The next day, some friends told me Canada Manpower wanted to see me. The guy there asked me if I would like to try working on a ranch. I told him I was willing to try anything. He phoned the ranch but there was no answer. He phoned Grand Valley and got an answer. The owner said, 'Tell him to come out on the Wolf Creek Stage and we'll pick him up.' And I'm still here.

"The people that knew the old me have said, 'You're a different person.' And that's the truth. Just like it says in the Bible, 'If anyone is in Christ, he is a new creation; the old has gone, the new has come.'" Willie swirled a fork of pancake through maple syrup and lifted it to his mouth.

"That's amazing. The first time I saw you I thought you were going to shoot me. I laughed out loud.

"Thirteen years ago, I likely would have." We pushed back our chairs and cleared the table. Through the window, twilight deepened, and a nearby owl hooted. Willie looked at me. "Did you hear that?"

"Owl?"

"Yes. My people believe the owl predicts a death. When you hear an owl, you know someone is going to die. If you are the only one who hears him, the death will be your own."

"What about you?"

"I used to believe that. But not anymore. Christ is Lord over the owls. He's Lord over all the creation. We never need to be afraid of an owl. He does only what God allows him to do."

"I like how you put that."

Willie stood. "You want to go to a Bible study tomorrow?"

"A Bible study? Around here?"

"You're surprised? Did you think we were all pagans?" Willie's eyes danced.

"Where?"

"Wolf Creek. In fact, I could use a ride. I'm supposed to pick up a truck from my cousin. Maybe you could drive."

SOMEPLACE NORTH, SOMEPLACE WILD

Grand Valley, Sunday, October 25

Ten long days after meeting Julie Stewart, we headed for Wolf Creek. The first snow of the season, five inches at least, blanketed everything in sight. Willie, against the other door, held his rifle and scanned the landscape for game. The evening was the perfect timing to hunt, but I hoped Willie would get skunked. The Bible study was my best chance to see Julie.

A big muley bounded from behind a juniper, cleared the fence, landed on the road, and sprung away into the trees above in less than three seconds, gone before Willie could put a foot on the road.

"Would you look at that." He shut the door and shook his head. "Just like last week."

CHAPTER 27

I SPEAK TO THEM IN PARABLES

Wolf Creek, Sunday evening

Three seconds after stepping into the bunkhouse at the Lazy S Ranch, my heart dropped halfway to my boots. A dozen people crowded the room, but no Julie.

I sat and scanned. The place was much like the bunkhouse at Grand. Wood floor, sparse furniture, walls bare except for propane lamps left over from pre-electricity days—now useful during frequent power outages.

I was thankful Willie had invited me, glad to be here—needed the encouragement. But disappointed at Julie's absence. I had no reason to expect her, just hope. And, like Solomon said, hope deferred makes the heart sick.

"Don't believe I've met you." A kind-faced, forty-something man stretched a hand my direction. I stood to shake it.

"No, first time here."

"I'm Dick. Good to have you with us."

"Thanks. My name is Cody."

"You must be new around here."

"That's right. I recently hired on at Grand Valley."

"Oh, that's good. I know Tom Holder. Great guy. So where are you from?"

"Texas."

"Long way from home."

"Yes, but I really like this country."

We stood for a few minutes, talking about Texas, ranching, weather, horses.

"In fact," Dick said, "I have a horse or two that always need riding, just in case you ever feel out of practice." He winked, stepped to the front, and picked up a guitar.

"Welcome everyone. Let's start with a song." He strummed a guitar chord. *Amazing grace, how sweet the sound...*

I mouthed along. On the third verse, the door behind me opened, cold spilled in, chilling my neck. I looked over my shoulder and smiled—there she was. She turned to close the door and didn't see me at first. I stood and moved a chair next to me, gesturing. She smiled and sat, and the world was right again.

"Didn't expect to see you here," she whispered softly.

"No, probably not. But I was hoping to see you," I replied in the same low tone.

"Tonight, let's look at one of Jesus's parables. Would somebody like to read Mark 4:26-29?" the study leader asked.

"This is what the kingdom of God is like," a woman read. "A man scatters seed on the ground. Night and day, whether he sleeps or gets up, the seed sprouts and grows, though he does not know how. All by itself the soil produces grain—first the stalk, then the head, then the full kernel in the head. As soon as the grain is ripe, he puts the sickle to it, because the harvest has come."

"Thanks, Carol," the leader said. "This is one of Jesus's many parables. He told many kingdom parables. This is one of my favorites. Let's do our typical study method, I ask, and you answer. So, what do you see here?"

"A farmer." The speaker was about my age, wife and baby beside him.

"Yes. And who else?"

Everyone looked at the verses. "No one," Willie answered.

"Are you sure about that?"

"Unless you include a seed as a 'who else.'" This from a lanky cowboy, red handkerchief around his neck.

The leader brightened. "Ah, good point, Ked. You may be on to something there." He waited a moment and then continued, "Let me rephrase the question. How many actors do you see in this story?"

"Actors?" an eager, preteen boy piped up. "I don't see no actors."

Everyone chuckled, and the leader continued. "Okay, fair enough, Nate. No Hollywood actors. And only one person. But something besides the human is acting, doing something."

"The seed." Willie jumped back in. "The seed is sprouting and growing."

"And the soil," the young husband and father added. "The soil is producing grain."

"Bingo. So, the farmer scatters the seed, the seed sprouts and grows, the soil produces the grain, and it ripens. Then what?"

"The harvest," Ked said. "The farmer brings in the harvest."

"That's right. Now, look closely, what does the parable say the farmer is doing while the seed is growing?"

I finally spoke. "He's sleeping or awake, that's all it says."

"That's right. And what does he understand about this process of the seed sprouting and growing?"

"Nothing," Carol said, "'the seed sprouts and grows, though he does not know how.'"

"In fact, how does Jesus describe the source of the action of the soil?"

Julie spoke for the first time. "'All by itself the soil produces grain.'"

"That's right. So, is Jesus a naturalist? Does he believe in a godless universe that operates on its own?"

"'Course not," Ked said.

"Then what's the explanation?"

"Maybe Jesus's point is that from the standpoint of the farmer, the seed and soil are acting on their own because he isn't doing anything," Carol said, "and doesn't even know how it happens."

"Excellent, Carol. Well said." The leader paused and pressed on. "So, who's invisible hand is at work in the seed and the soil?"

"God's." Nate said.

"Right. The farmer doesn't see God, but he sees what God is doing, through his creation laws. God built laws into the creation that play out all around us every day. A deist would say God set the creation on self-drive mode and went away. But the God of the Bible is intimately active in his creation.

"And I believe Jesus's point here is that God is at work in the seed and the soil. And the farmer is also at work." He looked around, "Everyone with me so far?" Our heads nodded and he continued, "Okay, we're almost through. What's the climax in Jesus's story?"

"The harvest," Willie said.

"Yes. This is one of several parables that points to a harvest. And what does Jesus's opening tell us the story is about?"

"The kingdom," Carol said.

"So, this parable is about the kingdom, God's rule on earth. It includes a farmer and his seed, and God's invisible hand working as well, with the result of a harvest. Now, here's the final question. How would you state this parable in your own words?"

Quiet settled on the group, the only sound the rustle of Bible pages. Moments ticked by before an epiphany swept my brain, and I braved a response.

"The kingdom grows as God and man work together?"

"Whoa, that's amazing, Cody. Yes, that's exactly the point of this parable. Let me unpack it a little more. God and man both work in the kingdom. Some things only God can do. Only God can make a seed grow and sprout. Humans cannot do what God does. But other things are for man to do. The man plants and harvests. God will not do the man's part, man cannot do God's part, but as they both work together, the harvest comes. The kingdom grows. And that's a very powerful truth."

The group discussed applications of the parable for twenty-five minutes before the leader closed in prayer, and then invited everyone, "Let's stand and sing the doxology."

We finished, and I turned to Julie. "It's good to see you again, Julie. I wondered if you might be here."

"You too. Yes, I'm generally here every Sunday evening. How are things at Grand Valley?"

I should have anticipated such an obvious question, had to think fast.

"New challenges, things to learn. But I'm doing okay. I reckon time will tell." Then, "How about you? How's it been for the Lower Mainland lady on the frontier?" I winked, and she lit up the room with her smile.

"You really locked on to that part of my story, didn't you?"

"I reckon. Not many girls I know are that brave."

Her eyes reflected my compliment. "And how many girls would that be?"

I fiddled with my shirtsleeves. "I know lots of girls. Just friends. Never known anyone like you."

She blushed and touched the chair. "Want coffee? We always have coffee and cookies after the study." We selected from the refreshment table and sat again, quiet for a moment in the buzz of conversation around us. I spoke first.

"You never answered my question."

Julie tilted her head, scrunched her eyebrows. "I'm sorry, I've already forgotten what you asked."

I grinned. "Just wondering how things have been with you."

"Oh, sure. Well, it's a good life. I like my work, love teaching. Of course, it has its challenges."

"What was a challenge this week?"

She searched my eyes and drew a breath. "Well." She glanced around the room and dropped her voice. "In a word, Danny."

"I'd like to hear about it. What more can you tell me?"

Julie bit her lip and looked at the floor.

She doesn't want to talk here. "Say, how about we go for a little walk?"

"Well, sure, okay. I mean, I walked here. My teacherage is a kilometer."

SOMEPLACE NORTH, SOMEPLACE WILD

"Well, how about I walk you home?"

"Sure."

CHAPTER 28

THEY WERE TALKING WITH EACH OTHER

We stepped out into the night. A riot of stars lit the heavens as if to compensate for the moon's absence. Cloudlets rose from our breath; our feet scrunched the snow-packed road.

"What else can you tell me about Danny?"

"He's a good kid, deep down. But he can be a handful. So many disadvantages. Tries to compensate for his home life."

"How old is he? Somebody said the school is through sixth grade?"

"That's right, but Danny missed a year from sickness. He's thirteen, and a big thirteen at that."

"Do you ever feel threatened by him?"

"No. Challenged, yes. But not threatened. You know, everyone has stress, every job has its challenges."

If only you knew.

"Have you worked on a ranch much?"

"I spent three summers on a ranch in Texas while I was at college, and then six months to qualify to immigrate."

"And you studied agriculture at A&M?"

"Yes, as a matter of fact, I did. On a baseball scholarship."

"You played college baseball?"

"I did, believe it or not. But you may have to take that by faith." I grinned and winked.

"What position."

"Just pitcher."

"Just pitcher? The pitcher is the most important."

"It's the position that gets the most attention. But baseball is a team sport. Not like, say, golf."

"I think I mentioned my friend Linda Adams who went there."

"Yes, I remember. Never met her. With thirty thousand students there, I reckon the chances of that are slim."

"Oh, sure. A needle in a haystack. A very colorful needle, though." She laughed.

"What do you mean?"

"Linda's one of the most outgoing people I've ever met. High energy, loves a party, drives her little sports car way too fast. We used to call her the Green Flash." Julie laughed, and I knew I had to spend more time with her.

"What made you choose teaching?"

"It was kind of a no-brainer. I've always loved kids and reading. My mom was a schoolteacher. It's probably in my genes." We stepped off the road into the deeper snow to allow a car to pass, then resumed our walk.

"Tell me about your family, Julie."

"Well, my parents and younger sister still live in the house we grew up in. It's in a little town called Langley, near Vancouver. My dad works for the government in housing. Mom's still teaching. My sister, Jessie, graduated from university last spring. She's living at home and working in an office while she decides what to do with her music degree."

"So how did you end up in a place like Wolf Creek? I don't know how big Langley is but I'm guessing it's not much like here."

"Langley is about twelve thousand people, a small town compared to Vancouver. But most people around here would consider it a city. It was a great place to grow up. Many good memories of school and friends. But I was ready for a change." She folded her arms over her chest and smiled. "I've always loved frontier stories, wanted to experience it, wanted to teach in a Native school. So, I applied, and Wolf Creek came up." She turned to look at me. "But I want to hear about Texas from a real Texan. Is it everything they say it is?"

"I don't know. What do they say it is?"

"You know, bigger and better than everything else." Every time Julie laughed, I wanted to squeeze her. I kept my hands in my pockets.

"That's hilarious. I didn't know the reputation carried this far." I shook my head. "No, Texas is like any place else. Great people, interesting history. But that 'biggest and best' stuff is mostly hot air. I love Texas, love our traditions. And I never forget the Alamo, for sure." I grinned, and she laughed again. "But I've wanted to ranch in the mountains for a long time."

"And how did you hear about Grand?"

"I met Willie. Literally in the woods, believe it or not." I told her the story. "Do you believe in God's providence?"

"Not sure what you mean." Her face invited me to continue.

"Often, people talk about coincidences. As if things happened by chance. But I believe things happen because God makes them happen."

"Well, sure, I agree with that."

"For example, I didn't mention the other day everything that happened to me when I was on the way up here."

"Oh?"

"Well, for one thing, my truck motor blew up in the middle of the night. I walked for two hours and finally got a ride with a trucker into town where I bought another pickup."

"Oh, wow, that's awful."

"But here's the deal. Because of that delay, I met Willie. I camped in the woods, prayed for direction, and slept. And in the morning God practically drops him in my lap."

"Oh, so God is provident, and he also answers prayer."

"Yes. The experience taught me to be more alert when something unexpected happens because he's up to something."

A coyote chorus suddenly rose in the distance, the barking and yipping crescendoed and fell away in the night. The village dogs took up the refrain.

"I'm still puzzled why Willie didn't mention he worked at Grand himself."

"I'm not surprised to hear that," Julie said. "I think it's part of the culture, especially the Native culture. Folks don't go out of their way to talk about themselves. Maybe they figure you'll find out eventually? I'm not sure."

We crossed a bridge over the frozen creek lined with dark woods. Village chimneys puffed wood smoke. I savored the delightful, dusky fragrance.

"What attracted you to BC?"

"Ah, yes. Look around. Wildness, winter, snow, wood smoke. Nights just like this. I also read Jack London's stories and dreamed about life in the north. The adventure of it, the challenge."

Julie smiled and nodded. "I know what you mean. I feel the same."

We arrived at Julie's teacherage, a frame building about twenty-five feet square.

"What did you think about the Bible study?" Julie said.

"It was interesting. Intriguing, in fact. I expect I'm going to be thinking about it for a long time."

At Julie's raised eyebrows, I continued. "I guess I've never thought about explaining the Christian life that way. I've always believed God has a purpose for every individual, of course. A plan for every believer. But I really liked how the leader put it, God won't do what I'm supposed to do, and I can't do what only he can do. But as he does his part and I do my part, good things happen."

"Yes, that's a fun thought."

"But it prompts another question."

"What's that?"

"How do I know what's my part and what's God's? In a given situation, I mean."

"Like?"

A window in my heart opened briefly. *Should I tell her I'd pulled a real boner and might lose my job.* No, it was too early in the relationship.

"I don't know." I cocked my head. "I think it applies to just about every big decision we make."

"And maybe the little decisions too."

"Could be." I shrugged. "Well, I reckon I need to start for Grand Valley. It's been real nice to get acquainted," I said as we shook hands. "Hope I'll see you again soon."

"That would be nice," Julie said. "You'll find me at the Bible study almost every Sunday night."

"I can pick you up next time. I could come early, and we could go riding. Dick told me I could ride his horses any time."

"Sure, why not?" Julie said with a nervous laugh.

The thermometer next to Julie's door registered twelve below, but I was warm all the way back to my truck.

Coeur d'Alene

Frank bit his lip, squinted, put lead to paper and scrawled. Then read what he had so far.

> *Joan was the dearest to my heart,*
> *Of all the girls I've known.*
> *And when we finally had to part,*
> *It cut me to the bone.*
> *Joan you were the very best.*
> *I hope you have a splendid rest.*
> *I'm sorry it did not work out.*
> *But be assured I will not pout.*

He wasn't as sure about the second stanza. "Very best" was pushing it. For that matter, "dearest to my heart" was pretty ridiculous too.

"But it's not like I'm intending to publish it, after all," he said to the empty room. "Just need a little more fuel to stoke the fires of grief."

He laughed and shelved the masterpiece for now.

CHAPTER 29

THEY SET A NET FOR MY STEPS

Kamloops, Monday October 26

Constable Seymour's desk phone rang first thing Monday morning. Chuck Harper, Double Bar Ranch, was on the line.

"You said to call you if I had any more information about Cody Brandon."

"That's right. What have you got?"

"On Friday night, I talked to someone who said he's a friend of Brandon's. Didn't get his name but he's a waiter at the Thompson River Inn. Young guy, blond hair, freckles, average height."

Thirty minutes later, Seymour parked his car at Rod Castle's address and knocked at the door. No one was home, but as he started to drive away, a man fitting the description Harper had given, with a black Lab on a leash, turned from the sidewalk toward the building.

Seymour stepped out of his vehicle and spoke to the man's back. "Excuse me, are you Rod Castle?"

The man turned. "Yes, I am."

"I'm Constable Seymour, RCMP. May I have a few minutes of your time?"

They sat down at Castle's kitchen table. Unpacked moving boxes perched here and there.

"Do you know a Cody Brandon?"

"Yes. He's a good friend. And I heard the police were looking for him. But why?"

"Mr. Castle, we are speaking today because the Idaho State Police contacted us in relation to a death they believe to be a homicide. They have compelling evidence to put your friend at the scene of the crime. Is there any reason you think such evidence would exist?"

Rod sat back and squinted at the officer.

"Do you mean do I think Cody murdered someone?" He shook his head. "Absolutely not. That's crazy."

"We're not saying that. But we need to talk to him. You can help him best by being completely forthcoming about what you know regarding his whereabouts. Has he said anything to you that would shed light on this matter?"

"No. Like I said, Cody isn't capable of murder, so, no, I can't think of any reason such evidence would exist."

"Well, we aren't saying he is capable of murder. That's why we need to speak with him. We've talked to the man he was planning to work for in Cache Creek, and to a waitress who spoke with him, but he spent less than five minutes with either of them. You're the one person we've found who actually knows him. You're his friend. It may sound ridiculous to you, and I get that. If you're right, there's another explanation for why such evidence would exist. But we can't know until we talk to him. What information do you have regarding his whereabouts?"

Rod lifted his palms. "Well, his heart was set on ranching in the mountains of British Columbia. That's all I can tell you."

Seymour wrote in his notebook. "Can you remember the last time you talked to him?"

"Yes, we talked by phone the day he crossed the border."

"What day was that?" The officer scribbled in his spiral notebook.

"The day before I left Winnipeg to come out here. I left home a couple of weeks ago." He went to a calendar beside the sink. "That was October fourteenth. So ... we spoke on the thirteenth."

"Anything you can remember of what he said will be helpful. Where had he been? What were his plans? Where did he say he was going? When did he expect to arrive? What was he traveling in? Anything you can think of that would help us."

"Well, he called because he was stuck at the border. Didn't have all his paperwork, and they grilled him for a while. He was waiting for a decision. He was determined not to call home. It's that important to him he does this on his own. And anyway, it was cheaper to phone me since he was already across the border."

"Where is home?"

"He's from Dalhart, Texas."

"Are his parents alive?"

"Yes."

"Did he say when he'd left home?"

"No, but he'd only stopped one night. I believe he said that was in Idaho. A campground. He mentioned a lake."

"Say anything more about that?"

"Said it was beautiful." He squinted at the floor. "Oh yes, he was sleeping on the ground, and an animal woke him up in the night. Scared him pretty bad, couldn't get back to sleep for a while, and overslept."

"Did he say what time he left the campground?" Seymour turned the page in his notebook.

"No. Just that he was behind schedule at that point."

"And what was he driving?"

"He had an older Ford pickup. Seventy something."

"Can you describe the truck? Or have any idea of the license plate number?"

"I can tell you it's red. A little beat up. But otherwise, sorry. Don't know the plate number."

"Is there anything else you can remember that might be helpful?"

Castle heaved a sigh through puffed cheeks.

"I can't think of anything." Then, "But can I ask you a question?"

"What's that?"

"How did you find me?"

Seymour forced a deadpan expression. "We're the Royal Canadian Mounted Police, Mr. Castle." He stood and fished a card from his pocket. "Here's my number. If you hear from him, or if you remember anything else, please call me."

CHAPTER 30

MY HELP COMES FROM THE LORD

Grand Valley, Monday, October 26

Afresh morning had never failed to lift my spirits. Today might be the first exception. My bunk had creaked and groaned all night, echoing my own mental torment. With the last of my coffee, I washed down one more bite of breakfast, set the dishes in the sink, and headed for the barn. I wasn't going to let Mr. Holder get there first.

New snow crowned the hills around Grand Valley. "I will lift up my eyes to the hills," I recited. "From where does my help come? My help comes from the LORD, who made heaven and earth." In the minute-and-a-half walk, I repeated that last sentence over and over.

Inside, I perched on a bale, drumming fingers on my knee. When Tom Holder came in, I stood, and kept my hat on. He stepped right up to me, his face sober but with a hint of kindness in his eyes.

"Well, Cody, I'm going to give you another chance. We all make mistakes, and you've shown promise, so let's move ahead."

I breathed, tried to shape the right countenance. He continued.

"But you should consider yourself on probation. Another careless performance and I'll have no choice but to let you go."

I opened my mouth but held my tongue when Holder put up a finger. "But I don't think that's gonna happen. In fact, I've got a special assignment for you. A tough one. If you succeed, we'll put all this behind us. If otherwise, you'll still be on probation. How does that sound?"

"Sounds more than fair, Mr. Holder. Thanks for giving me another chance." I shook Tom's outstretched hand. "What do you want me to do?"

"Like every ranch around here, we're missing horses. They're in the high country somewhere. I'm sending you with Gordon to find and bring them back."

"Really?" I leaned forward, eyebrows arched, mouth open. *Somebody pinch me.* I thought I had lost my job, and I'm getting a dream assignment instead?

"You'll be riding the whole way because you'll be checking all the meadows. The line cabins are a day's ride apart. The last one, Poison, is up high, so you'll need warm clothes. Plan to take an extra mount each and a pack horse. Make sure you have ammo. You'll be going into grizzly country. Should be a good adventure for you, but it will be a ton of work. There's a corral at every cabin so you can collect the horses you find and lead them back down here." He paused. "Any questions?"

"When do we leave?"

"You'll need a couple of days to get ready. Steve will help you choose horses. Gordon will teach you how to pack. You should be ready Wednesday morning. Poison is a three-day ride straight through, but you'll be riding plenty of extra miles. It could take you ten days."

"Sounds good," I spoke in a joy of disbelief. "I sure appreciate this, Mr. Holder."

CHAPTER 31

HE PLANS WICKED SCHEMES

Coeur d'Alene, Wednesday, October 28

Bleary-eyed, a wretched Marc Malone, Kootenai County Attorney, poured coffee in his kitchen and spoke in the silence.

"What a mess I've made of things." He sipped and shook his head.

"How did Johnson find out?" Sipped again.

"Who else knows?" He coughed up phlegm and spit in the sink.

"What now?"

Malone massaged his scalp, as if pressing his cranium hard enough and long enough would make everything go away. It didn't. He needed to think, desperately needed a plan.

Two-thirty a.m. wasn't his best hour, but the luxury of procrastination had dissolved weeks ago. His reputation, his career, his way of life depended on what happened next. With an election thirteen months away, he had to conquer this beast before it ate him alive.

He slurped coffee and shook his head again.

The affair was a bad idea from the get-go. He knew that, but in lust, he had smothered every second thought.

His title, power, and a full mane of silver hair lured women like hummingbirds to a red feeder. Not that anything was wrong with his wife. But after twenty-three years of marriage, no woman could be expected to compete with the glamor of females half her age.

That's how it all started with Debbie. When a clerical position opened on his staff, she was the second applicant. Her beauty could dazzle the blind—bronzed skin, shoulder-length blonde hair framing a perfect face, eyes to conquer Alexander the Great.

Malone had immediately told his secretary to inform the other applicants the position was filled. Debbie was the perfect fit. He had no idea if she could identify a file folder, type, or spell cat, but it didn't matter, he wanted this babe. And the attraction was mutual. They had dinner the first Friday night, and within two weeks the affair was in full bloom.

In another week, everyone in the office knew, and Malone had to protect his electability. Six weeks in he made a show of dismissing her for incompetence, and the office gossip died. Everyone believed she was out of his life. But that was hardly the case. He'd found her a job and apartment in Spokane, thirty miles away over the state line. The arrangement worked perfectly. For fifteen months.

Till Frank Johnson.

Now a tidal wave of folly mounted over him. Desire had morphed to danger, the potential death of his career.

He showered and headed for the office, still without a plan, except where to start.

Who was Frank Johnson?

Exactly what had happened at Bishop Lake?

What evidence had been uncovered?

There had to be a hole in the case somewhere, a weakness he could exploit to move the spotlight off Johnson and eliminate his threat of blackmail.

CHAPTER 32

THEY WENT UP INTO THE MOUNTAINS

Grand Valley, Wednesday, October 28

Two days later, Gordon and I mounted and rode west up into the hills. Gray clouds pushed down, sending white flakes to whirl around us, the soft blanket growing thicker as we climbed. I was leading a pack horse loaded with supplies, two extra mounts trailed behind Gordon. At the last ridge we stopped and looked back at the home place far below.

A lone figure strode toward the barn, wood smoke wafted from chimneys, a pickup headed out on the road, exhaust puffing in the cold. Twenty yearlings bunched against a fence like the A&M baseball team assembled for the pregame pep talk. Falling snow obscured the far side of the broad hay meadow, beyond that nothing was visible.

"Looks real nice," Gordon said. "Almost like a Christmas card."

"And it feels like Christmas to me. I can't believe Mr. Holder decided to send me on this trip. I feel like I've died and gone to heaven."

We turned west again and rode uphill into the wind.

"It's an adventure, that's for sure," Gordon said. "We'll see some wild country and probably game. But it'll be a lot of work, and maybe even dangerous."

"Dangerous?"

"Could be."

"Like what?"

"A person could get lost in a storm or break a leg. That's why we always go in pairs." Then, "And you want to stay on the lookout for bears, especially grizzlies." He reined to a stop, and I followed suit. I shifted in my saddle. "How much time have you spent up here?"

"Three summers. When the warm weather comes, we start pushing cows up here. Leave some at Relay Creek with a couple of cowboys. Take the rest up to Yodel and leave more cattle and cowboys. Same with Blackwater. The last bunch go to Poison." He tied his reins, dropped them over the saddle horn and sat back to fold his arms. His horse continued plodding. "That elevation only has grass a couple of weeks after the old snow melts and the new comes. Then we start back down."

"How do you keep track of so many head in country like this? How do you find them all when it's time to come back?"

"The older cows are smart. They know where the hay is. When a meadow is grazed out, and the snow starts flying, they're ready to head home. We don't lose many."

"But horses are different?"

"Yeah. They can be real knuckleheads. One rebel will gather a few head and they'll run off who knows where. And the snow doesn't push them down like it does the cows because horses, unlike cows, will paw through the snow to graze."

We turned onto an old jeep track that wound back and forth up the steep slope through the lodgepole pine. The snow stopped falling, two or three inches now dressed the landscape. As we rode, Gordon showed me how to read the tracks of marten and weasel, how to distinguish a coyote track from a fox. When he pointed to a deer print, I jumped in.

"That one I know. We have lots of deer in Texas. And I've hunted deer since I was thirteen."

"Here's a bear track." He pointed to a soft spot in the lee of a little hill without snow. "Not a grizzly, but a black bear is nothing to fool with. They can mess up a cow pretty bad."

"Have you seen that."

"Oh, man. Me and Duane were up at Yodel one summer and woke up in the middle of the night. Something out there was making the most awful noise, the sound of an animal in agony. Spooky as a ghost and didn't let up. We couldn't go back to sleep and were too afraid to go out in the dark, so we built a fire in the stove and drank coffee till we ran out of water. That horrible noise lasted all night."

I sat my horse, spellbound.

"At first light, we saddled up and headed toward it, guns ready, scared spitless but had to know what it was." He shook his head as if grieving the death of his best friend. "The sight will be with me till my dying days. A black bear had knocked down a cow and broke her back. She couldn't move, but was still alive, partly submerged in the creek and bawling in terror and pain as the bear ate her alive. Her entire hindquarters were nearly gone.

"We shot the bear and the cow. Couldn't quit shooting even after he was dead. Finally ran out of ammo, did without the rest of the summer."

I looked at the dark woods as we rode higher.

CHAPTER 33

THE CRAWLING THINGS OF THE EARTH

Wolf Creek, Thursday, October 29

Julie laid her books on the desk, hung up her coat and started a fire in the school's wood stove. Time to empty the mouse traps.

She never shrieked at a spider. Ignored every menacing dog on her daily walk. Had even been known to catch frogs by hand to entertain a kid she was babysitting.

And she trapped mice. Every morning she found at least one little critter who'd met an untimely end. Sometimes as many as three. Today, her trap line harvested just one victim. "Sorry, little fellow," she whispered as she lifted the trap spring and dropped him in the snow out the back door. Mice didn't bother her.

But she had one irrational fear, one she had managed to hide for three months, but in a ranching community she knew would eventually be discovered—Julie feared horses. When considering the offer to teach at Wolf Creek, she had thought about this, knew there would be horses, but figured she could just avoid them. She did not realize the horse population outnumbered humans by at least three to one.

Now the problem had risen to a whole new level. Horses terrified her, and Cody Brandon wanted to take her riding.

What was she going to do?

"Hi, Miss Stewart." Amy, one of the twin daughters of the village chief, bounced into the room, stamping her boots on the entry rug.

"How are you this morning, Amy?"

"Good. My cat had kittens last night."

"Oh wow. How many?"

"Four. Three mostly gray and one mostly white."

"Good for you. They'll make good mousers."

For her part, Julie wasn't convinced equinophobia was unreasonable. Fear of a tiny mouse was unreasonable, but fear of a thousand-pound, snorting, wild-eyed beast quivering with brute energy? That's irrational? On her first day in the village, she had to hold her stomach watching children climb on and carelessly race down the road, weave through the trees and splash across the creek.

"Hi, Miss Stewart." Bobby, the hard-working son of a single mom popped in and pulled off his wool toque. "Did you catch any mice?"

"Yes, one mouse this morning. How are you, Bobby?"

"Can I empty the trap tomorrow?"

"If you get here early, yes."

Of course, Julie was an outsider, a city girl. These folks had shown her much grace, and she wondered at times if that would extend as far as to accept her fear of horses, but she was afraid to go there, afraid the community would shun her if they found out. Better to be quiet and manage, work around the subject. That strategy had served her just fine, until now. Cody Brandon wanted to go riding, and she was about to be found out.

"Hey, Miss Stewart, I finished reading *Alice in Wonderland*." Millie, her only grade four student, approached Julie's desk. "What's another book I can read?"

"How about *The Very Hungry Caterpillar*? Have you read that?"

Her fear began when she was eleven and a friend, Michelle, invited her to go riding. Michelle's dad had dropped them off at a stable where the family kept two horses. They took a bucket of oats into the paddock to lure the old, gentle mare, but the young gelding pushed his nose into the bucket first. Michelle let him feed briefly and then took the bucket away to offer it to the mare. The gelding, squealing in protest, reared to an enormous height, a frightful tower of danger. Julie had panicked.

"I'll go get help," she'd yelled, and headed for the barn, running without thinking right behind the agitated horse. His kick caught her square in the chest and sent her flying several feet. She was bruised, had no broken bones, but over the years that seed of terror had grown into an ugly tree. She'd never been close to a horse since—until coming to Wolf Creek. And that was just fine with her.

She didn't want to tell Cody no, didn't want to say yes. She was stuck.

"Okay, children, let's stand and sing *O Canada*."

Back in her cabin after the school day, Julie went to the phone and dialed her sister.

"Jessie, do you have a couple of minutes? I need to talk."

"Always for you, big sister. What's going on? Is it about your new friend?"

"As a matter of fact, yes."

"Oh dear, bad news?"

"No, no. Well, not serious bad news, but I'm stuck."

"Okay. You've got me listening now, for sure."

"You know how I am about horses."

"Of course."

"Well ..."

"In fact, you remember I talked to you about that when you were making your decision about going up there, right?"

"Yes, I remember. I decided it would be workable, and it has been, until now."

"So, what's changed?"

"Well, Cody has invited me to go horseback riding."

"Ouch. You're in a real pickle."

"Telling me."

"Unless you just say no."

"That's just it. I'm still scared to death of horses, but I don't want to say no. I think he's growing on me."

"Oh, Julie, I'm so happy for you. Tell me about this guy. Except for smart, charming, and funny you haven't said anything."

"He's a real gentleman. Walked me home after Bible study Sunday night and had to hike back alone to his pickup."

"How far?"

"About a kilometer."

"And it's cold, right?"

"Yes. I think he wanted to spend more time with me but wasn't going to invite himself in."

"Okay. That's good."

"Oh yes, he graduated from Texas A&M. I asked him if he knew Linda Adams, but he didn't. He's kind and thoughtful. Asked all about my life. I'd be an idiot to tell him no, but I shiver to think about getting on a horse."

"I'm thinking the solution is right there in front of you."

"What do you mean?"

"He's thoughtful and kind, you like him, there's obviously chemistry. Why don't you just tell him the truth? Tell him you'd like to ride with him, but then tell him your story."

"You really think so?"

"I do. In fact, the more I think about the idea, the better it sounds. It's a great way to learn about his character. If he laughs and presses the invitation, he's probably not right for you. But if he truly has a tender heart, he won't laugh. He'll understand and respond with gentleness."

"Jessie, sometimes you amaze me. You're exactly right. My sister, the sage."

"Okay, so you owe me one. I'll be waiting to hear the rest of this story."

CHAPTER 34

DANGER IN THE WILDERNESS

Coeur d'Alene, Thursday

A disheveled Marc Malone lay a blank page on his desk and traced a vertical line down the middle. Above one column, he scribbled "Clear Frank Johnson," over the other, "Tarnish Cody Brandon."

The RCMP still hadn't found the guy, but they would, and the delay gave Malone time to dig for two kinds of evidence—what to disclose and what to hide. He'd long since abandoned any principled ethics—no constraint there—and his intellect was certainly up to the task. The challenge was merely discipline, mining for that one vein of gold to ransom his future. *Keep digging.* He scribbled, erased, crumpled, started again. Lost track of time.

Something thumped outside his closed door, and he glanced at his watch. 8:25. He closed his eyes. His admin assistant had arrived five minutes early as usual. The rampage of paper burying his usually clean desk would bear witness against him, and even worse, the pungent haze. He'd lit up again after quitting three years ago, from total abstinence to chain smoking overnight. She'd probably already smelled his cigarette. Her antennae would be straight up.

The best defense is a good offense. He reached for the Intercom. "Sue, come here right away." The door opened and she stepped in. He ignored the lift in her eyebrows.

"As you can see, I'm buried. The Johnson murder case. The lousy RCMP can't seem to find the guy, and I'll have the public all over me like hounds on a racoon till I have a conviction. Everything else must wait. Hold my calls and reschedule my appointments a week out."

When her jaw dropped an inch, he stuck up an index finger. "Call the Idaho State Police. Get Greg Barlow on the phone, the officer on the Johnson murder." He looked at his desk. "Also, bring me the record of my conversations with the US attorney in Coeur d'Alene and the Department of International Affairs in Justice in DC."

She melted back into her office, silent as a chastened puppy.

"I need an update from the RCMP," Malone demanded of Barlow after Sue buzzed the call through. "What do those guys have for me?"

Barlow sighed. "Well, Brandon reported late to the job he'd been promised and was fired. From there he disappeared. But they found a friend of his. Waiter at a restaurant in Kamloops, fifty miles from the job Brandon was heading to. He and Brandon graduated from university together. Says he knew Brandon was going up there to manage a ranch. Says he didn't know Brandon had lost the job and no idea what he might do next."

"That's all? That's pathetic. I need more, Barlow."

"I understand. So do I. Fact is, Brandon should have turned around and exited the country when he lost the job.

His work permit restricted him to that job. But we have no indication he's back in the US."

"So that puts him on the police radar for a second charge?"

"Yes. He's in the country illegally. The search is Canada-wide now. I have no doubt they'll pick him up soon, and when they do, the extradition will be quick."

"What about next of kin?"

"We have a call in to his parents, small town in west Texas. Expect I'll hear back soon, and I'll keep you posted."

"Yes, you will." The edge in Malone's voice sharpened. "I need to know everything you know the instant you get it. And I need action. We're sixteen days out from the crime and nothing to show for it. The press is camping outside my office."

"We're doing what we can, Mr. Malone. And of course, I don't need to tell you Johnson himself is still very much a suspect."

"Thank you for saying so. Let me be clear about something. We have no case against Johnson, no motive, no record, nothing. Any talk about Johnson sounds like excuses. I don't want to hear it."

"Do you mean to say you're going to let Johnson walk?"

"Wrong question. You're implying guilt on Johnson's part. I don't prosecute victims, I prosecute criminals."

"So, you've decided Johnson's innocent?"

"Another wrong question. I don't decide innocence or guilt, that's why we have judges and juries. I decide who to prosecute, and I'm not prosecuting Johnson. And I won't abide a law enforcement office that shrugs its investigative duty and takes the easy road. I've got two words for you— find Brandon."

CHAPTER 35

WILD BEASTS PASS THROUGH THE LAND

Grand wilderness, Thursday

Gordon and I climbed steadily, mostly in timber, sometimes breaking out into spacious meadows of grass, now brown where it poked through the deepening snow. Occasionally, the view opened toward the Fraser basin to the east, giving me some scope of our progress higher into the mountains. In the woods, squirrels—much smaller than those in Texas—barked their protest at us intruders. A gray jay followed, flitting from tree to tree, always watching.

We reached Relay Creek late, in the gray of early twilight. The cabin tucked into the timber, facing a broad mountain meadow four hundred yards across where a lone coyote watched us before turning into the dusky forest. The sun was down behind the higher ground to the west, but the snow cover pushed light against the darkening sky.

"You always need to check the condition of these cabin corrals up here," Gordon said as we curried our horses. "Once in a while a moose or bear knocks something loose. If you don't check, you might pay the price. A cowboy got up here late in the evening one time, put his horses in the corral without checking it and went to bed. Next morning, no horses. He walked twenty-six miles in his boots to get home."

"Are we in grizzly country now?"

"We could see grizzly sign any time. But they tend to hang out up higher. Up at Yodel we'll be more in their habitat."

We stowed the curry brushes in a small box next to the cabin's back wall, closed the corral gate and headed to the door for supper and sleep.

"Have you seen a grizzly up here?"

"I have. Last fall we were up here with Holder bear hunting. We baited for grizzlies."

"What does that look like?"

"You put down an old pack horse and wait for bears. Chain it to a tree or a grizzly will drag it deep into the woods where you can't see to shoot. A grizzly will move even a big horse. Mr. Holder said he'd seen a grizzly grab a twelve-hundred-pound horse by the shoulders and sling it over like you'd turn a blanket. That's when you realize how important it is to shoot straight."

I followed Gordon into the cabin and closed the door tightly.

"Did you take a grizzly on that trip?"

"No, we saw him through the woods but never got a shot."

I woke up in the middle of the night. I'd been dreaming about a grizzly devouring a dead horse, chomping and grinding. But now I was awake, and some kind of vermin was gnawing on something under my bed. I shuddered and didn't sleep well the rest of the night.

"Something was in the cabin last night," I said to Gordon over breakfast. "Did you hear it?"

"No, but there's always a pack rat or two hanging around."

"Can't you plug the holes?"

Gordon lifted an eyebrow. "It's just part of life in a line cabin. Does it bother you that much?"

I lifted coffee to my mouth, needed a moment to collect my thoughts. "Call me a wimp if you want," I shrugged, "but I can't stand it."

Gordon coughed all through breakfast, had to interrupt his meal. He stepped outside on the porch, hacking for a spell, before coming back to the table.

Later, we led our horses out of the corral. I swung up and looked across the meadow. "When I have my own place, the cabins will be tight. No rats, no mice."

"When you have your own place?"

"That's my goal. I want to own a ranch somewhere in the mountains. I've been working on that goal a long time."

Gordon mounted without comment, and we started the day's ride. Snow spirits scudded around the horses' feet in the cold breeze, and I pulled my collar tighter.

CHAPTER 36

THE YOUNG WOMAN WAS
VERY ATTRACTIVE IN APPEARANCE

Kamloops, Friday, October 30

Rod Castle grabbed his keys and stepped out on fresh snow. The hills around the town held up leaden skies, a white blanket softened the landscape and muffled the sound of a car passing on the street, its exhaust billowing in the cold.

He needed Heet for his gas tank against the dropping temperatures. While his engine warmed, he wondered aloud. "Cody, where are you, buddy? I hope you're okay."

Three blocks away, he pulled into the Husky station, and lost his concentration, narrowly missing the gas pump. A tall woman about his age, her face framed by long, silky blonde hair, stepped out of a car. A bright green Mazda RX7.

He parked on the other side of the pump, killed the motor, and sat. Was this the same vehicle and driver he'd already seen twice? How many bright green Mazda RX7s could show up in two days of driving? *Find out, Castle. Be cool. Don't come across like an idiot.*

He got out and reached for the gas nozzle. "That's a beautiful car."

"Oh, thanks." Her smile suggested pride of ownership and pleasure at the compliment. "I love this car. And I love driving it."

"I'm sure you do," Rod said, his own smile breaking out. "And I'll bet it goes zoom-zoom down the highway."

The girl laughed. "Oh, yes, that it does. The trick is to avoid the RCMP."

"Not that you would ever have reason to worry about that, though, eh?" He was finding his stride. *Be cool, Castle, be cool.*

The girl feigned offense, eyebrows raised, mouth open, fingers to her chest. "Who, me?" She busied herself with the nozzle.

"Well, I just wondered." Then, "Believe it or not, I saw a car just like that not long ago, traveling here from Winnipeg. Saw it twice, in fact."

Her head jerked toward him, mouth open. "Really? I've been driving from Winnipeg to Vancouver. When did you see it? I wonder if it was me."

"Three weeks ago," Rod said. "I saw it in Saskatchewan and again in Calgary."

"You're kidding. I left Winnipeg about three weeks ago and I've been calling on clients along the way."

"But the car I saw was going so fast it would have been here in about a day."

She laughed again, and Rod had never heard more beautiful music. "That was me, for sure. I love driving fast."

"But why are you just now in Kamloops?"

"I make lots of stops. In fact, I can't always manage to line up my customers in the right order. Sometimes I'm required to backtrack."

"What's your work?"

"I'm a product safety engineer. Medical field. I live in Vancouver and travel between home and Winnipeg a couple of times a year."

"Wow, impressive."

"Not really, just a sales job that requires a BS degree. But I love the job, love the travel, love meeting people."

"And love driving your car."

"Yes. That I do."

A driver in line behind her bumped his horn, and Rod turned. "Oh, my goodness. I've been standing here forgetting what I was doing." He looked down and frowned. Words failed him at the worst times. "It's been nice to talk. I ... I guess I'd better let you go."

"Nice to talk to you too. Have a great day." As she drove away Rod saw the decal on her rear windshield: TAMU. He sprinted to catch up, knocking on her window just before she pulled into the traffic.

"Did you go to A&M?"

"Yes, I did. Why? Do you know an Aggie?"

"Yes, me. Graduated last spring." Rod looked at his watch.

"You're kidding."

"No." Another waiting driver honked his impatience.

"There's less than a hundred Canadians at that school." Her eyes searched his face.

"Yeah, I know, I went to the Canada orientation. Um, listen, do you have time for breakfast? I have an hour before work. Hate to pass an opportunity to get better acquainted with a fellow Aggie." *Especially a beautiful Aggie*.

"Sure. Want to lead me to your favorite place?"

Fifteen minutes later, they sat at the White Spot café.

"I'm Rod Castle."

"Nice to meet you. I'm Linda Adams." They shook across the table. "So, tell me about yourself, Rod. Where are you from?"

"Winnipeg. Born and raised. But I wanted to study veterinary science. That's why A&M."

"And came out here from Winnipeg for a job?"

"That's right. I spent a summer out here and decided as soon as I could I was going to live in BC."

"That's interesting." They gave their orders to the waitress. "Know anyone out here?" she said.

"Funny you would ask that. My best friend came up here from Texas about the same time I got here. We were gonna connect, but I haven't heard from him." Not the time to elaborate.

"Really. Are you worried about him?"

"No, I'm sure he's fine. He's an independent spirit. You know, a Texan. I know I'll hear from him when he's ready to call. He's got my mom's number. He wants to own a ranch someday, and it's a huge priority to him to live in the mountains. Grew up on the high plains, ready for something, uh, rugged. Someplace north, someplace wild. Heard him say that a million times."

"Cool. Sounds a little bit like a friend of mine." Linda picked at her omelet.

"Oh?"

"I graduated high school with a girl who's teaching at a Native school in Wolf Creek. It's a tiny community in the middle of ranching country with plenty of mountains. At least that's how she describes it."

"Never been there?"

"No. I haven't. Someday, but it's an eight-hour drive from Vancouver." She looked out the window and frowned. "I need to call Julie. We haven't talked in a month."

"What about you, Linda? How did you end up at A&M?"

"Long story. Another time, maybe."

In the parking lot, they exchanged phone numbers before Linda jumped in her Mazda and drove off.

Rod slid into his truck. "Bo, I can't wait for you to meet Linda. And you will, old boy. You will." Bo wriggled and whined. He could hardly wait, either.

Wolf Creek, Saturday, October 31

Julie Stewart described her teacherage as cozy. Tiny, with everything within reach. Woodstove, loveseat, small desk, wardrobe, end table, bed, and kitchenette. A small table and two chairs between the woodstove and bed. She had placed rugs and hung family photos and artwork from the coastal Haida tribe.

She sat on her bed and paged through books, making notes. She'd learned the discipline of writing her lesson plan for the coming week before enjoying Saturday brunch.

The phone rang.

"Hey, Julie, it's Linda."

"Oh my goodness. It's been too long. I'm so glad you called." Julie sat back against the headboard. "How are you? Where are you?"

Linda laughed. "I'm fine and just home after another work trip. And I want to hear all about Wolf Creek. But I just met somebody and had to call you."

"Sounds interesting. So, are we talking about a new bosom friend?"

"No, silly, you're my only bosom friend. I met a guy."

"Oh, tell me about him." Julie brightened and sat up. "Where did you meet him?"

"At a gas station in Kamloops, believe it or not. I'd been on the road three weeks, on my way home from Winnipeg. I was filling my tank this morning, and this guy says he had seen me on the highway in Saskatchewan."

"What? I don't understand."

"I must have passed him on Highway 1. I may have been speeding, just a little. And then he said he saw me again in Calgary."

"This is too much, Linda. He saw you in Saskatchewan and again in Calgary?"

"Yes. And then we met in Kamloops. He was really friendly. We stood at the pump and talked for a minute, and when I was pulling out, he saw my TAMU sticker and ran up and knocked on my window. He also graduated from A&M. We went out to breakfast and had a wonderful time."

"Really? Another Aggie?"

"Who would've thought it?"

"Wait, Linda, listen to this. I met a guy recently who's on a ranch near here, and he's an Aggie. He moved up here from Texas to work on a ranch." The phone went quiet. "Linda? Are you still there?"

"Yes. I'm trying to process what you just said. Did I hear you correctly? Someone who came from Texas to work on a ranch?"

"Yes. Why?"

"Because Rod, this guy I met, said he had a friend who came up here from Texas to work on a ranch. But he didn't say anything about him being an Aggie."

"Well, how many Texans would come to BC to work on a ranch?"

"Actually, Rod said his friend wants to have his own ranch eventually."

"Linda, it must be Cody. Cody Brandon is his name. That's his goal, to have his own ranch. I can't believe this. What else did Rod say about him?"

"He called Rod from the border, didn't have all his papers together so he had a little trouble there. Rod said he hadn't heard from his friend after that but figures he must have made it or he would have called Rod's mom in Winnipeg."

"This is crazy. I met Cody, and you met his friend. And they haven't connected since Cody got up here."

"It's amazing. So, tell me about Cody. What's he like?"

"A real gentleman. He's working on a ranch about an hour away, but around here that's practically next door. He came to our Bible study here in Wolf Creek last Sunday, and I expect he'll be there tomorrow."

"I can give you Rod's phone number, and Cody can call him."

"Sure. Wow. This is unbelievable."

"I'll say."

"By the way, you've been saying you're going to come for a visit. So when will that happen?"

Wolf Creek, Sunday, November 1

The Sunday night regulars always enjoyed catching up on each other's news after the Bible study. Julie suspected some only tolerated the study so they could visit afterward. She enjoyed that part of it, too, but tonight she didn't linger.

"Big day tomorrow," she explained as she tugged at her wool coat. "I need to get to bed early." She said good night and stepped out into the crisp village air.

Maybe she would go to bed early, but the truth was she missed Cody. The empty feeling in her chest surprised her. He'd suggested he could pick her up, and she'd anticipated that all week. The prospect of another week without seeing him pressed heavily on her heart.

Could she be making too much of this friendship? *I wish I hadn't been so bubbly with Jessie and Linda.* She felt foolish and small and a little worried.

She had anticipated telling Cody Linda's story about meeting Rod. She'd delayed calling Rod, wanting to tell Cody first.

At her cabin, she tossed her coat on the bed and dialed Rod's number. When he didn't answer, she hung up rather than talk to a machine.

CHAPTER 37

He Knows the Way That I Take

Grand Wilderness, Monday, November 2

We sat our mounts, and Gordon studied the ground while I admired the splendid prospect. The Coast Mountains thrust up before us, north to south as far as one could see, a sawtooth ridge of rocky crests crowned the horizon. From those lofty pinnacles, the landscape cascaded in waves of lesser heights, flanked with timber, and crossed by deep canyons gouged out by icy rivers dashing over ancient boulders.

Here and there, mountain meadows lay under a foot of snow. A massive silence held a million acres in its brutal grip.

After five days of riding, pushing through every copse of pine and combing every mountain meadow, Gordon and I had finally found clear evidence of our prize, sixty miles west, and six thousand feet above, the ranch headquarters.

"They crossed this ridge earlier today," Gordon said between coughs. "Headed higher. Could be we'll see them at Blackwater. If not, you might get a chance to see Poison."

"How many, would you say?"

"Five or six head. About what we're missing. Look there. See their prints running parallel before bunching up here and heading straight for Blackwater?" He doubled over the saddle horn and coughed for half a minute.

"We've got to get you inside."

"Blackwater is about an hour ahead, I can make that."

"Are you sure we should keep pushing? I don't have a good feeling about that cough."

"It sounds nasty. And I'm feeling kinda rough, but I've had these symptoms plenty of times. Two days of rest and hot tea will put me right. And anyway, we've come too far to turn around."

We crossed the ridge and dropped down the other side, coming to a trail into the timber that descended into a deep valley. The haunting wind sang in the trees, and I buttoned my collar.

"So, what's the next step in that dream of yours to own a ranch?"

"I need to spend a year or two cowboying in this country. Need to know the weather and the seasons, how to operate up here." I shook my head. "Never seen country so wild and foreboding. Anyway, if Holder keeps me on, sometime in the spring I'll go to town and find a realtor, start looking at listings. I'm not in a rush—my dad says don't make a premature decision. New information may change the picture."

"Makes sense. Are your parents still alive?"

"They are. Have their own hardware and appliance business. Hope to retire early and travel. Tour Israel, maybe. Mom's eager to visit Scotland, and Dad wants to see the French Alps."

"I've heard they have some amazing panoramas over there," Gordon said, looking down at hoofprints.

An hour of riding brought us to the Blackwater cabin. Our quarry had been here, milled around, and moved on. We put our horses in the corral and went inside. Gordon lay down while I started a fire. I opened a can of stew to set on the stove and fetched water from the creek. The simple, hot meal warmed our bones and we hit the sack. I slept poorly, listening to Gordon coughing.

Tuesday, November 3

Gordon was no better after a bad night. We agreed he would stay put, and I'd go on alone.

"You'll have no trouble following their tracks now. It's a matter of time and work but not complicated."

"Well, I've never been afraid of work," I said, stoking the fire. "As for time, I reckon that'll be determined by how long the grub lasts."

I did not admit to my misgivings but was plenty anxious. Yet I'd told Mr. Holder he wouldn't be sorry for giving me another chance, so I couldn't quit now. The bitter taste of a serious failure back in Texas still ragged at my psyche four years later. The only way to be free of it was to take on an impossible task and see it done.

I was working at a ranch during the summer after high school graduation. The boss sent me to check a pasture fence where he wanted to place cattle. A simple assignment: find and fix any weak spots in the entire perimeter, be sure it was ready for any bovine knot head looking for greener grass.

At the end of a long, hot day, I was tired and ready for a cold drink in an air-conditioned kitchen. But I walked ninety minutes, covered almost the entire fence line, and found no problems. Where the fence went through a dry ditch full of high weeds and prickly pear, I stood at the edge and peered into the thicket. From where I stood everything looked copacetic, and I certainly did not want to wade into it. I went back to the boss, reported all clear, and went home for the day.

The next Friday, we put fifty head of black Angus calves into that pasture. The grass would provide three weeks of grazing.

That night, a family coming home late from a distant Little League game T-boned a thousand-pound steer standing on the road. The ball player's little sister, seven years old, was paralyzed and spent two years in therapy.

I wasn't sure I would ever recover. Add to that the disaster at the Fraser River bridge where my carelessness cost the ranch four heifers. Only one option would serve—I must not fail at an assignment again.

"We've got plenty of food," Gordon said. "There's always grub in these cabins. Just leave me some tea and a few oranges. And haul a little more water from the creek. Everything else I need is already here."

I fetched water and wood, started a fire, and set a kettle on the stove.

"The corral is tight. Anything else?"

"No, I'll be fine, just be careful. Don't forget what Holder said about the grizzlies. They mostly keep to themselves, but you don't want to surprise one. They'll be eating berries and fishing the streams, fattening up before they hibernate."

I opened the door and paused, sobered by the venture before me, a little fearful. *But isn't this what you've always wanted? Besides, your job is at stake.*

"See you in a day or two," I said, and walked alone into the wild.

New snow fell in downy flakes bullied by the whirling mountain winds as I rode higher. The horses' tracks, perfectly obvious even in the deep snow, continued up the trail from Blackwater. Per Gordon's guess, they were headed straight for the last line cabin. Why they called the creek Poison I had not thought to ask.

The trail ascended into thinner woods of shorter trees. Gray clouds pressed down over the higher peaks to the west. The trail took me out of the timber onto a broad plateau, a half mile across. Boulders the size of cars stood proudly, flung by an ancient volcano, I reckoned. The wind increased, whipping the snow, both falling and fallen.

Two hundred yards later, I was back in the woods. I constantly scanned the view from side to side and spoke aloud. "Hey, bear. Hey, bear." I could still hear Gordon, "You don't want to surprise a grizzly." The pans on the pack horse clonked and rattled.

A spruce grouse exploded into flight. I flinched and yelped, and my hand flew to my throat.

Four hours beyond Blackwater, the tracks ended at the Poison Creek line cabin. The horses had nosed around here, not long ago. I unloaded the pack animal, brushed both beasts down, fed them oats, and closed the corral gate.

I laid wood in the stove and lit it, fetched water from the creek, and opened a can of sardines. An old chair on the porch gave me a view of the meadow while I ate, and the stove warmed the cabin. By evening, it would feel pretty good.

Most of the afternoon, I followed horse tracks as they wandered around the woods. The day was pleasant, clear and cool, and the night promised to be cold. I came back to the cabin empty but didn't fret. I had one more trick to lure those horses.

First, though, time for sightseeing.

"A half mile west of the cabin is a great view," Gordon had told me. "Pay attention. You'll come right up to a cliff with a long drop. You can see down into the canyon there. Just be careful, it's a steep plunge."

Twenty minutes later, I was looking over a chasm deep enough to give me the spooks. I had never seen rimrock up close and found it magnificent. The opposite canyon wall resembled a red velvet cake cut through, reddish near the top deepening to chocolate further down, the layers interspersed with the "frosting," thin seams of pale stone. Juniper and sage populated the bottom where a creek meandered, rimmed with ice.

Wanting a better view, I swept snow from the rock with my boots, lay down and hung my head over the edge. The sheer wall dropped at least a hundred feet to a rocky floor dusted with snow, about three times that distance to the rimrock on the other side.

I dropped a stone to watch it fall and heard it smack at the bottom. The light was almost gone when I shoved back and turned around to head to the cabin.

An unmistakable, beastly huff froze me in my tracks, sending a thrill of terror through my gut. Somewhere out there in the gloom, between me and the cabin, a grizzly growled on the hunt.

CHAPTER 38

FROM THE PAW OF THE BEAR

Tuesday, November 3

My heels were ten feet from serious gravity, and a wild grizzly had caught my scent.

My great uncle had been a missionary in the Congo, hunted water buffalo and elephants with his African friends. "Never flee a charging animal," the old man had told me. "They won't run over you. They're bluffing."

He'd delivered that counsel with a conviction born of experience, but would I have the courage to heed it? How could I know if a grizzly would mimic an elephant?

"Dear Father, I'm in big trouble. I need you like never before. Please help me. Please deliver me from the paw of the bear."

For once, I found no comfort in prayer. Black dread smothered my soul, turned my gut to wax.

At that moment, a mountain of hair exploded from the edge of the timber before me less than a football field away, and a roar to shatter rocks turned my heart to ice. The bear raced toward me, and time stopped.

I left my rifle in the cabin. What an idiot.

Gary Brumbelow

I'm not going to own a ranch in the mountains. Or marry Julie. Or have a family.

Am I dreaming?

Mom and Dad will take this hard. Wish I'd called home.

Nobody will even miss me for at least three days.

What's he so mad about?

I should have been a better brother to Jerry. I wonder what he's doing right now?

What does it feel like to die?

The grizzly covered two hundred feet in seconds, roaring and snapping his jaws. Great gobs of spit flew from his mouth. The capricious mountain wind turned, washing me with his rank stink.

Death rushed to me as I stood in horror. I found voice for three words, "Jesus, help me."

In that instant, two things happened. I glanced down, spied a baseball-sized rock at my feet and snatched it. The beast stopped ten feet away and rose on his hind legs, towering above me like Goliath over David. He bellowed his rage, the terrifying bawl shaking the very landscape, and raised an arm for the blow that would either slash me open or crush my bones. One sweep of that deadly paw could kill me outright.

The bear stepped toward me, chomping and bellowing with a dreadful furor. From my brain, paralyzed by terror, came one vivid thought—this eight-hundred pound killing machine had one vulnerable spot. I hurled the rock at his nose and cried, "Jesus."

The missile struck its target, the mighty beast shrieked a horrible cry of agony, and collapsed. A subdued moan escaped its maw, and it lay still.

Surreal quiet descended over the scene. My heart thudded rapidly, and my lungs burned, chest churned in a turbulent mix of agitation, fear, and hope. I was beset with a trembling I could not stop, felt light-headed, ready to faint.

I gawked at the fallen monster before me. Was he dead or only stunned? I did not know, but resolved to put maximum distance between us.

A deep breath restored function to my quivering limbs, and I mustered my wits and ran. I fled like a deer before the hounds, heedless of fatigue, impelled by deadly fear, the crash of my boots in the undergrowth and the noise of my labored breathing the only sounds in the universe.

At the timber's edge where the grizzly had first emerged, I stopped and turned. Finding a climbable tree might be wiser than running for the cabin.

From this distance, the mass of fur seemed unmoving. I watched and counted to sixty, then turned to resume my escape, still trembling in body, but calmer now in mind and heart, and slower in pace.

CHAPTER 39

EVERYONE IS LOOKING FOR YOU

Kamloops, Tuesday, November 3

Rod got home from work Tuesday evening to find a message on his phone.

"Hi, Rod, my name is Julie Stewart. We haven't met but we have a mutual friend, Linda Adams. She gave me your number. I'm calling because I met someone you may know. Call me back, please."

He replayed the message and dialed.

"Hi, this is Julie."

"This is Rod Castle. You left a message on my phone."

"Yes. Hi, Rod. I got your name from Linda Adams. She said she met you recently."

"Ah, yes. My fellow Aggie at the gas station."

"Yes. She enjoyed meeting you."

"Me too. It was mutual. And she told me about you—you're teaching at a reserve, is that right?"

"Yes. I'm in Wolf Creek."

"Where's that?"

"A long way off the beaten track. Between Clinton and Williams Lake."

"Okay. I kind of get that."

"Anyway, I met someone you may know. Cody Brandon?"

Rod gasped. "Cody Brandon? Do I know him? My best friend I haven't heard from for weeks? Why do you ask?" The questions tumbled out like Legos from an upended toy box.

"I met him last month."

"What? You've seen Cody?"

"Yes. He's working at Grand Valley Ranch, about an hour from here. I met him at the local store three weeks ago. He was on his way to take a job at Grand. He came to a Sunday night Bible study about ten days ago."

"I'm so glad to hear this. I really need to talk to him. Do you have his phone number?"

"Well, sort of. The only phone on the place is in the rancher's house, but they would probably take a message. I've got it right here."

"Did he say anything about his plans?"

"His long-term plans to buy a ranch, yes."

"No, I meant more immediate plans."

"No. I thought I would see him Sunday. Don't know what happened, but I hope to see him this weekend."

"Well, I'm going to try to call his boss. But if you see him, would you please give him my number and tell him to call me as soon as he can?"

"Sure thing."

Rod hung up and dialed. The phone rang eight times and he moved to hang up, when someone answered.

"This is Tom Holder."

"Mr. Holder, my name is Rod Castle, and I just heard that my friend Cody Brandon may be working for you."

"Yes, that's right."

"Well," he cleared his throat. "I'm sorry to bother you but would it be possible to talk to him?"

"It would be possible if he were here, but he's away on a long ride."

"Oh, I see. When will he be back?"

"Hard to say. They've been gone a week. Could be back tomorrow, could be several more days."

"Oh, okay." Rod blew through pursed lips. "It's really urgent that I talk to him as soon as possible. I have some important information he needs."

"Well, give me your number and I'll tell him as soon as I see him."

Coeur d'Alene

Frank's fingers trembled. He had trouble reading the phone number in the clipping he'd just cut from the classifieds. "In crisis? Call for free counselling. All calls private and confidential."

"Gotta do this. It'll be okay. Just need to process with someone." Persuaded by his self-talk, he dialed. Someone picked up on the second ring.

"Free crisis line. This is James. How can I be of help?"

"I ... I need to talk to someone."

"Okay. You've called the right place. My name is James. Can I ask your name."

Caught unprepared, he blurted out his middle name. "Joseph."

"Hi, Joseph. I'm so glad you called. What can you tell me about your situation? Having trouble?"

"It's not me. I'm calling for someone else. I have a friend of mine who's in trouble."

"Okay. Do you want to give him this number?"

"I did. He doesn't want to call. So, I thought I might be able to help him by calling for him."

"Well, that's very kind of you. We can talk. But there's really no substitute for a direct conversation. Does that make sense?"

"Yeah." He paused. "But like I said, he doesn't want to call."

"Can you tell me about his problem?"

"It's not good. He's feeling guilty. He did something pretty bad."

"Okay. And he's talked to you about this?"

"A little. I don't really know for sure what he did."

"Has your friend struggled with guilty feelings before?"

"Not like this. No. I think he could be in big trouble."

"Like, in trouble with the law?"

"Could be."

"Did he hurt someone?"

"I'm pretty sure he did?"

"Is anyone else in danger?"

"No, he'd never hurt anyone."

"But didn't you just say he did hurt someone?"

"I mean, he'd never hurt anyone else."

"How can you be sure? It sounds like your friend needs help. It's good you're reaching out. But for all you know, he could hurt someone else."

"I doubt it."

"How badly did he hurt the person?"

Frank closed his eyes and hung up.

CHAPTER 40

THE WONDERS GOD HAS DONE FOR ME

Poison Creek

On the hike back to the cabin, I studied the trees and rocks, peered at the snow, stared at the darkening sky. Everything looked the same as before, yet different.

As my pulse returned to normal, my heart rose in thanksgiving to the One who made stones and muscles, minds, and nerves. I knew who had providentially directed my life for this day.

It was God who predisposed me as a toddler to chuck a ball. I'd heard Dad many times relate his astonishment at my early talent, throwing with remarkable force and uncanny accuracy as a young boy.

It was God who placed me in a community with a Little League coach known all over the Texas Panhandle for his skill at teaching.

It was God who had sovereignly put the joy of baseball in my heart, and led me to apply for that scholarship at A&M. He had made a space for me on the team, enabled me to throw fifty-thousand pitches in four years of college, honing that skill to a fine edge.

It was God who placed that stone of just the right shape and size at that very spot, God who directed my steps there, God who prompted me to look down at the very last second and see it.

Who sent the grizzly? God? Or the devil? The more I thought on it, the more I figured God at least had a hand in it. My pastor had said "The devil is God's devil. He can't do anything without God's permission."

The devil tried to destroy me, God permitted it, and then made a mockery of the devil.

I wasn't enough of a theologian to say, but I knew this— God had delivered me from the paw of the bear. I replayed the moment of salvation over and over. I'd sometimes wondered what it would be like to face death. Now, on this side of the experience, I knew I would never be the same.

Back at the cabin, I added water to a pot of oats and set it on the stove. Famished, I opened a can of stew and devoured it at room temperature, then put my horses in the lean-to. Back inside, I stirred sweet molasses into the oats and brought out the steaming pot to set on the ground in the corral, gate open, and went to bed.

Wednesday, November 4

The next morning, I started back down the trail toward home, leading my pack animal. Strung behind him were five horses who'd been waiting in the corral for more dessert when I got up.

At Blackwater, I found Gordon improved. But we stayed another night, for good measure, and headed out the next morning, arriving back home Saturday just after dark.

I'd grown older by much more than eleven days. The long hours of riding, the robust work of seeking lost mounts in rugged high country, the mentoring by a veteran cowboy—all these comprised at least a year's worth of maturing. This was truly life abundant. I knew I'd found my calling.

But defeating the deadly beast easily eclipsed everything else. That tale would endure. If Jesus tarried so long, my great-grandchildren would tell the generations to come how God and Cody Brandon, together, had despoiled an enemy's scheme to kill and destroy.

And I was a different man. That moment of terror, crowned by an unlikely triumph, had changed me. A new sobriety, a sense of the gravity of life, settled in my heart. I'd always been a fun-loving guy. People who didn't know my serious side sometimes labelled me the class clown.

Nobody would say that ever again. No more Mr. Entertainment. He was dead. Cody Brandon, the man, had replaced him.

And maybe it was time to start thinking about marriage. Maybe God was leading me to get better acquainted with Julie Stewart.

If that's what you're saying, Lord, I'm listening.

Grand Valley, Sunday, November 8

Early Sunday morning I found Gordon and Mr. Holder at the corral.

"Well, I see you found our strays, boys. Good for you."

Gordon filled Holder in on the story up to Blackwater, I finished from there. Holder listened without interrupting.

"Well, I thought I'd heard all the stories of grizzly kills, but that's a new one, Cody." He paused a long moment and looked west to the hills. "Good to have you guys safely back."

He turned to go, then stopped and turned back. "Oh yes, almost forgot. Cody, your friend Rod Castle called. He left his number and wants you to call him, said it's important. Stop by to use the phone whenever you're ready."

"Rod? Really? When did he call? Did he say where he was? Or why he called?"

"He called Tuesday. Didn't say where he was, or what he wanted, just that he had some important information. I told him I'd give you the message when you got back."

CHAPTER 41

THEY HAVE HEARD BAD NEWS

Grand Valley, Sunday, November 8

Ten minutes later, I was sitting in an alcove beside the Holders' kitchen dialing Rod's number.

"Hello."

"Rod."

"Cody. Boy is it ever good to hear your voice."

"I was gonna say the same thing. How did you track me down here?"

"Long story. I met a girl who knows someone you know, but that will need to wait. We've got lots to catch up on, but I have an important reason for calling you."

"What's going on, Rod? Mr. Holder said you had something urgent."

"Yes, I do." He paused, then pressed on. "Brother, I assume you don't know it, but the RCMP is looking for you."

"What?" I lowered my voice, my mind racing. "The RCMP? Something must be wrong back home."

"No, it's not about your folks. It's about you."

"What do you mean?"

"Well, I don't know how to say this, and I don't understand it." Another pause. "But they said they wanted to talk to you about a murder in Idaho."

I stood. "What are you talking about, Rod? This sounds crazy."

"I know. It's bizarre, man. That's all I can say."

"When did they tell you this?"

"Two weeks ago tomorrow. I got home from work and a cop was waiting for me."

"What else did he say?"

"He said there was 'compelling evidence,'—those were his words, to put you at the scene of a homicide. He wanted to know if I could think of any reason why such evidence would exist. That's what the cop told me. Does any of that make sense to you?"

"Evidence that put me at the scene of a murder? I have no idea what that could be." I squeezed the phone cord in my fist.

"That's what I figured you'd say. They must have made a mistake, eh?"

"What else could it be? How could there be any evidence that I was at the scene of a murder?"

"Did anything unusual happen while you were in Idaho?"

"Not that I remember. The only time I even thought about the police was when I abandoned my truck, and that was in BC. My motor blew up, and I pushed the truck off into the bushes to get it out of sight. I wondered at the time if I should call the police. But anyway, that was in BC. I was in Idaho overnight, hardly saw anybody. I don't get this. I don't know what to make of it."

"Well, doggone it, I'm so sorry. I hate to be the bearer of bad news."

"Not your fault, Rod. In fact, if I had to hear it, it's better to hear it from a friend." I shook my head. "But how did the police know that you knew me?"

"That was crazy. My vet job is part-time, and I'm moonlighting as a waiter. I overheard a customer say something about firing a young man who'd come up from Texas to take a job on his ranch. I asked him if it was you and he said yes."

"Wow. That was Chuck Harper, Double Bar Ranch."

"If you say so, I never heard his name. Anyway, the police had already contacted him and said to call with any further information, so he told them where to find me. The constable that interviewed me said to call him if I got any information about you. But I wanted to call you instead. Not sure if I'll be in trouble or not."

"I really want to talk, Rod. We've got more to talk about later. I wouldn't be able to concentrate anyway."

"Sure. I'm in Kamloops. Working at a vet clinic and waiting tables. You've got my number now, call me any time."

I hung up and sat, confused, rubbing my head, trying to think. *What's the next step here?* I needed to call home. *Should I find Mr. Holder and ask permission to make another call?* I didn't feel free to wander around the boss's house looking for him.

My forehead wrinkled and I dialed.

"Hello?" At the sound of Mom's voice, I stood.

"Hi, Mom."

"Oh, Cody." She immediately sobbed. "Are you okay, sweetie? I thought you would never call. Oh, Cody. Thank you, Father. Thank you, thank you, thank you. Hold on a minute. Honey, it's Cody."

Dad picked up. "Cody, it's so good to hear from you, Son." My chin quivered; tears came.

"Oh, Mom and Dad, I feel so bad. I'm okay, I'm just so sorry I put y'all through this. I should never have made y'all wait all this time to hear from me. I'm so sorry, I haven't been anywhere near a phone for ten or eleven days or I would have called sooner."

"Well, we're talking to you now," Dad said. "That's all that matters. Are you okay?"

"I'm fine. Well, I've *been* fine. I'm working on a ranch, and it's been a good fit for me. Much to tell you, but I just talked to Rod Castle, my A&M friend. Do you remember him, from Winnipeg?"

"Of course, we remember Rod," Mom said. "You brought him here a number of times."

"I knew he was from Canada but didn't remember where," Dad added.

"Well, anyway, he moved to BC, to a town a couple of hours from here to take a job. I hadn't seen him or talked to him since I got here, but he tracked me down and told me something crazy. Just now. He said the police want to talk to me. At first, I was afraid there might be bad news from home, but he said it's about something in Idaho."

"Well, that fits with a call we got here, too," Dad said. "The Idaho police are looking for you. Your mama was already worried sick, and it didn't help to get that call."

"Oh, man, I can't believe it. They called you, too?"

"They did. We've been genuinely concerned for you. Did something happen in Idaho?"

I took off my cap and scratched my head. "I'd need to think about it. So much has happened it seems like years since I was in Idaho."

"Just talk to us, Cody," Mom said. "We've waited so long to hear from you. You might recall something while you tell us your news."

"Well, okay." I sat down. "I got to the border about three hours after I called you from Idaho. It took a little time at the border, but I got through. Then in southern BC the motor on my truck blew up and I had to hitchhike into town and buy another one."

"Doggone it, Cody." My dad jumped in. "That's Mike's fault."

"Well, doesn't matter now. Replacing the truck set me back several hours, so I was late getting to the ranch in Cache Creek and lost the job."

"You lost the job?" Mom interrupted.

"Yes, can you believe it? The guy said I should never have started off in such an old truck. He needed someone he could count on."

"What did you do?" Dad said.

"Got back in the truck and kept driving, headed north. Found a place in the woods to pray and met a guy hunting. He told me about this ranch, and the Lord provided a job here.

"I'm at the Grand Valley Ranch, way out in the middle of nowhere and just got back from a ride up into the mountains to find some horses. We were gone eleven days, and as soon as we got back, the boss said Rod had called. I don't even know how he found out where I was. Said he talked to someone who knew I was here. Anyway, as soon as Rod said the RCMP wanted to talk to me, I hung up and called you."

Mom spoke. "Cody, you don't know what it means to hear your voice and find out you're okay, Son. In my heart I was so afraid something terrible had happened to you."

"I'm so sorry, Mom." *And something terrible did happen, which I'm not going to tell you about right now.* "But I'm just fine. Except I need to figure out why the police want to talk to me. I really want to talk to you, but I've had this phone tied up, and I'm a little nervous about it. This is the only phone on the place, in the Holders' house. They let us use it, but I don't want to abuse the privilege. Plus, I need to call the RCMP."

"Sure," Dad said. "Now that we've heard from you, we can rest better."

"But please call back soon," Mom added.

"As soon as I know something about this Idaho thing. Oh, and take this number down. I'm never in this house, but you can always leave a message."

I hung up and sat in silence. I needed to straighten the clutter in my head. I couldn't just call the police without talking to Holder first. More than anything I needed to pray.

I stood and walked quietly through the kitchen toward the back door, not sure whether I should speak my thanks aloud. No other room was visible from where I stood, but as I opened the door to leave, I caught the sound of Holder's voice and felt free to speak up.

"Thanks for letting me use the phone. I wrote the numbers on the pad."

"Hold on, Cody." Holder's voice floated into the kitchen. "We need to talk." The rancher came into the room and pulled a chair from the table. "Have a seat, son."

I sat down opposite my boss. Without his cap, Holder looked old—had to be crowding forty.

"I told you this assignment would determine your future on the place. So, we need to close the loop on that."

"Okay." *Be still my heart.*

"You did an excellent job up there, all by yourself when the crunch came. You've redeemed your reputation with me. The job is yours."

"Oh, thank you, Mr. Holder."

"No more probation. You'll make more mistakes, we all do. But I can see what you're made of, and I'm happy to keep you on."

"Thanks, Mr. Holder. I really appreciate that." I glanced down at the table for a moment, took a deep breath and looked directly at him. "But I need to tell you about something I just heard from Rod."

"Sure thing. What's that?"

"I don't know how to say this, and I don't know what it's about, but he said the police are looking for me."

"Oh?" Holder's eyebrows lifted, the first indication of surprise I'd seen from the rancher in the three weeks I'd known him.

"Yes, sir. I don't even know how Rod found out where I was, but the RCMP talked to him two weeks ago. Said they want to speak to me about something that happened in Idaho. I don't know what it was, we didn't even talk after he told me that. I hung up and called my folks in Texas. They said the Idaho police had called them. Something's wrong, and I can hardly think about anything else until I know what's going on." I couldn't bring myself to say "homicide." They had to be mistaken about that.

"Well, sure, anybody would feel that way. We're just reading in the living room. Feel free to use the phone as much as you need. Let me know what you find out."

"Yes, sir, I sure will."

Back at the phone, I found the number for the Williams Lake RCMP office and phoned.

"You've reached the Williams Lake detachment of the RCMP. Our business office is currently closed. If you are reporting an emergency, please hang up and dial 911. Otherwise, please leave a message after the tone."

"My name is Cody Brandon. My friend Rod Castle just told me the RCMP wants to talk to me. I'm at the Grand Valley Ranch. 800-555-1212."

CHAPTER 42

MUCH MORE TO SAY TO YOU

Monday, November 9

Dawn was straining to defeat the dark as I drove out of Grand Valley just after seven o'clock Monday morning. Low, bulging clouds spit heavy flakes. I was anxious to meet with the police to solve this mystery, and Williams Lake was two hours north on dry roads. Three inches of new snow would double the time. But no matter, I was going to stop in Wolf Creek. I had to see Julie. Whether I should tell her the bear story I wasn't sure. Would have to play that part by ear. But as for the change wrought in my heart, no question. She needed to know my true feelings for her.

Hopefully her school schedule would allow time to talk.

But what would she think about my news? I suspected she felt something for me, but we'd only talked twice. She was probably wondering why I'd missed two Bible studies.

Would the relationship survive my news? Or would she back away like a fox from a porcupine?

Then again, maybe I shouldn't hurry to tell her. Clearly, somebody in Idaho had made a mistake. If so, better to tell her on the other side of the interview. It could even be a fun story to share, a can-you-believe-that-happened moment.

Gary Brumbelow

But what if it wasn't so easily resolved? What if I had to leave the country suddenly without the opportunity to tell her? That would surely be the end of our relationship.

"Father, please help me. Please show me what I should say to Julie."

Nobody else was on the road all the way to the Fraser River bridge. Ice cakes formed on the river, slowly bumping into each other to form perfect circles. My truck slipped here and there climbing Wolf Creek Mountain, but I managed it without having to chain up. Coming down the steeper eastern side into the village I braked carefully, slid a couple of times but stayed on the road.

Julie's teacherage revealed dim light inside. So far, so good.

My headlights swept across her window, and she looked out. My foot was on the bottom step of the stoop when the door opened.

"Hello, Cody. Good to see you."

"Hi, Julie. Nice to see you too."

"I wasn't expecting you. How are you?"

"I'm mostly fine. On my way to Williams Lake and thought I would stop by for a minute. I was hoping to catch you before your school day started."

"Actually, the power is out in the village. They called for an electrician, and I'm free until the lights are back on. So I have time. I'm glad you stopped, let me get my coat."

I stood in the open doorway while she wrapped herself in a heavy coat, hat and scarf, and pulled on bunny boots, the oversized, white footwear famous for their warmth.

"Looks like you're outfitted for the weather," I said.

"I love the snow and cold," she said as she came back to the door. "I can't look out at a new snow without my heart taking a leap."

She was as beautiful as I remembered, even more beautiful. Men had fought wars, armies had perished over women of inferior loveliness, I was sure.

We walked toward the village. Every roof wore a thick white blanket. Smoke rose from every stovepipe, children played in the snow. I almost forgot my troubles.

"So did you hear from your friend Rod?"

"Yes. Are you the one he was talking about?"

"What do you mean?" Julie cocked her pretty head.

"He called me yesterday. I had to get off the phone before he finished, so I don't know how he got my number. He just said he'd met a girl who knew someone who knew me. I never heard the rest of the story."

"Well, I can tell you." She smiled and I bit my lip. "You remember I told you about my friend Linda who graduated from A&M? The one who drives fast?"

"I remember."

"Well, believe it or not, they met." She related the serendipitous encounter at the Husky station in Kamloops. "Linda was so amazed to meet a fellow Canadian Aggie. They went out for breakfast. He said he'd recently moved to BC from Winnipeg, and the only person he knew out here was a friend who'd come up from Texas to ranch in the mountains. Wanted to live in a remote area. She said she had a friend who was teaching in a little community in ranching country. They hit it off and exchanged phone numbers.

"Linda called me the next day and told me about Rod and what he said. I knew it had to be you. She gave me his number, I called him, and voila, the connection was made. That's how he got your number—from me."

I gaped. "What? So, let me be sure I have this straight. Rod met Linda. He mentioned me without naming me. She mentioned you without naming you. Linda called you, told you the story, and you knew he had to be talking about me."

"That's it. So I called Rod and gave him your number." We stepped out of the road for a moment for a passing vehicle and resumed our walk before I responded.

"That's amazing. The providence of God, I reckon. By the way, reckon you could give me your number?"

"Well, let me think." She closed her eyes and put a finger to her temple. "Okay. I guess I'm ready to do that." With a big smile, she pulled a paper from her coat pocket. "Oh, how about that. It's right here." She handed it to me.

"Thank you, Julie. As we say in Texas, I'm much obliged."

"We missed you at Bible study two Sundays in a row," Julie said. She looked up with a smile that invited, without demanding, an explanation.

"I wanted to be here, believe me. The boss sent me and another cowboy on an errand up into the high country to find some stray horses. Had to go all the way to the last cabin before we found them and didn't get back till late Saturday. Took eleven days." *Should I tell her why I missed the study last night, that I was too overwhelmed by the news I'd received that morning to go anywhere?*

"Oh, wow. Sounds like quite the adventure."

"It was, Julie. I loved it, almost all of it." I told her about the splendid scenery, about Gordon getting sick, and going on alone, seeing the canyon.

I wasn't sure how much to say about the bear, didn't want to sound dramatic. But I was pretty sure I was falling in love with this girl. *Maybe I should tell her. Especially since I'm not sure I should tell her about the RCMP story.*

"There was some part you didn't love?"

"I reckon you could say that." I related the bear tale, detailing every part of the terrifying incident.

I got so caught up in the story I forgot my manners. "Oh, Julie. What am I doing? I'm sorry, I've been going on and on. I guess I just got lost telling the story. What a horrible bore."

"No." She turned to look directly into my eyes, touched my arm and spoke quietly. "No, you're not a bore. I want to hear this. I want to know about your life, and this story is anything but boring." She paused and spoke again. "If I had found out later that you hadn't told me, I would be hurt."

I silently thanked God for providing the sign I'd asked for, breathed deeply, and plunged in.

"Well, since you say that, here's the bigger news." I bit my lip, looked down at the snow and heaved a sigh before continuing. "Julie." We faced each other and she searched my eyes. "I, uh, that is, well, here it is." I hesitated once more. "Rod told me the RCMP is looking for me." I paused and studied her face but couldn't tell if I was seeing fear, confusion, or rejection.

"What's it about?"

I sighed again. "I'm not sure how much I should say." I looked off in the distance, tried to collect my thoughts, reconcile my mixed feelings. My heart rode a tidal wave of desire, captured by such beauty, yet my gut was a roiling black pit of dread.

"You don't need to say anything, Cody." She winced. "I care about you. I'm willing to keep a confidence if you want. But I'm not going to pressure you to tell me anything."

I took her mittened hands in mine. "I have so much to say to you. I feel like Jesus talking to his disciples in the upper room. Remember? 'I have so much more to say to you, more than you can now bear.'"

She shocked me with a big smile. "More than I can bear? As in grizzly bear?"

We laughed together. Relief from the humor soothed my soul.

"Touché. I owe you one after that, Julie."

"I'll be expecting it." She smiled again. "But anyway, yes, I do know that passage. But I would rather try to carry it than be left wondering."

"Okay, here goes. First of all, I've thought about you a lot since we met. I enjoy being with you, and I really want to get to know you."

"Okay. I'm good with that."

"Okay, here's the hard part. Rod told me that the RCMP want to talk to me about something that happened in Idaho. Not just something, a murder. He said they told him they have compelling evidence I was at the scene of a murder."

She squinted. "What? What happened? I ... I don't understand, Cody."

"Me neither. I can't think of what this could be. I was only in Idaho overnight and nothing happened, nothing that could explain that."

"But how did the police find Rod?"

"That's another unbelievable piece of the story. Rod was waiting tables when he overheard a customer talking about firing someone who'd come from Texas to work on his ranch. Rod asked this guy if he was talking about me, and of course, he was.

"He's the rancher that fired me when I got there late after my truck blew up. The police got his name from the immigration office. They'd already been to see him and told him to call if he had further information. He must've called the police and described Rod, and they tracked him down at the restaurant where he's moonlighting."

After a long moment, Julie broke the silence. "What are you thinking about this? What are you feeling?"

I shook my head. "I'm still processing it, don't know what to think. Except that somebody must've made a mistake. But I also called my folks, and they said the Idaho police had phoned. They're looking for me too."

"Want to tell me everything you can remember?" She tilted her lovely head, raised her gorgeous eyebrows, and I wanted to kiss her.

"Sure." I released her hands, and we turned to resume our walk. "I was traveling on Interstate 90 through Montana. Got to Coeur d'Alene Idaho late in the afternoon. That's the only town of any size, and I don't remember much about it, didn't even stop.

"I would've crossed into Washington there and gone north, but our neighbor back home had made me promise to see Bishop Lake. It's a couple of hours further north off the main road. I got to a campground after dark, cooked supper, and slept under the stars. I hadn't stretched out since leaving home almost twenty-four hours earlier."

"You left home that late in the day?"

"I did. I was ready to go and too excited to sleep."

She nodded.

"Anyway, in the middle of the night, an animal woke me up, and I stayed awake for a long time, and then slept till almost noon. I jumped in the truck and took off. A few miles down the road a guy was stranded, and I helped him push his car out of the way. Got gas in a small town and an hour or two later, I was in Washington. That was it."

"That's crazy. I see what you mean. How could any of that relate to a murder?"

"I sure don't know, but I'm on my way to find out."

"You're going into the RCMP office now?"

"Yes. I phoned last night but their office was closed. Left the ranch phone number on the machine. But this morning, I decided not to wait to hear back. I want to know what this is all about."

We walked, our footsteps scrunching in the snow, two troubled hearts silent for the moment.

"Do you think you'll be in Williams Lake very long?"

"I hope not. Probably not. Somebody's made a mistake, so I'll probably be back through later today."

Julie slipped her hand into my offered arm for the last few steps to her teacherage. I reached to open her door. "Thanks for listening, Julie. It means a lot."

"Here's an idea. How about I invite the Brownings over and we have dinner, just the four of us, at my place?"

"The Brownings?"

"Sure, don't you remember them from the Bible study? A young couple with a baby boy, missionaries at Weedy Lake?"

"Oh, yeah. Sure, that's a great idea. Even if it takes several hours, I can be back here for dinner. What time?"

"How about five?"

"Sure thing. I'm looking forward to it already."

"Me too. Cody. Be careful. I'll be praying."

I drove away with a lighter heart. What a girl. "Thanks, Lord, for introducing me to her. Please allow us to spend more time together."

CHAPTER 43

WHEN YOU HAVE FOUND HIM, BRING ME WORD

Williams Lake, RCMP detachment

Monday morning, RCMP Staff Sergeant Dave Pruitt whistled as he walked into the office. With his butch haircut and beefy frame, he had the classic cop physique that intimidated criminals.

"Good morning, Maggie," he greeted the receptionist. "How are you? How was your weekend?"

"Just fine. At least I got to work on time." She rolled her eyes playfully, tongue in her cheek.

Pruitt looked at the clock. "Had to drop the kids off at school. Claire's not feeling well today."

"I'm sorry to hear that." She pushed a memo at him. "A call came in over the weekend."

He read silently, lips moving. "Is the message still on the machine?"

"Yes, sir, of course. Want to hear it?"

"Please."

She handed him the receiver and punched the buttons. He listened, then went to his desk and called provincial headquarters.

"Major Crime Unit."

"Staff Sergeant Pruitt in Williams Lake. I need to talk to Tremblay." He drummed his thick fingers on the desk while he waited.

"Tremblay."

"Pruitt here, Williams Lake. I just listened to a message from a homicide suspect."

"Name?"

"Cody Brandon."

"What'd he say?"

"He's at a ranch about three hours from here. Said he was told the RCMP wanted to talk to him and left the number."

"Hold on." Pruitt tolerated the Muzak for five minutes.

"Okay. He's in the country without a valid work permit. The border guys have already issued a warrant. I'm going to call them right now. I'm sure they'll send someone to bring him down here, but in any case, you can expect to hear from them.

"In the meantime, you need to send a car to get him. Our friends south of the border are very anxious to get him back. We don't want to take the chance he might run."

Coeur d'Alene, Idaho State Police building

Greg Barlow wanted coffee and a donut. He was reaching for his hat when the phone rang. He checked his watch and picked up the receiver.

"Barlow."

"Officer Barlow this is Superintendent MacDonald, RCMP liaison in the Vancouver headquarters. Our detachment in Williams Lake, about seven hours north of here, has heard from Cody Brandon, and I knew you would want to know."

He dropped into his chair. "You've got that right. What can you tell me?"

"I think you're aware that our Kamloops office found a friend of Brandon's. He told us he didn't know where Brandon was. But about ten days later, he tracked him down and called him, and Brandon called Williams Lake. He'd found a job at a remote ranch three hours from town."

"Okay, so what now?"

"He's in violation of his work permit which restricted him to the job in Cache Creek. When he lost that job, he was supposed to leave the country. He's here illegally. The border security agency has already issued an immigration warrant. They've been alerted to his location and are sending someone to take custody."

"Is he in detention already?"

"No. They have dispatched a car and will arrest him when they arrive at his location, probably about an hour from now."

"Thanks, major. This is good news. Glad to get it."

Barlow hung up and found County Attorney Marc Malone's cellular phone number.

"Malone."

"Mr. Malone this is Greg Barlow, Idaho State Police."

"I know who you are," Malone cut him off. "Tell me you've got something for me."

"As a matter of fact, I do."

Gary Brumbelow

Sleep fled from Frank Johnson like litter in the wind. He finally got up and found the poem. Maybe the mental effort of adding a stanza would do the trick.

> *Joan was the dearest to my heart,*
> *Of all the girls I've known.*
> *And when we finally had to part,*
> *It cut me to the bone.*
> *Joan you were the very best.*
> *I hope you have a splendid rest.*
> *I'm sorry it did not work out.*
> *But be assured I will not pout.*

The murder was four weeks ago. He was tired of the mental games, tired of the pretense of grief. He doodled and decided to take a new direction for this ode to a dead wife.

In a half hour of scribbling and scratching, he'd added four new lines.

> *It's not my fault, you were to blame.*
> *I couldn't live with all the shame.*
> *But now you're gone, and all is well.*
> *So how are things down there in hell?*

CHAPTER 44

THEY HAVE HIDDEN A TRAP FOR ME

Grand Valley, Monday, November 9

Tom Holder, coffee in hand, walked into his living room and saw an RCMP car stop at his gate. Two uniformed constables got out and headed toward the door. Holder stepped out on the porch.

"Good morning, gentlemen." His tone was friendly, his countenance open.

"We're looking for the owner of the ranch. This is Grand Valley, right?"

"That's right. And I'm the owner, Tom Holder."

"I'm Corporal Clark, this is Constable Williams."

"Glad to meet you, gentlemen. How can I be of help?"

"We're looking for a Cody Brandon. We were told he works for you."

"Yes, he does. But he's not here."

"Oh? He phoned the Williams Lake office last night and said he was here."

"And he was. I think he's eager to get this thing straightened out. He left here over an hour ago on his way to see you."

"Really? What was he driving?"

"Sixty-five Chevy pickup. Black."

Clark and Williams exchanged puzzled looks. "We didn't meet a vehicle of that description on the way here. Are you sure he was going to Williams Lake?"

"That's what he said. And he's never given me any reason to doubt his word in the slightest."

The Mounties looked at each other, as if a second mutual stare could clarify things.

"Could you have missed him in Wolf Creek? He may have stopped there."

"Why would he stop there?"

"Who knows?" Tom said.

Clark frowned. "Plate number on his truck?"

Holder shook his head. "Don't know. But I'm confident he's on his way to your office. Sorry you came out here for nothing, but you don't need to worry about losing him. He'll be there before you, I expect."

Holder watched them drive away. When he went back inside, Carrie was standing at the window.

"They came after Cody?"

"They did. Apparently they want him bad."

She sighed. "Tom, I feel so concerned for that young man."

"Me too. He needs our prayers."

They knelt at the love seat opposite the huge stone fireplace where juniper logs were cracking and popping in the flames.

Williams Lake

The trip from Wolf Creek to Williams Lake took eighty-five minutes. I got directions at a service station and found the RCMP headquarters, a single-story brick building. I parked and checked my watch, 11:25.

Inside, I went to the reception window and spoke through the port in the bulletproof glass. The receptionist was a younger version of my mom, groomed to perfection and smiling.

"I'm Cody Brandon. Left a message on the phone last night."

"Oh yes, Mr. Brandon. Please wait a moment." She switched off the speaker and picked up the phone. A forty-something burly man with close-cropped hair and a thin mouth blew through the door to my right about fifteen seconds later. He reached me in two long strides.

"Cody Brandon?"

"Yes, sir."

"Mr. Brandon, I'm Staff Sergeant Pruitt. Please don't be alarmed but I need to frisk you. Strictly routine for anyone who comes beyond this public lobby. Okay?"

"Sure."

"Spread your feet a little, please." The moment was weird, felt like being in a crime show. But the pat-down took less than ten seconds.

"Very good. Can I get you to step this way, please?" He gestured toward the door, held open by a younger officer.

For a split second, I froze. Something didn't seem right. Did they think I was guilty?

But a lifetime of obeying parents, teachers, bosses, and law enforcement kicked in. By default, I trusted legitimate authority, regarded it as an institution from God. *I have nothing to hide, and nothing to fear.* Within a second, I was moving toward the door.

The officers ushered me through a big room into a corridor to a small room on the right, visible through a large window in the hallway. The room was spotless, the table and six chairs gleaming, no window to the outside. A black phone hung from the wall; its coiled handset cord reached the floor.

Pruitt gestured me toward a chair, and I sat. The officers stood, Pruitt across from me and Junior near the door.

Pruitt spoke. "Mr. Brandon, is it correct that you entered Canada a few weeks ago from the US?"

"Yes, sir."

"Do you have on your person the permit that was issued to you at the border?"

"No, sir. It's back at Grand with my things." I looked from one face to the other. "Was I supposed to bring it?"

"I have a faxed copy of it here." He pushed it across the table. My name and birth date appeared at the top. I looked up and opened my mouth, but Pruitt cut me off.

"Mr. Brandon, do you understand the permit authorized you only to work at the Double Bar Ranch in Cache Creek and any other employment was unauthorized?"

"What?"

"Look right here." Pruitt pointed to a list of statements near the bottom. "Read number four."

"Not authorized to work for any employer other than stated." I read aloud and looked at the constable. I bit my lip.

"Sir, you are being arrested for being in Canada without a valid work permit. Do you understand?"

Time, and my heart, stopped. Arrested? I squinted and blinked. This couldn't be happening. I tried to breathe. Arrested? I got fired and found another job and now I'm under arrest? The whole thing was crazy. Panic tore at my brain.

"No, I ... I don't understand. I was told you wanted to talk to me about something that happened in Idaho."

"Mr. Brandon, it is my duty to inform you that you have the right to retain counsel in private without delay. You may call any lawyer you want. There is a twenty-four-hour telephone legal aid service available which provides legal advice without charge. If you wish to contact this legal aid service, I can provide you with the telephone number. Do you understand?"

I pushed the fingers of both hands through my hair. "Can you give me just a minute to think?"

Pruitt nodded.

Was I dreaming? I'd had one brief experience inside a police headquarters, two years ago, for a trivial infraction. That was the closest I'd ever been to this moment.

I mustered my thoughts. "Yes, I think I would like to talk to a lawyer."

"Okay, we'll get the number for you. You are not obliged to say anything, but anything you do say may be given as evidence, do you understand?"

"Yes, sir. I understand."

Pruitt looked at Junior who walked out.

"What happens now?" I said to Pruitt.

"You will be put in a holding cell here overnight. The warrant for your arrest was issued by the Canada Border Security Agency. They are sending someone tomorrow from Vancouver to take custody of you. You will be taken to a detention center at the Vancouver airport while arrangements are made to deport you to the US."

Junior walked in with a paper. "Here's the number of the legal service. Would you like me to dial it for you?"

I nodded, mute with anxiety and shock. The officer dialed and spoke into the phone.

"This is Constable Brown. I have an accused here who would like to talk to a lawyer." He handed the phone to me.

"Hello?"

"Please hold." I waited and descended slowly into smothering fear.

"This is Philip Killingsworth. To whom am I speaking?" After two minutes of conversation, I handed the phone back. "He says he'll be here in about an hour."

"You are allowed one phone call to anyone of your choice on the North American continent. I will dial when you're ready."

"Can I call my parents in Texas?"

Pruitt nodded and stepped out. Junior dialed the number I recited. "You got five minutes."

Mom answered.

"Mom, it's me."

"Oh, I'm so glad you called. We've been wondering how things are turning out for you."

"Not so good. They a ... I'm in ... I just got arrested."

"Oh, no. Oh, Cody. Arrested? Oh sweetie, I feel so far away. What's happening? Why did they arrest you? Did they come to your ranch? Where are you?"

"Okay, Mom, I only have a few minutes. Is Dad around?"

"He's sleeping, Cody. He hasn't been feeling very good. Should I wake him?"

"No, no, it's okay. You can tell him later. Here's the deal. I didn't remember I was supposed to leave the country when I lost that first job. That's why I've been arrested. I'm in a town called Williams Lake. Tomorrow, they'll take me down to Vancouver. I don't know how long I'll be there. Eventually I'll be deported to the US. I don't know exactly what that means. I'm sure I'll be able to call you again from down there."

"Oh, my, this is such a nightmare. I feel so sorry for you."

"I'll be okay. But Mom, can you make a couple of phone calls for me?"

"Sure, Cody. I'm ready to write."

"Okay. Please call Mr. Holder at Grand Valley. And if you could call Rod, and ..." I hesitated. I hadn't told them about Julie, and this wasn't the ideal moment, but I didn't want her to be left in the dark. "I met a girl. Her name is Julie." *Does that cop really need to stand right here*? "Anyway, I would sure like her to know what's happening."

"Of course, sweetheart." I knew her number by heart.

"I don't have Rod's number, but Mr. Holder has it. Or else you'll need to call directory assistance, Rod Castle in Kamloops."

"I love you, Cody. We'll be praying."

"I know. I love you too. Thanks. I gotta go."

Pruitt returned, carrying a clear bag. "Mr. Brandon, please put your watch, any other jewelry, and everything in your pockets in here. This will be secured until you are no longer in the custody of Canadian law enforcement. And hand me your coat." My knees went weak. I had the sensation of falling into a deep, dark hole.

"We'll take you to your cell now and bring you back when your lawyer arrives."

Junior took my elbow and guided me into the hall, through doors, around corners, me moving in a scummy daze. They put me in a tiny windowless cell, a concrete bench and stainless-steel toilet along one wall, said something about mealtime, clanged the door shut, and vanished.

I sat and stared at the floor, alone, helpless, and scared. What would happen to me? Was I about to leave Canada forever? Would I never see Julie again? Or own a mountain ranch?

And what about Idaho? Why had the police officer ignored my question about that?

None of this made any sense.

Then a terrible truth emerged from the murk in my head, a ghost too ghastly to look at but too compelling to ignore. If I got booted from Canada, a quarter million dollars was down the tubes, and without that money, I had no way to buy a ranch. The stipulations on the inheritance were suffocating my dream.

The whole thing would seem impossible to someone who didn't know my grandpa, a sheep in wolves' clothing, with a heart big as Texas and a head like an anvil. At my high school graduation, he'd pounded up to me, an envelope in one meaty fist, Grandma's hand in the other.

"Now, Bud, your grandma and I want to see you get a good start. We've got somethin' here that could make that possible. We done the same thing for your brother and made him promise not to tell. Wanted it to be a surprise for you same as him."

Mute as a rock, I pinched the paper from Grandpa's outstretched hand with a glance at Dad, who winked and smiled. Grandma caught the puzzle on my face and caressed my cheek, "Oh honey, you'll like it." I pulled out the card and squinted at Grandpa's scrawl.

Dear Cody,

We are proud to have you as a grandson and look forward to watching you succeed in your future. We've been mightily blessed and want to share that with you. We've set aside $250,000 in a minor's trust available on your twenty-fourth birthday.

SOMEPLACE NORTH, SOMEPLACE WILD

Congratulations on your high school graduation.
Love,
Grandpa and Grandma

Grandma squeezed Grandpa's arm, he grinned like a kid at Christmas, Mom bit her lip and Dad winked again. I opened my mouth, hoping something appropriate might come out, but Grandpa headed me off.

"Now don't be thinkin' I mean easy livin'. We've worked hard all our lives, and you need to do the same. I figure one way to teach you that is to put two strings on this money. You'll get every dime on your twenty-fourth birthday if you've finished your university program and if you've been at the same job for a year. Otherwise, it will go to charity. I don't cotton to laziness or shiftlessness in a man, and I ain't about to reward either one."

Three weeks later, when a sleeping trucker crossed the center line and sent Grandpa and Grandma to their eternal reward, the stipulations in the minor's trust hardened to stone. Grandpa was gone, and some faceless legal authority controlled the fund.

That was five years ago. Now, eleven months before my twenty-fourth birthday, I sat in a jail cell facing deportation. There was no wiggle room in the condition about working at the same job for a year, no chance to make any appeal, no way to argue the interruption in my employment did not mean I was irresponsible or lazy.

The capital required for a down payment on a ranch would be lost forever.

I couldn't breathe. My entire future was dissolving before my eyes, spilling like sand in an hourglass.

Gary Brumbelow

For the third time in less than a month, a hollow pit opened in my stomach, more consuming than before. I felt myself falling into dark despair.

I dropped to my knees beside the bench and agonized in prayer, pleading for assurance God had not forgotten me. I stood and paced the floor, then sat and rocked. Time stood still. I'd never prayed so hard. I recited Scripture I'd memorized in my teens.

"Be merciful to me, O God, for men hotly pursue me; all day long they press their attack.

My slanderers pursue me all day long; many are attacking me in their pride.

When I am afraid, I will trust in you.

In God, whose word I praise, in God I trust; I will not be afraid. What can mortal man do to me?"

CHAPTER 45

Pray For One Another

Wolf Creek, Monday, November 9

Julie's teacherage, sometimes cluttered but never dirty, sparkled. She'd spent a day free from school preparing for the evening and looking forward to seeing Cody and hosting the Browning couple. She'd made only superficial connection with them in the Sunday Bible studies. How delightful it would be together around her table, especially with Cody beside her.

No word from him yet, but it was only one o'clock. She'd invited the Brownings to arrive at five.

She set a skillet on the stove and put a moose roast on to brown. A student family had gifted her with the roast, and she hoped it would taste good. The sizzle pushed a robust aroma through the little cabin. The phone interrupted her quiet thoughts.

"Hello."

"Is this Julie?" A woman spoke, the voice not familiar.

"Yes."

"Julie, we haven't met, but I'm Cody Brandon's mother. He asked me to call you."

Julie put a hand to her chest against the sudden rise of fear. "Oh, nice to, uh, meet you, over the phone. Is he okay?"

"Well, yes and no. He's okay, he's not hurt. But he's in jail."

"Oh my. Oh, I'm so sorry to hear that." Julie sank to the bed. "He was here earlier today on his way to the police station. What happened?"

She listened as Cody's mom relayed the news.

"He asked me to call you, Julie. He wanted you to hear this sooner rather than later."

"Thank you for calling, Mrs. Brandon," She fingered the phone cord. "It's hard to hear this. If you get a chance to talk to him again, please tell him I'm praying for him." She stood and paced between the stove and the bed. "Do you think he would mind if I shared this at Bible study so others could pray?"

"I know he would want that, Julie. Thanks so much for sharing this burden with us. And now that I have your phone number, I'll keep you up-to-date."

"That's very kind of you, Mrs. Brandon. Thank you so much."

Julie turned the roast over in the pan and sat trembling at her table, head in hands. From that first collision at the village store, she'd enjoyed being around Cody. He was such a gentleman, very mature for a young man, had a great sense of humor. And she could tell he cared for her.

Before now, she would have said she liked Cody a lot, even had affection for him. But the possibility of losing him clarified things—she was falling in love with Cody Brandon.

She knelt by her bed.

"Father, please hear my prayer. I come with a broken heart. Please look on me, Lord, and grant my prayer. Please give Cody courage. If he's anxious, give him peace. Please give him hope. Show him your great power. Father, please give him favor with everyone who has authority to make decisions.

"If he has to leave the country, please give him the opportunity to return. That's probably selfish of me, Lord, but I'm praying from my heart. You led us together, didn't you, Father? Didn't you cause our paths to cross that day at the store? Aren't you the providential God who directs the affairs of your children?

"God, please don't let him slip away. Please protect him, exonerate him in the eyes of the law, and return him to me. For your own glory. For Jesus's sake."

She stood and wiped her eyes. *I'm glad the Brownings are coming.* Being alone this evening would be too hard.

Poor Cody. Alone was exactly what he was experiencing right now.

CHAPTER 46

OPEN TO ME THE GATES

Williams Lake, Tuesday, November 10

If the holding cell had a mirror, I might have frightened myself the next morning. I'd never spent such a miserable night—the thin mattress afforded little cushion on the concrete bench, especially in my current state of mind. Misery and anxiety had ruled, sleep fled away.

The lawyer's news included a glimmer of hope: I would not be charged with a crime and might avoid being deported. A border agent would accompany me to Vancouver by plane where I would stay in a holding facility. I could appeal my deportation and wait weeks for a hearing. If I waived the hearing, I would be set free, but required to leave Canada inside a week.

On the Idaho matter, Killingsworth could shed no light.

Over the long, sleepless night of mourning at the certainty of losing the minor's trust, I had composed a mental list of reflections. I paced three steps forward and back and rehearsed that list for the twentieth time. Tempting as it was to wallow in despair, I strove to exercise mental discipline, to salvage whatever was in reach of my exhausted psyche.

First, I must slow down and pay attention to details. How many times had I told myself that? Like after the Fraser disaster, not even three weeks ago, when I hurried, got sloppy, and cost Mr. Holder four heifers. And almost lost my job.

I should have known about that work permit requirement. If I'd called Immigration from Cache Creek and explained what happened, they might have allowed me to find another job. At the worst, they'd tell me to leave, but I wouldn't be in jail and threatened with forced deportation.

But I wouldn't have met Julie, either. Wasn't sure how to score that one. If this was the only way to meet her, it was worth it. How to recover if I lost her, was another question.

Second, even though I had lost the inheritance, I was not ready to consign my dream to dust. I had decent grounds for an appeal—Canada needed good people to contribute to the welfare of the nation, and that's exactly what I intended to do. A simple oversight on my part did not deserve getting kicked out. Somehow, I would own a ranch in British Columbia. I would pursue Julie, persuade her to marry me. Just had to get through this first and find a way back.

Or was all this nothing more than empty self-talk?

Third, I still have no idea what happened in Idaho that could be described as a murder scene. That's the biggest mystery in this whole story.

The slot on my door opened and a tray slid through. Overcooked oatmeal, but I could've eaten more. At least my appetite was intact.

About an hour later—it was weird being without a watch—my door opened, and Pruitt came in.

"Good morning, Mr. Brandon. Please come with me. You're going to Vancouver."

Vancouver, BC

Three hours later, I was in my new digs at the Canada Border Security Agency, Vancouver, one step closer to leaving the country, my heart heavy with dread as that fate loomed larger every hour.

The RCMP had handed me off to a uniformed CBSA agent at the Williams Lake airport. We landed seventy-five minutes after our departure, and I spent thirty-two hours in the detention facility, thinking while sitting or pacing and sleeping as much as I could.

Wednesday, November 11

Late Wednesday afternoon, I was awakened by a knock. The door opened and two uniformed officers walked in, a woman dressed like the CBSA guy on the plane and a male cop.

"Mr. Brandon, I'm Officer Tobin with the Canada Border Security Agency. This is Constable Green, RCMP. Would you kindly step into the next room?"

The adjoining room was no bigger than my own cell but furnished with a desk flanked by a chair on each side. While Tobin sat and opened a file, Green quickly frisked me and directed me to sit opposite Tobin.

"Mr. Brandon, do you understand why you were arrested?"

"Yes, ma'am."

"This conversation is to determine what happens next. If you want legal representation, we can arrange that. It will add a day or more to the process. Would you like to have a lawyer?"

"Can you tell me a little bit more about what to expect before I decide?"

"Of course. You have two options. If you believe you have been arrested without cause, you can have a hearing in court to establish a final ruling on your immigration status. By law, this hearing must be within thirty days, it usually takes about half that.

"The other option is to waive the right to a hearing and voluntarily exit the country. That process takes about twenty-four hours and gives you seven days to cross the border.

"In either case, you have the right to contact your embassy if you want to talk to someone there."

I almost blurted, *I want to appeal* but surprised myself by remembering the first item on the list. *Slow down. Think things through.*

"I understand that I violated my work permit, I get that. I think I want to appeal, but I have a question."

"Yes?"

"I still want to immigrate to Canada someday. If I appeal and lose, would that affect a future application to come back?"

"Not at all. With reference to a future application, the outcome of either option—appealing or waiving your appeal—is the same, unless the court were to determine that you were treated unfairly."

"What are the chances of that?"

"Well, you are hearing this from a CBSA officer, not a lawyer. But I have reviewed your file, and I would say the chances of that are quite small. In fact, a waiver on your part would likely accrue to your favor in a future application to return."

"If I waive my appeal, how long must I stay out of the country?"

"The process is similar to your original application for a work permit. Right now, from ninety to one hundred eighty days."

With a quarter million dollars at stake, I knew immediately I had to appeal and pray it succeeded. "How do I appeal?"

"If you wish to appeal, I strongly recommend you get a lawyer. If you can demonstrate you can't afford a lawyer, one will be provided."

I assured her that was my situation.

"Very well. If you want a lawyer to be provided, please fill out this form. And these forms are necessary for the appeal." She laid paper and a pen in front of me and waited while I wrote. After I signed, she pulled off a copy of each triplicate, and handed them to me.

"Our office will start the process, and you will be kept informed. You will remain in the custody of the CBSA, not in jail, not under arrest, but not free to go. You have liberty within this facility but are obliged to obey any orders." She stood. "You can expect to hear from an attorney within twenty-four hours. Constable Green will brief you on the rules and expectations of residents in this facility."

She left and Green sat down. "This shouldn't take long. First off, you are allowed two phone calls per day—please sign up in advance for a fifteen-minute slot."

He talked, and I tried to listen.

Coeur d'Alene, Wednesday, November 11

Greg Barlow grabbed the ringing phone, eyes still on his paperwork.

"Barlow."

"Officer Barlow, this is Superintendent MacDonald, RCMP liaison in Vancouver. We spoke Monday. I've got an update on Cody Brandon."

"Okay."

"He was arrested Monday in Williams Lake. Spent the night in jail, was flown down here Tuesday by the Canada Border Security Agency and processed. He claimed his right to a hearing, so he may be here another thirty days, but probably about half that."

"What? You guys can't do that. We need to put him on trial for homicide. I've got a county attorney breathing down my neck. What am I supposed to do with this news?"

"Sorry, that's what our procedures call for."

Barlow swore. "We were hoping for a much quicker extradition."

"I know. But extradition is complicated, as I'm sure you're aware. Don't know about you guys, but up here we're required by law to use the courts."

Barlow sighed through pursed lips. "Same here. I guess it's the best we can expect."

"We will contact you when his appeal process is finished. At that point, he'll be issued a deportation order and given a few days to get his house in order and cross the border. After that, he's all yours. I assume his passport number will be flagged on your national database, and he'll be detained."

"That's assuming his appeal is denied."

"His appeal will be denied." He chuckled. "But you didn't hear me say that."

CHAPTER 47

IN THE MIDDLE OF MY DAYS, I MUST DEPART

Vancouver, Wednesday, November 25

If two weeks in jail could be worse than two weeks in a holding facility, the distinction was lost on me. Time crawled, punctuated by a couple of sessions with the lawyer they assigned me. As the days passed, my hope to return to Grand Valley Ranch, resume the job, and save the inheritance slowly faded like a jet contrail in the wind.

The rules prohibited international phone calls, so any communication with the folks back home had to go through Rod or Julie. As I descended further into a depression, my energy to punch a phone pad dissipated.

As for the hearing, a barely coherent defense and a sleepy judge combined to crush any hope of reversing the deportation order. The entire process almost seemed rigged, but I had no recourse. The gavel dropped, the court intoned "Denied," and in an instant, a quarter million dollars evaporated.

A grim Officer Tobin turned to me. "Here's a document you will need." She pulled a single page from a file and pushed it at me. "Don't lose this. Show it to the border office upon exiting the country.

"You have seven days to cross the border. If you do not produce this document at a border crossing within that time, another warrant will be issued for your arrest, and this time, you'll receive an exclusion order, which effectively prevents your return to Canada for one year."

One year or one month made no difference. The money was gone and my future with it.

They took me back to my room in the holding facility. An hour later, an RCMP constable showed up with my bag of personal effects Pruitt had confiscated two weeks earlier.

Fourteen soul-shriveling days in CBSA custody ended with a failed appeal. I was legally free, emotionally crushed, mentally empty, and materially impoverished—fifty-three dollars in my wallet and seven days to tie up loose ends and get out of Canada.

Outside, I looked around. The airport was less than a mile away, and I wanted exercise. I didn't need a plane, but whatever public transportation I required would probably be found there.

The fifteen-minute walk, longest by far I'd done in three weeks, began to clear my head. I stepped onto the curb in front of the terminal with a new resolve to put behind me, for now, the burden of a lost fortune. Maybe a way forward would appear, I could not say, nor could I envision an alternative route to my dream. But I could see the next step, and the one after that. In such measure I would create a future, God helping me.

I stepped inside, found a phone, and had Rod on the line in five minutes. We'd not spoken in the last week.

"Hey, bro, I'm so glad you called. I've been praying and wondering. What can you tell me? Where are you?"

"I'm at the Vancouver airport, was just released." I sighed and watched the pedestrian traffic. "They turned down my appeal. That's final. I have to leave."

After a moment of quiet, "I hate to hear that, Cody. I'm so sorry. I wish I could do something."

"Just hearing you say that gives me a measure of comfort, Rod. Thanks for being there." I moved over to put space between me and another caller at the next phone. "Anyway, I have seven days to get to Williams Lake, fetch my truck and all my stuff from Grand Valley, and leave the country. I'm guessing the bus to Williams Lake will leave tomorrow, so I'll probably sleep on a bench tonight."

"Then what?"

"All I know is I must go to Coeur d'Alene and clear things up. It's going to be one day at a time for the foreseeable future. But enough about me. You haven't told me anything about your world. The job still going okay?"

"Well, yes. In fact, I believe there's a strong future for me here. Things have been slow lately, but I'm managing. I'm making good tips at the restaurant where I work nights."

"Julie tells me you met her friend Linda."

"Yes. She's a great girl, we really hit it off. I mean, two Aggies from Canada, what are the chances of that?"

"Really. Think you'll see her again?"

"Oh yes, count on it. I'm watching for a twenty-four-hour window to get down there."

"Down where?"

"She lives in Vancouver. Didn't Julie tell you?"

"No, I guess it didn't come up."

"Yeah, she's in Vancouver somewhere, don't know where."

"Listen, Rod. I'd sure like to see you somehow before I have to leave the country."

"That would be great. Let's see, you need to leave by, uh, next Wednesday?"

"I'm shooting for Tuesday, so I have some margin in case of trouble. In fact, given my truck, I may try to leave Monday."

"I could probably swap shifts with someone at the restaurant and get up to Williams Lake."

"To Wolf Creek is more like it, I won't stay in Williams Lake. As soon as I have my truck, I'll be headed for Grand. But we have the Bible study every Sunday night at Wolf Creek. Reckon you could make it for that?"

"I think so. As long as I start back by nine or so, I could get home in time to sleep a bit before work Monday morning."

"Let's try for that, Rod. It would be good to see you, and you could meet Julie."

"Okay. Let's keep in touch."

"And Rod, one more thing. I'm short on cash and need to call my folks. Would you mind calling Julie and explain why I couldn't call and bring her up-to-date?"

"Sure, no problem."

"Thanks. Tell her I hope to see her tomorrow night or Friday."

I got change at the information desk. An international call was a dollar a minute, so I'd have to be efficient.

"Hi, Mom, it's Cody."

"Oh, thanks so much for calling again, son. How are you?"

"Well, I have an answer, even if it's not the one I wanted." I caught her up with the news and related my plans for the next few days. "How's Dad?"

"Well, he's doing okay. Where will you go once you're in the US? You couldn't get here tomorrow, but we'd happily hold off Thanksgiving dinner till you arrived."

"That would be wonderful, but I can't. I'm headed to Coeur d'Alene—going to show up and find out what in the world happened and get it straightened out."

"I'm sure that's the right thing to do, son. I just wish you could come straight home."

"Well, I'm planning to as soon as I'm finished in Idaho. I need to reapply to enter Canada, so I'll be home for a while. A few weeks, I reckon."

"That sounds so wonderful. We could all be together for Christmas."

"That would be good. I haven't seen Jerry since, what, August? Listen, I gotta go, Mom. The international rate is eating me alive. I'll be in touch. Love you."

Wolf Creek

Julie walked into her cabin, dropped an armload of books on the table and picked up the ringing phone.

"Hi, this is Julie."

"Hi, Julie, it's Rod, Cody's friend."

"Yes, Rod, how are you? Have you heard from Cody?"

"Just hung up. He's at the Vancouver airport, short on cash, and asked me to call you and tell you the news."

Julie listened, holding her breath. When Rod said Cody was coming the next day and hoped to see her, she couldn't suppress a "Yesss." *Thank you, Lord.* She surprised herself with this outburst, but it confirmed the feelings for Cody she'd recognized two weeks ago.

"He's planning to sleep in the airport tonight and take the bus to Williams Lake tomorrow."

Something clicked in Julie's head. "Listen, Rod, I'm going to call Linda. I have an idea, but I need to call right now. She may call you real soon."

In fifteen seconds, the girlfriends were on the line.

"Linda, listen, I have a crazy idea." She quickly related Cody's news. "What are you doing right now?"

"Reading. But I'm always ready for an adventure."

"Perfect." She shared her brainstorm, Linda agreed, and they hung up. Five minutes later, a green Mazda raced out of the parking lot at her Richmond apartment complex.

Julie called her parents' home in Langley. When her sister answered, she indulged a tiny moment of chit chat and then told Jessie why she was calling.

"It's a great idea," Jessie said. "Hold on while I check with Mom." She was back in half a minute. "Mom and Dad both think it's a wonderful idea, Julie. I'm so excited."

"Me too. Tell them thanks so much. See you, little sister." She hung up and dialed directory assistance, got the number for the airport information desk, hung up and dialed one more time.

CHAPTER 48

HIS FATHER-IN-LAW PRESSED HIM

Vancouver International Airport

I waited at the information desk while the agent spoke on the phone. The man's tightly wrapped scarlet turban set off his sculpted features and bronzed skin. He hung up and turned to me.

"I apologize for the delay. How can I help you?"

"Can you tell me how to take public transportation to Williams Lake?"

"Of course. You can purchase a ticket for the shuttle to a bus terminal downtown. The fare is sixteen dollars." He consulted a schedule on his desk. "From there, you can catch a bus to Williams Lake. That fare is twenty-five dollars."

"What's the schedule for the shuttle to town?"

"It leaves every hour on the hour. But the next bus to Williams Lake leaves tomorrow at 4:50 a.m."

My hunch was right, another night on a bench. But wood is softer than concrete.

"And where do I buy the ticket for the shuttle?"

He pointed. "Walk that way until you come to the sign for transportation to the city. Turn right there and go to the end of the walkway."

Halfway to the shuttle desk I heard my name on the PA system.

"Cody Brandon, Cody Brandon, please pick up a white courtesy phone. Cody Brandon, go to a white courtesy phone."

I spotted an old man with a mop and asked, "Can you tell me where I can find a courtesy phone?" He pointed without smiling across the busy terminal. I weaved through a crowd of arriving passengers to pick up the phone.

"This is Cody."

"Oh, Cody, it is so good to hear your voice."

"Oh, hey, Julie. I'm sorry I didn't call you myself, I just ..."

"I understand, Cody, no problem, we can talk later. I need to tell you something."

Two minutes later, I was at the arrivals curb watching for a bright green Mazda RX7. After a short wait I spotted it, weaving around traffic like a coyote darting through inattentive sheep. When it pulled to the curb and the driver stepped out, I could see why Rod was attracted to this young woman. She stood behind her open door and spoke.

"You look like Julie's description of Cody Brandon."

"That's right. And you must be Linda."

"Yes, Linda Adams."

"Real nice to meet you."

"You too. Ready to go?"

I climbed in and she pulled into the terminal traffic creeping at a sloth's pace.

"Thanks for picking me up, Linda. Sorry to meet you under these circumstances. This all happened so fast."

"You're welcome. Glad to help. Glad I was available."

"You must live near the airport."

"Ten minutes away."

"And a fellow Aggie, I understand."

"Yes. We need to start a BC Aggie's club or something." She scanned her mirror for the slightest opportunity to maneuver left into the fast lane. I was impressed with her handling of the five-speed stick, the wheel, and the accelerator. She was clearly at home.

"So, Rod told me about how you two met."

"Isn't that a scream? And then to find out that you knew Julie. It was too much."

"So how do you know Julie?"

"We met in school, both grew up in Langley, went to different middle schools that fed into the same high school."

"Middle school? Is that like junior high?"

She flashed a puzzled look. "Yeah. Grades six, seven and eight. Don't they have middle school in Texas?" She smiled.

"I don't think so. Just Jr. High. Seventh and eighth grade."

"Oh, well, middle school is much, much better." Her voice and eyes teased.

"Oh, I'm sure it is. What year did you graduate from TAMU?"

"Eighty-six. Came back and found a job that suits me well."

"Rod said you travel quite a bit."

"I do, that's one reason I love the job so much."

"He said you called it a 'sales job that requires a BS degree.'"

She laughed. "Yes, that's about it. What about you? It's one thing for a Canadian to go to school in Texas. It's another thing for a Texan to move to Canada permanently, eh?"

"I've dreamed about it for a long time. It's a long process, I can tell you, a lot longer than I realized." *As in maybe never.*

We spoke over the high whine of the motor as Linda glided through traffic on the four-lane. I had never taken to sports cars but found this ride therapeutic. The green indicator on her radar detector grew brighter as the daylight faded. I started to ask about it but didn't. Fifteen minutes wasn't long enough to earn the right to inquire.

"Tell me about your family, Linda."

"Not much to say, really. My parents got divorced when I was twelve. Dad remarried and lives in North Vancouver. He's a lawyer, works in a big firm. Mom is a prof in the childhood education department at UBC. I'm the only kid. How about you?"

"My folks still live in the house we grew up in. They own a hardware store in a little town in the Texas panhandle. I have an older brother, Jerry, who lives in Chicago. Just earned his CPA and works in a big firm there."

"Chicago. That's a far cry from the Texas panhandle, eh?"

"It is. But he found fascination in the big city. For me, it's all about the wilderness."

"Interesting. Do you see him much?"

"No, that's the downside. But we make the most of it whenever we're together."

"Thanksgiving and Christmas, like that?"

"Pretty much."

We had driven out of the city into the suburbs. The last bit of light revealed residential neighborhoods and commercial parks through the bare branches of trees and bushes in the wide shoulders.

"So, what can you tell me about Julie's family? She's talked about them, but now that I'm going to be their overnight guest, I feel like I should know more."

"They're wonderful. I've never known a family so hospitable. Julie has talked about you, so they'll be so excited to meet you. They'll make you feel right at home."

"It'll be good to meet them." *I wonder what Julie said about me.* "And I haven't had a home-cooked meal in a month. Plenty of bunkhouse grub, pancakes for supper, you get my drift."

"So how do you like the cowboy life?"

I turned to look out my window, then back. "It's good. It's an adventure. I find great freedom in it. Kind of ironic, I guess."

She bit her lip. "How is this jail stuff going to affect your future, do you think?" When I didn't immediately respond, she continued. "I'm sorry, we don't have to talk about it." She swerved to miss a brave, darting rabbit.

"No, it's okay. I'm trying to understand it, still processing it." I sighed through my nose. "Course, I don't know for sure, time will tell. I tend to be an optimist, think everything's going to come out okay. Guess that's how I'm looking at this whole thing."

"It caught you by surprise, I imagine?"

"Yes, for sure. Never been a careful planner, tend to go with my gut." I drummed fingers on my knee. "But from what they told me today, my chances of getting back into the country should be good." *If I don't mind cowboying the rest of my life.*

"Well, then, it's just a matter of time, eh? And homework."

She doesn't know about Idaho. "For the immigration part of it, yes, that's what it looks like. I get home, make a new application, and wait."

"Well, could be that's not so bad. Your folks will be happy to have you home for a while."

"It will be good to get home. Don't know when that will be, but I'm ready for it."

Langley, BC

Ten minutes later, we parked in front of an unpretentious bungalow in south Langley.

"Looks like somebody pays attention to details," I said. The grass and shrubs were groomed to perfection.

"Oh, yes. Mr. Stewart is in his yard every Saturday unless it's pouring rain. His girls tease him that he's trying to compete with the Butchart Gardens." My puzzled look prompted her to elaborate. "That's a world-class flower garden in Victoria."

"Victoria? The capital of BC. On the island, right?" She nodded.

At the door, Linda knocked once, and we walked in. "Anybody home?"

"Yes, we're home, Linda." A moment later, a pleasant-looking woman emerged from the kitchen, an older version of Julie, with charming crow's feet at her eyes and salt-and-pepper hair. She went to Linda, and they embraced.

"Hi, Linda, so good to see you." Before Linda could respond, the woman turned to me, her smile wide and warm. "And you are Cody. Julie has told us all about you, and we are so happy to have the chance to meet you and have you in our home. I'm Elizabeth. So glad to meet you,

Cody." She came right to me and took my hand in both of hers.

"I'm glad to meet you too, Mrs. Stewart."

"Oh, fiddlesticks. Just call me Elizabeth. Come on in. I'll find Harry. Jessie's on an errand and should be back soon."

We followed her through the kitchen. A wonderful aroma smothered me with waves of comfort.

"Are you baking salmon?" Linda's face lit up.

"Yes, as a matter of fact, I am."

"You're in for a treat," Linda said to me. "This woman is famous all over the Lower Mainland for her salmon recipes."

"Oh, Linda, I've told you a million times, don't exaggerate." Elizabeth patted Linda's face and winked at me, "But I hope you like salmon."

"I've never had it, except for the stuff that comes in a can. My mom makes salmon patties, but this smells wonderful."

"Never had fresh salmon?" I turned to see a slight man with gray, thinning hair, wearing glasses, and carrying a book. He held out his hand. "Harry Stewart."

"Cody Brandon." We shook. "Glad to meet you, Mr. Stewart."

"You, too, Cody. Welcome to our home."

"I don't know how to thank the both of you," I looked from host to hostess. "It's an unexpected treat to meet you and stay in your home. I figured I'd be sleeping on a bench in the bus depot. Thank you so much."

"Sleep on a bench? I should say not." Mrs. Stewart added, "It's such a pleasure to meet you, Cody. We're looking forward to hearing more about you."

"I want to apologize for my appearance. I've hardly slept for a couple of nights."

Gary Brumbelow

"No problem at all, Cody, you're just fine," Mrs. Stewart said. She smiled and laid a hand on her husband's arm. "If you two will give Linda and me a little space, we'll have supper on the table in fifteen minutes."

Mr. Stewart led me into the den.

"Have a seat, young man." He waved at a couch facing his recliner and we sat. "Why don't you tell me about yourself."

Away from the kitchen and Mrs. Stewart's cheerful warmth, the room felt cool. I shifted in my seat, seeking a comfortable yet respectful posture.

"Well, as you know, I'm from Texas. Born and raised in the panhandle, a small town on the railroad called Dalhart. About eight thousand souls." He nodded without comment.

"My folks have owned and operated a hardware business since shortly after I was born. I have an older brother in Chicago who's an accountant. We lived in town, but I spent as much time as I could on my friends' farms and ranches."

Stewart leaned forward, bent his head to listen. I shifted on the couch.

"I love my family and had a great childhood. But I didn't want to be a merchant; I've always wanted to be a rancher. I love Texas, but I knew I couldn't spend my life there. Too tame, no wilderness. I wanted to go someplace north."

"Well, you're certainly north of Texas here. So, what's happening now? Julie tells us you saw the inside of the Williams Lake jail and spent time in a detention center."

I blushed and bit my lip, looked out the window for a moment before facing Stewart again.

"Mr. Stewart, I was raised to respect the law. My folks taught us to obey authority. I've never flaunted the law, although I have had a couple of speeding tickets." I looked at the floor and back. "Yes, sir. I spent a night in jail and

252

two weeks in the border holding facility. But not because I intentionally broke the law. It was more like an accident. You could say an oversight."

I related my story starting at the border crossing. Stewart focused as I recounted the truck breakdown, the firing at Cache Creek, meeting Willie Joe in the woods, bumping into Julie, and getting hired at Grand Valley.

"The boss sent me and another cowboy out to the back country, and when we got home eleven days later, I found out the RCMP was looking for me. I went straight to Williams Lake the next day, and they put me in jail just like that."

He frowned and looked at the floor. The cool was moving toward frigid.

"Believe me, I was shocked. I mean, they were just doing their job, I don't object to that. And the fact is, I should have been more careful to note my work permit didn't authorize me to stay in Canada or take another job. But to tell you the truth, after all that had happened ..." Mr. Stewart nodded, his lips parted, but I wasn't done.

"Well, I mean, it took me four hours to get through the border, and then my truck breaking down, then getting fired, my head was spinning, and I forgot I was supposed to leave Canada. It was careless of me, I'll admit that, but I'm no criminal. They even told me today at the border agency I could apply to come back, which I will. And I'll mind my p's and q's this time if you get my meaning."

Stewart's silence and inscrutable look unnerved me. Had Julie told her parents about Idaho? I opened my mouth but was interrupted by a young woman bouncing into the room. She walked straight to me.

"You're Cody, of course. Hi, I'm Jessie, Julie's sister." She stuck out a hand.

I stood and shook. "Nice to meet you, Jessie." *Your timing was perfect.* "Julie has told me about you."

"Same here," she said, smiling and still shaking my hand. "It's just so cool you can be here and meet the family. What do you think about my sister?"

Before I could respond, Linda stepped in from the kitchen, "Supper's ready."

Coeur d'Alene

After two weeks without a news team lurking outside, Frank finally felt free to sample the evening broadcast. He grabbed a beer, dropped onto the sofa, and found the remote. Five minutes later, the commercial break finally ended, and a familiar female face appeared on the screen.

"The Idaho State Police have issued an update on the Joan Johnson murder. Mrs. Johnson drowned in Bishop Lake on October 13. ISP spokesman reported that Cody Brandon of Dalhart, Texas, was apprehended recently in Canada and is expected to be extradited to the US to face charges in the murder of Ms. Johnson."

Frank slumped to the floor and wept. Huge, heaving sobs poured out in a catharsis, two parts relief, one part grief. Maybe the end of his torment was in view.

CHAPTER 49

WE MUST LEAVE OUR LAND

Hope, BC, Thursday, November 26

Astunning winter landscape lay open through the window as the Greyhound bus growled up a long, steep grade out of Hope. The hills rose and fell, fuzzy with thick woods. Snow covered the highway. The pavement was surely slick, but the driver seemed unconcerned. I gazed at the scenery, my mind bouncing from the grief of a lost inheritance to my visit with the Stewart family. Except for my conversation with Mr. Stewart, being with them was almost like being home for Thanksgiving.

Not that I blamed him for wanting to know more about me, grilling me, even. I'd be the same if some stranger was interested in my daughter. Especially somebody who'd been in jail. *I wonder if I passed the test.*

Mrs. Stewart, on the other hand, was all sweetness and hospitality, the perfect hostess.

"Please come again, Cody. Please be sure to let us know if you're in the area. We would love to have you any time." My own mom treated guests like that—to get the same reception from Julie's mother was great.

Jessie was the classic little sister, pumping me for anything she could get out of me.

"What's your favorite band?"

"Believe it or not, Chicago,"

"Why did you choose Grand Valley?"

"It was more like God directed me there." I related the *Reader's Digest* version of my tale since Mr. Stewart had already heard my story.

"What do you like to do in your spare time?"

"Hunt. Read. Play baseball. But I don't get much opportunity for any of that on the ranch."

"What was your favorite subject in school?"

I had to think about that. "Math, I suppose. And science. And English too."

"How many girlfriends have you had?"

That one had drawn a "Jessie." from her mom, but I didn't mind. She was cute, and getting to know her could only enhance my relationship with Julie.

Jessie saved her biggest question for this morning, driving me to Abbotsford to catch the bus. I was lost in thought, studying an abandoned farmhouse, and wondering what had happened to the family that once lived there and what would happen to me, when she popped it.

"So, what do you really think of my sister?"

I turned and smiled. "Your sister is a very special girl. I'm looking forward to getting to know her better."

"She is special. Even if she is my sister." Jessie's laugh sounded like Julie's, and I couldn't wait to see her again.

At the bus depot, I turned to Jessie. "Thanks for the ride, Jessie. It was fun to talk. And please thank your folks for me again. That was a million times better than sleeping on a public bench."

"No problem, Cody. I'll tell them. Hope we get to see you again soon."

As the bus traveled north, the valley grew deeper and steeper until the road dropped into the Fraser River Canyon. The highway hugged a sheer rock wall on the left, rising at least a hundred feet. On the other side, the foaming river crashing over granite boulders below put me in mind of my life, my dreams dashed on the harsh realities of unfair accusations and indictments.

We crossed a bridge, and now, the cliff rose on the right. At Hell's Gate, where you could ride a tram to the bottom, all was river, rock, and sky. We finally left this striking landscape behind at Lytton, where the road turned away from the Fraser and skirted the Thompson River.

An hour later, the bus pulled into Cache Creek, where Chuck Harper had fired me just six weeks ago.

How was the old boy, Chuck Harper, doing I wondered? Had he found a manager good enough for him? I doubted it. Looking back, I was glad I didn't get the job. The country around Wolf Creek and Grand Valley was much more to my liking. Besides, I wouldn't have met Julie. That right there was adequate reason to be happy I wasn't managing the Double Bar. Funny how God's providence works bad things out for good.

What will you do with my mess now, Lord?

Williams Lake

Three and a half hours later, we pulled into Williams Lake. I found the bank where my first Grand Valley paycheck had been deposited, and from there it was a half-hour walk to the towing yard. A Chevy pickup had never looked so good.

I drove south up the hill out of Williams Lake, the same hill I'd descended seventeen days earlier, naïve, and confident of my future. Who would have thought, when Gordon and I returned from the back country, how fast my world would turn around? Who would have guessed I'd spend two weeks in the custody of law enforcement, would watch my future get sucked down the drain?

I suppose it could have been worse. At least, they'd given me time to prepare. What if they'd deported me immediately?

I was far from home and family on Thanksgiving Day, but I had reason to be grateful.

"Thank you, Lord, for saving me from myself. You are a faithful heavenly Father. Please give me wisdom. I need to grow in my awareness, in my ability to think through a situation. And please work a miracle with that money, Lord." Tears welled up and I had trouble seeing.

I pulled my head together to think through the next few days. If I left Monday, I should be able to get out of Canada with two days margin and still allow time to talk things over with Holder. But what would I say? He was a great boss, and I loved the Grand Valley operation, but I was not willing to be a cowboy on someone else's ranch for the rest of my life.

And I was about to see Julie. I needed to talk to her, needed to secure the relationship. I couldn't know when I might return. Would she wait for me?

One month ago, I was wondering if I should pop the question. I knew more than one happily married couple who'd gotten engaged within a couple of weeks. I'm sure many of those marriages had failed. But I knew Julie was the one for me. Did she feel the same?

All that had occupied my thinking for the eleven-day ride to the mountains and back. But then everything changed.

What could I offer her now?

Wolf Creek

The fields were heavy with powder, but on the road the snow was mostly packed. I drove as fast as I dared and pulled into Wolf Creek an hour and fifteen minutes after leaving town at 6:25 p.m. Julie's cabin was dark, but the school was lit. I knocked and stepped in. Wearing jeans and a heavy sweater—and lovelier than Venus—she was pinning a poster to a bulletin board.

"Cody." She laid down the poster and came to me. "It's so good to see you."

I took her offered hands and tried to read her eyes.

"You're a sight for sore eyes, Julie."

She smiled and broke my heart. "Jessie called. Sounds like you had a good time with my family."

"They were great, Julie." She started to let go but I held on, wanting to draw her to me but unsure about the timing. "Your mom is a wonderful hostess, made me feel right at home." I released her hands, but we stood facing each other.

"What did you think about Jessie?"

"She's a hoot. Such a kid sister. Adores you and wanted to know everything about me."

"I'm not surprised to hear that." She leaned back against a desk. "How about Dad?"

"He was exactly like I would be in his shoes."

"What do you mean?"

"If I had a beautiful daughter, and a stranger just out of jail was showing interest, I'd ask plenty of questions."

She flushed, went to the bulletin board, and picked up another push pin. "Did Dad cross-examine you?"

"Let's just say he wanted to know about my past and what I'm planning for my future."

"And what did you tell him?" She pinned giant snowflakes to a blue poster, each labeled with a different day of the week.

"I made a careless mistake, but I've always respected the law. That I intend to come back, and I've learned a big lesson."

"So, how did that conversation end?"

"It didn't really. Jessie showed up right then, and we got interrupted. Never had a chance to come back and finish it."

Julie completed the bulletin board and stepped back to check it out before turning to me. "So, what's your schedule right now?"

"I'm on my way to Grand. But I've got no deadline. What are you thinking?"

"Are you hungry?"

"Starved, yes. Haven't eaten much more than an apple all day."

"Okay, I've got stew on the stove. How about we have supper together here in the classroom?"

"Sounds good to me. Let me help."

Julie told me about her happenings of the last two weeks as we put the meal together. Twenty minutes later, we sat beside each other at a table in the classroom, bowls of steaming stew and a basket of warm bannock before us.

Julie started to speak, but I interrupted her with an uplifted finger and a nod. I took her hand, and we bowed our heads.

"Father, thank you for this moment. Two weeks ago, I didn't know when I would see Julie again, and here we are together with good food before us. This is your gift to us, Lord. Thank you for the opportunity to meet Julie's family. Thank you for hope. Thank you for the time we've had together.

"Please help Julie as she faces the challenges of teaching. Lord, please grant us the privilege to continue our relationship. Please open a door into the future and help me to see what you want me to do.

"Thank you for this good food. In Jesus's name."

"How long can you stay, Cody?" She smoothed a napkin on her lap.

"I'm leaving Monday. They gave me seven days, so technically I would have till Tuesday or even Wednesday, but I'm taking no chances. I'm learning to put margin in my life, if you get my drift." Her face told me she was counting the days. *That's a good sign.*

"Well, we've talked about my news. I want to hear yours."

I finished a bite of stew and replaced the spoon in the bowl. "The moment in the Williams Lake RCMP office when they said I was under arrest was the new low point of my life."

"I can only imagine."

"Nothing could have prepared me for that. I was stunned. The officer asked me if I had my work permit, and when I said no, he showed me a faxed copy of it and had me read the place that said I wasn't authorized to work anywhere except the job I'd been offered in Cache Creek."

"Didn't they tell you that at the border?" She broke off a piece of bannock.

"I know they said something about it, but I didn't think it was a big deal." I slathered butter on bannock. "I guess the effect of everything—my motor blowing up, replacing my truck, getting fired—all that pushed the work permit out of my mind. All I could think about was where do I go now. You know the rest of that story, of course." I paused.

"You know, I still believe God led me to Grand, but does that mean it was God's will I get arrested? Doesn't that seem strange?"

"Not to me." She set down her spoon. "Think about it. Isn't it better the law caught up with you sooner rather than later?"

"I'm not sure what you mean."

"It just seems to me the longer this remained unknown, the bigger it would grow. And meanwhile, you'd be getting more invested in a life here. And it would be more painful to deal with an interruption like this."

"Wow, that's right, Julie. I see what you mean. Yes, it's definitely better. Good point. That's good to remember." I crumbled bannock into my stew. "I can tell you, getting arrested is no fun, especially when you haven't done anything wrong. At least, not intentionally."

"Oh, Cody, I feel sorry for you just hearing it. I can't imagine actually experiencing it."

"Well, if I had to experience it, at least it's in the past. I don't expect anything like that again." I went back to my stew.

"So, what happened after that?"

I related the night in jail, the flight to Vancouver, two weeks of boredom in the CBSA detention center, the stress of the hearing. "They returned my stuff, and I was free to go. I walked to the airport and called Rod."

"And met Linda."

"She's a character, that girl. Did you know she uses a radar detector."

"Oh yes, she's famous for her fast driving. Remember, we call her the Green Flash."

"I remember. You know, I think Rod likes her."

"There's a mutual interest there, Cody. Believe me."

"Ah, interesting. What more can you tell me about that?"

"Promise not to pass this on to Rod?"

A bite of bannock was halfway to my lips, but I laid it back on the plate. "Hmm. Is it better to know it and keep it from him, or to not know it at all?" I drummed fingers. "What do you think?"

"Up to you. I don't think anyone but you can answer that." She pinched a crumb to her lips. "Or, maybe Linda will tell you herself. She's coming this weekend."

"What? That's crazy. Rod is planning to be here for our Bible study Sunday night—we wanted to spend time together before I leave, and that was the only day it could work."

"Oh, what fun, the four of us all together. I'm so excited." She stood, did a quick dance of joy, and picked up our dirty dishes. "Wait right here. I'll be just a second," she promised, and walked out.

I looked around with admiration at Julie's orderly classroom, a sign of a well-organized teacher. The opposite wall held three rows of cubby holes, each with a student's name, patiently awaiting the next school day. A map of the world hung on the front wall, and next to it, a calendar with a movable magnetic frame to show the current day. A

Canadian flag graced the other side of the blackboard, and under it, a multiplication table through ten times ten.

Julie came in, stomping the snow from her feet and carrying a plate.

"A little bird told me you might be here today, so I baked some cookies. Hope you like chocolate chip." She set down the plate and took her chair again.

"My favorite." I happily dug in.

"So, you and Dad didn't finish talking?"

"Not really. Jessie bounced in and saved the day. But I found him a little intimidating, to tell you the truth."

"What, my dad, intimidating?" Her eyes sparkled. "I've never seen that side of him."

"He's your dad, Julie. He loves you. It's his job to protect you."

"Well, sure, that makes sense." She bit into a cookie. "I never thought about it like that. To me, he's always been tender. Indulgent, even."

"I'm not surprised, but you've probably never seen him talking to a guy who's interested in his daughter."

Julie looked into the distance. "You know, I think you're right." She faced me again. "He always insisted on meeting guys who wanted to date me, but I was never part of those conversations, and none of those guys ever said anything about it."

"So, just how many conversations would that have been?" I grinned. "Roughly, I mean."

Julie blushed and pulled a cookie from her lips. "Not that many. Why?"

"Curious. Just wondering how far down the line I come."

"Well, you go first. How many girls have you dated?"

"Hmm, let's see." I closed my eyes and mumbled while unfolding my fingers one at a time. "I can't remember. I only have ten fingers." I grinned and snickered.

"Cody. You're bad." She made an impish face, but her eyes were smiling.

"Just kidding. I don't need five fingers for that. I took a girl to my senior prom. We'd been friends since grade school, but there was no attraction. It was more about finishing school together. That was it in high school."

"And A&M?"

"Believe it or not, I didn't really date anyone. I was busy with school and work. Our Fellowship of Christian Athletes group used to go out for pizza, but it was always as a group. To tell you the truth, I had decided not to pursue a relationship until I'd finished school. I didn't want anything to get in the way of my dream."

"But you still haven't reached your dream."

"That's true. I'm closer, but I won't be satisfied until I have my own place."

"What is that going to take, Cody?"

No further sidestepping, no more ducking what I had dreaded for two weeks. With that simple question, Julie forced me to disclose the painful truth.

"That's the sixty-four-dollar question, Julie, and everything has changed." I took a deep breath. "I need a place that can run three hundred cows, about thirty thousand acres in this country. Could cost a million dollars."

Her hand flew to her mouth.

"You're probably thinking I was crazy to take this on in the first place, but here's something you don't know. When I graduated from high school, my grandparents told me they had set aside an inheritance for me. Two hundred fifty thousand dollars."

Her jaw dropped again.

"That was my response. Amazing. They said they'd done the same for my brother but made him promise not to tell." I ran fingers through my hair and plunged ahead. "It's in a minor's trust, kept by a guardian till I turn twenty-four. And it came with two conditions.

"First, I had to finish a university program. Check.

"Second, I had to work at the same job for a year. If those two conditions were met by my twenty-fourth birthday, the money would come to me."

I stood and walked to the window. The village children sledded on a hill in the distance, the moonlight and snow illuminating their play. But my heavy heart refused to respond to the beauty. I turned to face the one I wanted most and was least likely to win, now that I had nothing but myself to offer her.

"I have to leave the country. I can't keep this job. I can apply to reenter but in a best-case scenario, it will be at least ninety days before I can return. By that time, my twenty-fourth birthday will be only months away." I came back and sat across from her. "For that matter, I couldn't qualify even if I just went home and took a job. I'm three weeks into my twenty-third year. Plus, it might take time to fix the problem in Coeur d'Alene."

Julie thumped a womanly fist on the table and stood, her eyes flashing a strange anger.

"No. That cannot be. That's ridiculous. I simply cannot believe anybody would deny your inheritance because of three lousy weeks. Surely your grandparents would be willing to flex that much, especially given the circumstances. Right?" Her fiery defense warmed and charmed me at the same time. This Julie I had not seen.

"Well, I don't know. My grandpa had a reputation all over the county for his stubbornness. He worked harder than anyone I've ever known and insisted on the same from his family. He made that extremely clear when they gifted this at my high school graduation."

"But, Cody."

"Hold on, Julie, there's more." She sat, still simmering. "Grandpa and Grandma were killed in a car accident three weeks after my high school graduation. They have no more say in the matter. It's in stone."

The wall clock ticked. "I'm sorry, Julie. I was dreading to tell you this, ever since I realized it that first night in the Williams Lake jail."

"I'm sorry about your grandparents, Cody." Her soft, sweet voice soothed my hurting heart. I nodded, and she went on. "So, who's in charge of this money now?"

"Grandpa appointed a lawyer as guardian—somebody in Dallas I've never met."

"But you could try to talk to him, right?"

"He wrote a letter a month after my grandparents died, went out of his way to firm up the stipulations to the money, said grandpa had instructed him to do that in the event of his death."

I reached to take her hands. "I'm not giving up on my dream, Julie. I have no idea how it can happen. Maybe I can find a property that's undervalued, something that needs work, a place that would allow me to use sweat equity to make up what I lack in cash."

"How many places like that are there around here?"

"I haven't had time to look. But even then, I would need a sizeable down payment."

I hated to leave her in such dreariness, but it was time to go.

"I have to go. I've got two days to tie up the loose ends at Grand and get ready to leave the country. And this isn't goodbye. I'll be back on Sunday."

"I'm so glad you stopped, Cody. I missed you. So much has happened in two and a half weeks."

"Yeah, it seems like way more than that." We stood and went to the door. "Thanks for a great supper, and even more, for a great time, Julie." I put a hand on the doorknob and with the other, gave her arm a squeeze.

"Julie, I ..." *Kiss the girl, you idiot.* She looked up at me, her dark hair on her shoulders, lips slightly parted. The classroom fell away, time stopped, we stood alone in a strange, wonderful place I'd never visited. "Julie, is it okay if I kiss you?"

"It's okay." She smiled, and my insides turned to water. With my hands on her shoulders, I bent my head, and we kissed. When we parted, she wiped an eye. "See you soon."

CHAPTER 50

I WILL SEE YOU AGAIN

Grand Valley, Friday, November 27

Flames danced and pitch pockets popped from the Ponderosa pine logs in the ample stone double fireplace of the Holder home. I sat on the sofa opposite Mr. Holder in his recliner in the living room. In the kitchen, Mrs. Holder was visible through the flames, cleaning up after a wonderful roast beef dinner.

Friday evening, I surprised my fellow cowboys when I showed up at the bunkhouse, and they'd insisted on hearing all about my time away before hitting the sack. We had spent the day reconfiguring the barn for more hay storage.

I'd given Holder the *Reader's Digest* version of my story that morning. The rancher insisted I join his family for dinner—his invite warmed me all the way through. I'd learned all about the family, and my hunch about their testimony had been right—they were strong believers.

They told me about their home in New Mexico, about moving the operation up here, their first years at Grand and some of the challenges of running a three-hundred-thousand-acre operation.

The Holder boys, Thad and Cale, were quiet but responded to my probing.

"How old are you, Thad?"

"Ten."

"And what's your favorite thing to do?"

"Oh, ride my horse I guess."

"What's your horse's name?"

"Which one?"

"You've got more than one horse?"

He looked at me and then at his dad, processing for the first time, after a decade of life on the ranch, the idea that anyone might have only one horse.

The younger boy looked about eight.

"How about you, Cale. Do you ride, too?"

"Oh sure. But I like my ATV better."

"Where do you go?"

"Looking for snakes and rats to shoot with my .22."

Mrs. Holder grinned at Cody. "As you can see, they're all boy."

She was a gracious hostess whose love for her husband and sons was obvious, whose cooking rivaled my own mom's. We feasted on a superb dinner of roast beef, mashed potatoes and gravy, home-churned butter on homemade bread, topped off with warm cinnamon apple pie in a bowl swimming in fresh heavy cream. The scrumptious meal around this family's table lent a peaceful rest to my troubled mind.

Now relaxed on the sofa, I was happy to let Mr. Holder lead the conversation.

"What do you expect the next few days and weeks to look like, Cody?" Holder held a cup of coffee near his face with both hands and studied me from the overstuffed recliner that bespoke "king of the castle."

"Well, tomorrow I need about an hour to sort through my stuff and pack for the trip. I'll pull out Sunday and head to the border. Going straight to Coeur d'Alene to find out what's going on with this homicide thing. Then, I'll head to Texas."

"You don't expect to spend much time in Idaho?" He silently sipped from his cup.

"No, I don't. Somebody's made a mistake, and I reckon we'll get it straightened out pretty quick. I know one thing—I wasn't anywhere close to any murder. Either a mistaken identity or maybe somebody spotted my truck and assumed I was involved. Something like that."

"Well, I hope it all turns out okay. Are you thinking about trying to get back into Canada?"

"Yes, sir. Absolutely. Would I still have a job here?"

"Yes, you would. I'd be happy to have you back."

"Great. If I had a job offer, I think that would just about guarantee a new work permit."

"Are you still thinking you want to get your own place?"

I looked at my boots for a moment. "Yes, sir, that's my long-term goal. But I've lost a big piece of the puzzle, and I'm not sure if I can put it all together now."

"Oh?"

A big sigh, then I forged ahead. "I told you about my A&M program and all that."

"He nodded."

"Those credentials were one necessary piece of the puzzle, and the learning another piece. But there was a money piece that's gone now." I elaborated the sad story as he listened with the intensity of a mentor wanting to help.

When I finished, he set his empty cup on the coffee table, a restored Conestoga wagon rim fitted with smoked glass.

"Do you have any advice for me?" I said.

"Starting out from scratch is tough, Cody."

"I thought you'd say something like that. Not surprised to hear it. But I'm not afraid of hard work."

"I wasn't thinking only of the work." He looked out at the dark. "How big a ranch are you figuring on buying?"

"Need to run about three hundred cows, so about thirty thousand acres. Does that sound right?"

"Yes, deeded and leased acres combined. Depending on the grazing leases, the location, the winter range, the general condition ..." Holder looked at the floor. "You could be looking at a million bucks."

"That's about what I figured. And without the two hundred fifty thousand, I don't know how I would get a loan for the rest."

"No, that's pretty much a minimum down payment for a place you described. And ag loans are getting tight. It might be hard to find a bank to finance seventy-five percent of the value. And even at that, the payments could eat you alive."

"Kind of like my grandpa used to say, 'If we had some cake, we could have cake and ice cream if we had some ice cream.'"

He smiled with me, "That's it exactly."

The room grew quiet, a low wind moaned through the chimney, and I shivered in spite of the warmth of the snapping, crackling fire. The mountain between me and my goal loomed larger. A long moment passed before I spoke.

"Well, I figure I need to find a place that's undervalued. I've got more energy than money. I could start from there and build it up."

Holder exhaled through his nose. "Probably not an operation of the size you're thinking. You might need to settle for a smaller place, something you can operate on the side and get a job in town."

Something happened in my heart when he said that. I remembered my tenth birthday. My folks knew my dream for a Remington automatic .22. I had talked of little else for weeks. When Mom set a long narrow gift on the table at my party, I knew what it was.

After dinner, before the cake and ice cream, Dad handed me the present, a strange light in his eyes. I shredded the gift wrap like a hungry dog pouncing on a bone—it was a Daisy BB gun. The disappointment on my face lasted a half second, long enough for both Mom and Dad to detect. How does a ten-year-old kid celebrate a BB gun when he wanted a real rifle?

I pondered the same question now, only the size and value of the asset had changed. I managed the same half-smile response to Mr. Holder as to my parents, but the hidden wound struck deep.

CHAPTER 51

YOU SHALL NOT HAVE AN INHERITANCE

Grand to Wolf Creek, Sunday, November 29

Two days later, I drove out of Grand once more, wondering if I'd ever return, sobered by the scattered jigsaw pieces needing to be sorted before the puzzle could be assembled. The only strategy in reach of a weary brain and wounded heart was to focus on job one—get to Coeur d'Alene and clear my name. Idaho was a long way, with one last Wolf Creek visit intervening.

I started early. Snow had fallen all day Saturday, and a half-foot covered the road. My tire chains thumped against the wheel wells, muffled by the soft powder.

The world dazzled. Cedar boughs bent low, trying not to break. A six-point mule deer bounded over the road and down the hill toward the Fraser, hooves flicking snow.

Every time I topped another ridge, a new, frosty panorama opened. At the lip above the river, hoary hills twenty miles north rose, enthroned above the fork where the Chilcotin River joined the Fraser. My eyes feasted on fifty thousand acres of pure, splendid white, even more enchanting given the probability the scene would never appear before me again.

At one-thirty, I rolled into Wolf Creek. On the phone yesterday, Rod had estimated he'd get to the village about two. "I'm running the sound board at the first service, so I should be on the road by eleven."

But when I rounded the last turn to Julie's teacherage, a pickup sat at the cabin. Before I killed my ignition, Rod's head poked out the door.

"Well, look at you, Rod. How about that." We grabbed each other in a manly bear hug.

"Good to see you, too, Cody. Been too long."

"I'll say. We've got some catching up to do."

Julie stepped out. "Cody, I'm so happy to see you." I hugged her before she spoke again. "And of course, you know Linda."

"Hey, Linda. How's my rescuer and fellow Aggie?"

"Come in, you guys." Julie swept her hand toward the door. "It's nice and warm inside and I've got hot cider on the stove." Rod and I stepped into the little cabin. I touched Julie's face, and whispered, "So good to see you." Her simple smile thrilled me.

Linda spoke before I had my boots off.

"Okay, Cody, I want to hear about this dream of yours. How does a guy from Texas get interested in ranching so far from home? You mentioned it the other day but didn't really tell the story. I've been curious ever since Rod told me about you."

"Whoa," I replied, stepping away from the door in my socks. "Let's back up a second. I want to hear about you and Rod meeting. And where's that famous RX7? Did you actually stoop to ride in Rod's lowly Ranger?"

Everyone laughed.

"You didn't think I was going to drive it on these gravel roads, did you? That's why I always have a friend with a four-wheel drive pickup." She winked at Rod.

We squeezed around Julie's little table as she set a steaming mug of apple cider in front of each guest. I circled my cup with my hands, "This feels great, Julie. Didn't realize how cold my hands were." Already, less than three minutes after my arrival, the ache settled in my chest. I tried to ignore it.

"'Course they are," Linda said. "Did you suppose your thin Texas blood would keep you warm up here? Which brings me back to my question." She lifted her eyebrows and grinned at Julie.

"Well, think about it," I replied. "If a Canuck can spend four years in College Station, why can't a Texan survive in BC?"

"Didn't you notice most Canadians at A&M disappeared in the summer."

"To tell you the truth, I never realized there were so many Canadian Aggies. I knew Rod had a couple of buddies there, but I didn't run in those elite, northern circles."

Rod chuckled. "Well, that was then, this is now." He lifted his mug, "Here's to a new Canadian. Here's a welcome for my favorite Texan into the elite Canuck circle. Welcome to Canada, Cody. May your life north of the border be long and fruitful."

"Here, here." The girls joined in. Four ceramic mugs met with a clink—four apparently happy friends carefully sipped a toast. But my smile faded quickly.

"Let's just hope I have a life north of the border. Right now, things are looking grim."

Linda lifted her eyebrows. "But didn't you say the border office indicated you could apply to come back?"

"Yes, they did. In fact, they made it sound like being deported wasn't a big deal. I'm not worried about that." I looked at Julie, she dropped her eyes, and I changed gears on the fly. She clearly did not want me to talk about the lost treasure. What did that mean? "But the more I think about Coeur d'Alene, the more uneasy I am about what's waiting for me there."

"Would you like to talk about that?" Rod said.

"No, not really. Let's don't spoil a fun evening." Your fun, that is. Whatever joy I had brought to the party had vanished with Julie's silent signal. What did that indicate? Was she afraid I would lose face? Or was she already losing interest?

I was ready for the festivities to be over, wanted to talk to her, reassure myself of her affection. But my painful secret had to stay between Julie and me—we had to carry on for Linda's and Rod's sakes. I swallowed my anxious grief and settled in for the duration.

"But Linda's serious." Julie broke in. "She really does want to hear more of your story."

"I guess a big piece of it comes down to personality. My brother is a serious, careful guy, the classic accountant type. For my part, I've always been drawn to adventure in the outdoors. My folks gave us a great childhood and worked hard in their retail business, but I'm too restless to settle into that kind of life."

"Remember the day we met in class?" Rod spoke up. "I knew from the get-go you weren't going to work in a store."

I grinned. "No, sir. I mean, at eleven, I was tramping the woods with a .22, hunting squirrels. Loved the feel of a rare Texas winter storm, tracking animals in the snow. Reading adventures about the north, Jack London, Robert Service, stuff like that. We camped in Colorado, and I loved hiking in the mountains."

Julie went to the stove and added a log.

"Then, too, all my friends grew up in ranching families, and I liked nothing better than spending the weekend on a friend's operation, riding, working cattle, even doing chores. When you put those three things together—mountains, northern adventure, and cattle ranching—all roads lead to British Columbia."

"So," Rod spoke, "sort of John Wayne meets Jeremiah Johnson, eh?"

"Yes." I said with a chuckle. "I loved that movie."

After the Sunday night Bible study ended, Rod and Linda headed home, and Julie and I walked toward her cabin in the frosty night.

"Cody, I have a question about something you said on Friday."

"Sure."

"I know so much has changed for you. You can't predict your future with the loss of your inheritance. But laying that aside for a moment, how come you're not worried about a girl interfering with your dream now? You said you avoided girls in college. You didn't want anything to get in the way of your dream. Aren't you still worried about that?"

"Well, first of all, the dream hasn't vanished entirely, even though I can't see it with anything like the clarity of before. But as for your question, no I'm not worried about that."

"Why not?"

"You don't know?" I looked down for a moment. *Father, please give me the right words.* We stopped and I searched her eyes.

"You know how I said your dad wants to protect you because he loves you?"

Julie nodded.

"Well, I understand that. I get that one hundred percent." I framed her face with mittened hands. "Because I love you. I want to be your protector." Our eyes locked, a Texas-wannabe-mountain rancher gazing at the perfect picture of pure feminine beauty. "I want to marry you."

Her mouth opened, her eyebrows lifted, but she said nothing.

"Julie, I have to leave Canada. I'll be back as soon as I can. But I don't know when that'll be, and I can't take the chance some random cowboy might move in and sweep you off your feet before I can return."

She swallowed. "Are you proposing?"

"No, not yet. Just clarifying." I slowed down, spoke carefully. "I'm not asking for anything from you right now—just making sure you know my intentions."

We reached her cabin, I pulled off a glove, and placed my hand gently against her cheek. Her dimples, lit by the moon, turned my knees to jelly.

"Can I kiss you again?"

She nodded, and I did.

"Cody, I have strong feelings for you too." She bit her lip. "But this is all happening so fast. We met just a little over six weeks ago. I mean, don't get me wrong. It would break my heart if you could not come back. I don't want you to go." She looked away for a moment. "I just don't know if my feelings match yours. How can a person know they love someone? How can you be so sure."

I took a deep breath. "It's a fair question. Not sure I have a satisfactory answer." I pushed snow off the stoop with my boot. "I just know it. Sorry I can't be more convincing." I shrugged.

"I don't doubt you. I just wish I could be as sure."

Her plaintive tone made my heart swell with affection. "Dear Julie, true love can wait. You must not feel pressured. That's a horrible thought—that you would have anxiety about it. If it's real, God will show you. If it's not, he'll show me." I held her hand as I went down one step. "I'll be praying about it. And I know you will too." I smiled, winked, and squeezed her hand. When her countenance brightened, I knew she was at peace.

An ache of sorrow grew in my chest. I wanted to stay, to be with her, dream together of the future, cultivate the relationship, to talk, to revel in her warm glow. Maybe kiss her one more time.

But my epic journey had to begin. I must head for the border and on to Coeur d'Alene, to face what awaited me there.

Two hours later, I stopped at the Frontier Motel in Clinton and slept hard.

CHAPTER 52

ON DRY GROUND THROUGH THE SEA

Southeastern BC to the US/Canada border, Monday, November 30

Early Monday morning, I drove south out of Clinton into the Okanagan district, through miles of fruit orchards, their bare limbs stark against the snow-dusted ground.

Seven weeks earlier, I'd taken the scenic route and entered Canada at a tiny border crossing in the wilderness. This time, I stuck to major highways to cross at a big office where they'd likely be too busy to catch any irregularities in my paperwork. I had no way to know that God was leading in that decision. But it soon became apparent.

At the Canada Border Security Agency office in Osoyoos I parked and went inside. The agent at the desk opened my passport and checked the photo against my face. He scanned the exit document issued to me in Vancouver and looked up at me while I held my breath and resolved not to blink.

"Looks like you've had a little excitement."

"You could say that."

"Well, things should be back to normal for you now. Have a nice day." The officer stamped my passport and handed it back.

A minute later, I pulled into a line of nineteen vehicles inching toward the US border facility a few hundred feet south. A moment of truth was about to unfold. I fidgeted, turned on the radio, looked for a station, gave up, turned it off, drummed my fingers on the dash, and prayed. I reminded myself, *you'll be okay. You'll be okay.*

Thirty-five minutes after getting in line, I stopped at the window.

"Passport, please." The thirty-something agent wore a beard and long hair and a name tag "T. Hague." Six weeks earlier, I had watched him swearing as he attacked an unresponsive computer keyboard. He did not smile then. He was not smiling now.

I handed off my passport and held my breath. Had my record been flagged? Did Idaho have an APB out on me? Were the feds involved? Would I be detained? Had the Canada authorities called ahead? Was I about to fall into a net?

The customs officer tapped at his keyboard and frowned. *What's wrong? Why is it taking so long?*

"Something wrong?" I mustered my best nonchalant pose.

"Computer went down. Hold on a minute." He stepped away to talk to another agent. A third stepped to the computer and sat while the first two looked through the window at the growing line of vehicles. The guy at the computer shook his head and spoke to Hague. The three talked for a couple of minutes before Hague came back to the window.

"We need to move the line to the other window. But you're already halfway through, so I'm going to wave you on."

He shoved my passport back and turned away. Three seconds ticked by before I realize what had just happened: God had parted the Red Sea. I stuck my passport in my pocket and drove into America.

So far, so good.

CHAPTER 53

I Have Escaped by the Skin of My Teeth

Coeur d'Alene, Monday, November 30

Kootenai County Attorney Marc Malone loved to flaunt his silver mane, the perfect frame for his radiant smile, a device he employed frequently to disarm opponents, charm the ladies, and generally schmooze his way through the grind of an ambitious professional life that depended on guile.

His hairdo was intact, but Malone had not smiled in forty-seven days, since Frank Johnson's rude confrontation at the No Place Bar, the encounter that imperiled his world. Even worse, despite his prodigious labors ever since to find salvation from blackmail, prospects had not improved.

He climbed out of bed, went to the window, and swore. His trash can, which he'd parked at the curb last night, lay on its side, and a mangy, lean hound was rooting through the garbage strewn halfway across the yard and into the street. He pounded on the window and shouted, "Get out of here," but the animal looked at him and went back to his feeding. A thick snowfall was quickly covering the ground, complicating the mess of cleaning up after this mutt. *Just what I needed.* He slammed the glass and swore again.

I drove into Coeur d'Alene at five minutes after six p.m., stopped at a pancake house and took a booth with a newspaper on the table. Over a waffle, I browsed the local stories till a headline jumped off the page, Suspect Still at Large in Johnson Drowning. I read the brief story and lost all appetite.

> Almost seven weeks have passed since Joan Johnson drowned in Bishop Lake, yet police have been unable to locate the suspected killer, Cody Brandon. The Idaho State Police say Brandon fled to Canada after the incident, where he was eventually apprehended by the Royal Canadian Mounted Police to be deported to the US. The US border patrol has no record of Brandon reentering the country. His whereabouts are still unknown. Anyone with information on this case is asked to phone the ISP at 800-555-1212.

I put a shaky hand to my forehead and closed my eyes, feeling dizzy. The room closed in, breath failed me, a knot of dark dread formed in my gut. My attempt to reassure myself that nothing was new—except the details—and there was no reason to panic, failed utterly.

I looked around the diner, empty except for the waitress fiddling with the coffeepot, and wondered if she'd seen my picture on TV. I took a couple of deep breaths and stepped quietly to the till where I laid a ten on the counter and turned for the door before saying, "Keep the change."

The door opened just as I reached it. I stepped back, looking down, to admit a fifty-something guy with thick, silver hair wearing a suit. The stranger glanced at me, his mouth open, and stopped.

"You're Cody Brandon."

I scrunched my eyes. "How do you know who I am? Who are you?"

"I'm a lawyer. My name is Mark Ma ..." He stopped mid-sentence and covered a cough, then stepped backwards and held the door open. "Maybe we should come out here." I followed in a daze and heard the man say, "My name is Mark Morgan. I recognized you from ISP police reports. I know about the charges against you. You're a wanted man, Mr. Brandon. There's a warrant out for your arrest."

Twenty-three years of life had not prepared me for such a surreal moment. Hearing about the warrant was one thing. Reading it was even worse. But a real, live person standing before me and announcing my criminal status was too much. I stepped back to lean on the alcove, knees threatening to buckle, opened my mouth to speak and closed it again.

The guy spoke again. "I'm surprised to see you here. The ISP has been looking for you." He stuck his hands deep in his coat pockets. "Don't know how you can be walking around, but they will find you." He looked around and lowered his voice. "If you don't have a lawyer, you're going to need one and the fact is, I'm a public defender. I can help you."

Words failed me. Where was I? What was happening? "I don't even know what to say." I looked off into the distance. Then back at Morgan. "I don't even know you. Who did you say you are?"

"Mark Morgan." He raised his palms toward me and stepped back. "You need time to think. I'll be in my car if you wanna talk." He pointed a thumb over his shoulder at a burgundy Fifth Avenue. "No obligation. If you care to hear me out, just come and listen and then decide." He took two steps toward the vehicle and turned. "But if I were in your shoes, I'd want a lawyer, for sure."

Morgan walked to his car while I studied the dark, almost empty parking lot. Cold sweat formed on my forehead. I started toward my truck. This was too much, overwhelming, none of this made sense. I walked faster, but then stopped, trying to think. I was desperate to know what this guy could tell me, and afraid to hear it at the same time.

I gritted my teeth, shut my eyes against the burning in my chest. Should I get out of here, or hear him out? Had God provided this guy at just the right time? I looked at my boots and tried to pray. I didn't feel like God was listening. What to do?

Curiosity finally won over panic. For three weeks, I had stressed about Idaho. The paper had given me a victim's name and method of death, but why were they after me? Here was a chance to find out. *What have I got to lose?*

I headed for the Chrysler. Morgan opened the passenger door from inside.

"You know, it's an amazing coincidence we would meet tonight," Morgan said as I got in. "I never come here and wouldn't be here tonight except my usual place is closed for a family death. Anyway, you made the right choice, Mr. Brandon. You need to hear me out at least."

"You said you know about the charges against me."

"Yes, I was just coming to that. But may I ask you a question first?"

At my nod, he went on. "You're wanted by the Idaho State Police. They have an APB out on you. Your record was supposed to be flagged. Customs should have stopped you at the border. How did you get through?"

How much should I tell this guy? After a brief silence, I spoke. "Believe it or not, the computer died when I was at the window at the port of entry, and the guy waved me through."

"You're kidding me. Serious?"

"No, I'm not kidding. That's the truth. I could have gone anywhere, but I knew something was brewing down here. I didn't know there was a warrant for my arrest but was told the law wanted to talk to me. So, there's no way I would've skipped town." The slightest sense of calm rose in my heart, a level of reassurance from finding my voice. "What's going on, anyway?"

Morgan blinked and rubbed the back of his neck. "Well, you ... you know about the charges, right?"

"I just read something in the newspaper," I gestured with my head toward the restaurant. "Three weeks ago, my friend said the police told him they have evidence I was at the scene of a murder. The story in the paper was about a woman drowning in Bishop Lake, but I had nothing to do with that. Don't even know what happened."

Morgan's eyebrows lifted. He studied me.

"Did you camp at Bishop Lake?"

"Yeah."

"Drove out about noon on a Tuesday?"

"About noon, yes. I'd have to think back what day it was."

"Never mind. Mr. Brandon, let me ask you a question. Are you an impatient driver?"

"Sometimes, I guess." I lifted my shoulders.

"Ever seen red when someone cut you off? Ever tailgated someone you couldn't pass?"

"Probably. Not lately, not in a long time."

"Didn't get frustrated driving along Bishop Lake?"

"In fact, I was frustrated because I'd overslept."

"Anything happen on that road beside the lake?"

"No." I paused. "Wait, yes. I came on a guy stopped in the road. Asked me to help him push his car off to the side so vehicles could get around him."

"What happened?"

"I pushed him. Just a little way. There wasn't much room on the narrow road, but we got it over enough to let cars pass."

"And then what?"

"I asked him if he needed help. He said no. I got in my truck and left." I frowned. "Why? What's the big deal about this anyway?" Fear was morphing to irritation.

Morgan looked out his window. He took a big breath and exhaled slowly through puffed cheeks. "Well, Mr. Brandon, that guy tells a different story."

"What does that mean? What'd he say?"

"He told the police he was the victim of an extremely angry driver. Said you had tailgated him for a mile or two before he could pull over to let you by. And you were so mad, instead of driving off, you got out yelling and kicking and pushing his car and the next thing he knew he was going into the lake and barely had time to get out. Said you knew his wife was unconscious in the backseat, and she drowned."

My face scrunched. I snorted. "What? That's a ridiculous lie. He completely made that up." My voice betrayed a growing anger at such a stupid, manufactured story. Who was that guy?

"Could be. But your prints are on the trunk of the car, and you just admitted you've gotten angry when driving, and you were behind schedule and frustrated that morning. A woman is dead. At a minimum, that's voluntary manslaughter, up to fifteen years. You're also facing a charge of assault with intent to commit murder, one to fourteen years in the pen." He turned to look directly at me. "And the woman's family is very influential in Coeur d'Alene. You're in big trouble, son. You're going to need help."

My hands were shaking, bile was rising in my throat. I wasn't sure I could stifle the ragged scream growing in my chest.

"I'm guessing you don't have much experience with criminal investigations, but most of the time a criminal trial isn't about the truth, it's about the counsel. Listen carefully, son. Do you have a lawyer? I'm a public defender. I can help you."

"You listen, mister. This is the biggest pile of horse dung I've ever heard."

"Could be, but that doesn't change anything in the immediate offing for you. I think you'd better bring me in to your confidence."

"I'm not ready for that. I need to think."

I drove away, but within three minutes realized I had nothing to hide. Retaining this lawyer and turning myself in seemed the way of wisdom. God must have sent him. And besides, no way could I be found guilty. Hiding would create another delay to the bigger question of my future career. But I would have to plow through this problem, not try to go around it.

His car was gone by the time I got back to the restaurant, as I expected. I figured I may as well turn myself in and call him from jail.

Fifteen minutes later, I parked at the Idaho State Police headquarters on Wilbur Ave. The glass front door was locked, the sign read "8:30 a.m. to 5:00 p.m." Across the dimly lit lobby the reception counter showed no sign of life. I stood a moment, grasping the handle, before returning to my truck. Five minutes later, I found a convenience store where a pay phone hung outside, next to a window. The clerk on a stool inside watching the news must have been deaf. I could clearly hear the TV through the glass. I dialed 911.

"911, what's your emergency?"

"My name is Cody Brandon." I had to speak loudly to hear myself over the TV inside. "I'm trying to turn myself in to the Idaho State Police, but the police station was closed. How am I supposed to do this?"

"What is your location, Mr. Brandon? We'll send a car."

As she spoke, I saw something on the TV through the window that riveted me. There was Mark Morgan speaking into a microphone, holding a press conference, talking about a fraud crime. But the caption identified him as "County Attorney Marc Malone."

Seconds passed before I could put into words what I was seeing. "He lied to me. He's not a public defender. He's the prosecutor."

"Your location, Mr. Brandon?" I heard the ISP dispatch repeat her question, but I paid no attention. Something was very wrong. That guy was no public defender. And his name was not Mark Morgan.

"He lied to me." My eyes narrowed. I forgot someone was listening and spoke aloud. "He lied to me."

"I beg your pardon?" The dispatcher's confusion landed on a deaf ear as my mind raced. My A&M program had included a class in law, I knew what a county attorney did. This guy was a prosecutor. I had stumbled right into a trap, and the net was closing fast.

"He intentionally misled me, then milked me for information, and he's probably on the phone with the police right now."

"I'm sorry, sir, I'm not following. Can you give me your location?"

I hung up and walked away, my hands clammy. What did it mean? I sat in my truck, closed my eyes, and made myself think.

The guy with the car at Bishop Lake—that was a total setup. I knew something was fishy about that guy.

I recalled the driving gloves, the limp. Which was probably fake. I put my head to my hands and thought out loud. "Maybe my gut recognized the limp was fake, but it never made it to my brain."

The guy could easily have pushed that little car into the lake all by himself as soon as I was out of sight. The whole thing was a trap, and I had walked right into it.

No wonder the RCMP had told Rod they had evidence. "I set my hands on the trunk and pushed and gave him just what he wanted."

Where the county attorney fit in that scheme I could not guess. But less than a half hour ago, he had lied to me and used the deception to wrangle incriminating information out of me. Yes, I had been frustrated that day and in a hurry. Yes, I'd gotten angry in traffic in the past.

For three weeks, since Rod first told me the RCMP had evidence I'd been at the scene of a homicide, I was so confident they were wrong. Somebody had made a mistake. All I needed was to show up in good faith, get exonerated, and head for Texas.

But my confidence was gone now. Extinguished like a match in a thunder shower. Something like ice rose in my gut. I wiped clammy palms against my jeans.

One thing was clear. I needed to move. Now. I fired up my engine and pulled into the street.

Where to? Where do I go? My eyes filled. I drove without aim. My brain was jelly, but I had to think. *Get out of here, fast.* I saw a sign, Interstate 90, and drove there, to head west on the freeway. A mile later another sign read "State line, 13 miles." Of course, get out of the state. Washington was right next door.

I looked over my shoulder, saw headlights but no red or blue flashers. I stayed just under the speed limit and spoke aloud.

"What's happening? Am I really running from the law? A Brandon avoiding arrest?" Until three weeks ago "Brandon" and "arrest" had never appeared in the same sentence. Now, twenty-two days later, I was a fugitive.

I replayed the scene of the crime in my mind. "I knew something was weird about that guy. That whole thing was a con. Should've trusted my gut."

The rearview showed emergency lights, and I panicked— then realized it was only an ambulance and breathed again. I slowed and steered to the shoulder to let it by. Back on the road, I drew my wits together and reviewed again those five minutes by Bishop Lake.

He parked right there so the next driver would have to stop.

His wife was in the back seat all the time. But I never looked in the car. I had no reason to.

And so, what if I had? A woman asleep on the seat. I couldn't know what he was planning.

Who is this guy?

I felt sick and angry. How could somebody be so vile, heartless, cruel?

I watched the eastbound traffic, glanced in my rearview, alert for any sign of law enforcement. Guilt and fright played tug of war in my chest. "I can't believe I'm doing this."

The truck's muffled growl hurt my head. I tried the radio but couldn't stand the noise.

"One step at a time. Do the next thing." But what was that? I looked around me.

"Gotta replace this truck. Gotta find a dealer before the news gets across the border."

CHAPTER 54

BETTER A NEIGHBOR NEARBY
THAN A BROTHER FAR AWAY

Spokane, Monday, November 30

If you're trying to hide, the dark is good. If this trouble had to befall me, at least it wasn't high noon. The cover of night offered a measure of comfort. And another level of relief washed over me as I crossed the Spokane River and entered Washington. Dozens of questions flooded my mind, but I had cleared the first hurdle.

At the first exit, I pulled into a Phillips 66 station and went to the yellow pages hanging in the phone booth. I felt guilty tearing out the page of used car lots, but there wasn't time to write down a list of numbers.

Three used car dealerships were already closed, but the light burned at Friendly Al's, a corner lot with about twenty vehicles. Al was out of his office and nearly to the truck by the time I stepped out. "Well, you just caught me before closing, son." He pumped my hand. "How can I help you?"

"Just looking to trade. This truck is hard on gas." My conscience reminded me it was a deception if not exactly a lie. But how could I tell the whole truth?

I kicked tires as Al looked over my pickup. We settled on a straight-across trade and I crammed my stuff into a 1965 Chevy Impala.

"All my sales are As Is, you got that, right?" He shoved a receipt at me as I nodded.

"Actually, I give a two-day warranty on everything I sell, yesterday and the day before." Al's laugh had to serve for both of us.

"One more thing, here's a temporary permit." He signed and dated it and handed it to me. "Put this in the rear window. It's good for thirty days."

I took the keys and permit and headed for the door. "You know, you barely caught me," Al said as he flipped the "Closed" sign around and locked the door. "Leaving early in the morning for a fishing trip. Way up in Canada. Closing up shop here for five days." I nodded without speaking and drove off.

At a freeway truck stop, I bought a cheap razor and went to the men's room. Twenty minutes later I emerged, my face clean-shaven for the first time in three years and sporting wrap-around sunglasses.

The deep rumble of diesel motors and fragrance of exhaust filled the lot. I found an inconspicuous place to park and tried to sleep.

Grand Valley, Tuesday, December 1

Tom Holder laid down his *Cattle Today* magazine and picked up the ringing phone to hear Pete Andrew's greeting.

"Hey, Tom, how are ya doin'?" Pete operated the ranch bordering Grand to the south. After the usual small talk about the beef market and the weather, he got to the point. "You missing some heifers?"

"Well, as a matter of fact, we are, yes. A few weeks ago, at the Gang bridge, one of our new guys had trouble and three head got away from him, ran down the hill and fell in the river. I figured they drowned. Why do you ask?"

"Well, that explains it. We were down in the bottom hunting coyotes yesterday and found three with your brand. They were a little wild, but we managed to get 'em up here. They took to the hay pretty quick and looks like they're gonna be okay."

"Well, I'll be doggoned. Who would've thought we'd ever see those girls again?"

"I bet. Just when you think you've got a cow figured out, she surprises you, eh?"

Tom laughed. "Yes, sir, that's for sure."

"Well, we've got 'em penned up whenever you're ready."

"That's good news, Pete. I appreciate hearing this, thanks for your efforts."

"It's nothin', really. I figure that's what neighbors are for, eh?"

"Much obliged, my friend. We'll be down tomorrow to pick them up."

He hung up and spoke loudly enough for Carrie to hear him in the kitchen where she was preparing dinner.

"Did you hear that, honey?"

She came into the front room. "What's that?"

"That was Pete Andrews. He found my lost heifers in his bottom land and has them in his corral."

"Really? That's wonderful. Praise the Lord."

"I'll say, I had written them off as lost for good. Oh me of little faith."

"Cody would be happy to hear this. I wonder how he is doing."

"Me too. I hope everything's turning out okay in Idaho."

Spokane, Washington

Whoever designed the front seat of a Chevy Impala certainly never slept in it. Neither did I. Long before daylight, I gave up and went into the truck stop cafe. Over bacon and eggs, I penciled on paper what I'd mulled over through the long cold hours in the car.

First stop after breakfast, a thrift store to put a disguise together. I would need to find a pawn shop. The Clinton motel room and gas had eaten most of the partial-month paycheck I'd earned at Grand Valley. I needed to fill my tank, buy clothes, rent a room, and get groceries. The saddle, chain saw, and guitar should fetch three or four hundred dollars.

After that, hunker down and figure out how to expose the real villain.

I had also thought long in the night about the ethics of running. One week ago, I had assured Mr. Stewart, Julie's dad, I was taught to respect authority. I remembered the conversation clearly.

But this was different. I'd been framed by a killer, and lied to by the county attorney who would prosecute my case. I refused to believe that running away from a trap was flaunting the law. I was innocent and in survival mode.

And besides, I had biblical precedent—another takeaway from the long, miserable night. I recalled the story of David running from Saul and pretending to be insane. The narrative didn't exactly justify David, but it certainly didn't condemn him either. I figured I was on neutral ground with God.

Most urgently, I had one week before Al got back from his fishing trip. If the police were on the ball—and I had to assume they were—I would go on their radar as soon as he registered the title change.

"Warm up?" A tired waitress held the pot ready to pour.

I tugged at my cap bill and spoke without looking up. "Sure, thanks."

Armed with a second yellow page from the phone book, I canvassed the second-hand stores for a new look. Something to drastically change my appearance without making me stick out. In a couple of hours, I had what I needed.

Ten minutes in another bathroom at another truck stop and I couldn't recognize myself in the mirror. Bellbottom jeans, tired silk shirt, worn leather jacket, and a mullet wig. My trial run was a trip to the grocery store; nobody gave me a second glance.

A map and the classified ads from the local paper guided me through Spokane streets looking for a room. Had to be cheap, four-hundred fifty dollars was all I could wring from a stingy pawn broker.

I meandered around an industrial area until I found a suitable place on Crown Avenue—railroad tracks on one side, vacant lot covered in dead weeds on the other, and an interline trucking outfit across the street.

Twenty-five bucks a week for a tiny, stale room with a foam rubber mattress. The place needed air, but I couldn't get the window open. Mom would be appalled, but what she didn't know wouldn't hurt her. At least the hot plate worked. I stirred noodle soup for lunch, its spicy aroma setting off my appetite, and thought aloud.

"Have to figure out how to communicate with the folks." Julie and Rod, too, after that.

December 1 evening

I climbed west on Interstate 90 six-hundred feet out of the Spokane Valley. Four hours of driving through irrigated farms, a magnificent canyon and over the Cascade Range, the road wound down into Seattle.

Inside the city limits, I found a post office and mailed an envelope addressed to Mr. and Mrs. Bob Brandon, Dalhart, Texas.

Portland lay just a hundred seventy-five miles south, and I wasn't due there till after midnight, so I had time to burn. I toured the Washington State Capitol, stopped at every rest area along Interstate 5 and arrived at the Jubitz Truck Stop near the Portland airport at eleven.

I parked and tried to sleep, but the traffic noise and headlights conspired against me. A little after four in the morning, I downed two cups of coffee, dropped another envelope to the same address into the Jubitz mailbox and drove out again, wipers slapping rain, tires hydroplaning on the pavement.

In downtown Portland, I turned east at Interstate 84 and traveled beside the Columbia Gorge for an hour before crossing into Washington. At the Tri-Cities, the Snake River joined the mighty Columbia and the road bent northeast, through dryland wheat farms.

The snow started before Ritzville. At Fishtrap, three inches lay on the road. I fought the snow for three hours and was back at my new digs in Spokane at six p.m.

I had burned thirty hours traveling eight hundred miles and figured it was time and money well spent. The folks would have heard from me without being compromised when the ISP called again.

Now to find the killer.

In my room, I knelt by my bed and opened my Bible to Psalm 22. "Do not be far from me, for trouble is near and there is no one to help. Many bulls surround me; strong bulls of Bashan encircle me. Roaring lions tearing their prey open their mouths wide against me."

"Father, please look on me with favor. You know my desperate condition. I need your help. Please give me some notion of what to do. Please send me help."

I dozed, woke, dropped onto my bed, and let weariness take me into a deep, dreamless sleep.

CHAPTER 55

A STRANGER IN THE LAND

Thursday, December 3

December dawn comes late in eastern Washington. By seven, I had prayed, showered, and breakfasted. The day was breaking as I started my car and scraped frost from the windshield with a piece of discarded cedar shingle. The car's exhaust billowed in the still, frigid air.

Any clear plan had escaped me, but Coeur d'Alene seemed the starting point to catch the culprit. From there, I'd have to take things one step at a time.

As I turned on to the eastbound ramp to Interstate 90, a hitchhiker stood on the shoulder. He wore a ball cap and fleece-lined jacket, a worn saddle lay at his feet. Looked about my age. I pulled over and stepped out.

"Hey, partner, where you headed?"

"Montana. Great Falls."

"Well, I'm only going thirty miles that way, but you're welcome to hop in."

"Sure, thanks." The stranger shoved the saddle and bag into the back and climbed into the front passenger side. "Appreciate it. I started for home yesterday when my truck broke down."

"Well, I was hitchhiking a few weeks ago, so I know how it feels." I checked my mirror and pulled back on the ramp. "What's going on in Great Falls?"

"My family lives there, Mom, Dad and two sisters. Just finished cowboying in the Okanagan." At my raised eyebrows he continued. "Ranching country up in north central Washington."

"Oh, okay. Seasonal work, then?"

"For newcomers like me, yes. They keep a couple of hands over the winter, but this was my first summer, and I felt pretty good staying on this late, to tell you the truth."

"How big a place?"

"Ten thousand acres, two hundred cows. Half dozen cowboys."

"Hay?"

"Yeah, pretty good alfalfa. They kept me on for a couple of weeks to be sure the feeding operation would work for them."

"So, what brought you out here to cowboy?" I passed a snowplow clearing the last of yesterday's powder, now soiled from the tires of a thousand vehicles. "Aren't there enough cowboy jobs in Montana?"

He chuckled. "Ever seen a cow standing in good grass with her head poked through the fence?"

I laughed. "Got the picture. I reckon we all have a bit of wanderlust." I stuck a hand in his direction. "I'm Cody, by the way. Cody Brandon."

"Billy Clay," the hitchhiker said. "Real good to meet you, Cody."

"You too, Billy. You wouldn't know it from this getup, but I've been cowboying too. Up in Canada. I'm kind of on an assignment right now. Needed a disguise." I turned away, looked out my side window, before throwing a glance at my rider. "I'm not at all the hippie I appear to be."

The silence was broken only by the thump of cold tires against the road.

"Well, that sounds interesting, but it's none of my business," Billy said, studying the snowy hills to the south.

I drummed my fingers against the wheel. *Should I tell him? No, that's crazy. I don't know anything about him. But I just asked God to send me help. Maybe this is God's answer.* I bit my lip and shot a furtive glance. Billy was looking straight ahead, impassive.

I sighed through my nose. What've I got to lose? He's just headed through.

Then I remembered meeting Willie in the woods, hearing about Grand Valley from a complete stranger. A clear answer to prayer. I turned toward my passenger.

"It's like this. I'm a wanderlust kind of guy too. You went west to cowboy, I went north. From Texas to British Columbia."

"Really? Texas to BC? Sounds like a big trip." He smiled. "Another greener grass story?"

"You could say that I reckon." I nodded. "Started while I was at Texas A&M." I told Billy how I'd met Rod at A&M and heard about the mountain ranches of BC. About landing the job at the Double Bar, leaving home. I hit the high points of the trip—pushing a stranger's car to the side of the road, trouble crossing the border, motor blowing up, hitchhiking.

"Wow, walking in the dark. Doesn't sound like much fun."

"It was not, but I survived. Prayed a lot." I thought I saw Billy's eyebrows lift and kept on with my narrative. I held off the grizzly story for the time being.

"So, I came back down here to get this straightened out. That's when things really got interesting. I no sooner got here when a lawyer told me I was wanted for voluntary manslaughter and assault with intent to commit murder."

Billy flinched. "What? I don't understand."

"Exactly my response. But this lawyer explained it. The driver I helped told the cops his sick wife was in the back seat, he was trying to tend to her so he couldn't go very fast, and I was behind and couldn't pass. Said I was honking and in a rage. And when he stopped to let me go by, I jumped out and pushed his car into the lake. His wife drowned, and the cops pegged me for a murderer."

Billy drew a breath and pursed his lips. "Wow. What a story." He turned to me. "What are you gonna do?"

I told him about my initial attempt to turn myself in, getting 911 on the phone and what I saw on the TV at the convenience store.

Billy's jaw dropped. "You've gotta be kidding. Unbelievable."

"You're telling me. That's why I decided flight and fight was the way of wisdom. Who knows what might happen if I fell into this guy's clutches. He may be the county attorney, but he's also a big liar."

"When did this happen?"

"Day before yesterday." I told Billy about my quick trip to Seattle, Portland, and back. "I wanted to alert my folks I was alive and try to throw the police off my trail in the bargain. I knew the police would talk to them, and if I called them, they'd be duty bound to admit they'd heard from me. And before that, I found this sappy outfit in a secondhand store and rented a room. I figure this is going to take a few days."

"What's going to take a few days?"

"I've gotta find a way to put the law back on the right trail."

"How do you do that?"

"I'm not real sure, to tell the truth, but I have to try."

Now in Coeur d'Alene, I took an exit and parked on the shoulder. "Here you are, Billy. Sorry I can't take you any further, hope your trip goes well for you."

Billy stepped out and opened the back door. "Nothing to apologize for. And anyway, you've got plenty to think about."

He pulled out his saddle and bag, closed the door, stepped back and spoke. I heard words but they didn't register at first. I was thinking about the lost inheritance right then, the grief never far from mind. I nodded and pulled on the road. Then it struck me what he'd said.

I whipped my head around to look at Billy. He stood on the shoulder getting his stuff together. I pulled off again and got out.

"What did you say?" I hollered over the freeway traffic.

"Huh?" Billy looked up. "What's that?"

"No, what did you say just now? I couldn't hear you well, but did you say you're going to pray for me?"

Billy smiled and nodded. "I did. And I will."

"That's great. Thanks." I got back in my car. Then out again, "Listen, can I ask you a question?" My new friend nodded, and I continued. "Are you a Christian? Like, do you really know and love Jesus? Know what I mean?"

Billy grinned wide, "I know exactly what you mean, yes." He chuckled. "And yes, I belong to Jesus. No thanks to me, it's all his grace."

"Cool, brother." I rubbed my arm and looked at my shoes. "Listen, I, uh." I kicked a stone. "You don't suppose?" My mouth opened without words, but I finally found my voice.

"I know this must sound crazy, but is there any chance you could spare a couple of days? Now that I know you're a believer, it would just be amazing to have someone with me. Two are better than one, after all."

Billy smiled again. "Had the same thought but didn't want to push in on somebody else's business. You know, code of the West, and all that." We laughed. "I've got the time, Cody. No hurry for me."

"Wow, that would be unbelievable. Don't know how to say thanks."

"Never mind that, where do we start?"

CHAPTER 56

A Friend Closer Than a Brother

Coeur d'Alene, Thursday December 3

Two index fingers clinched two coffee cup handles at a ham-and-egg café along Northwest Avenue as Coeur d'Alene morning traffic slid by. Other than a busy waiter, no one paid attention to a strange pair, a cowboy and a hippie, sharing a booth and talking between sips as we waited for breakfast.

"You believe in God's providence, right, Billy?"

"Of course."

"I think it's amazing that just last night I asked God to send me some help, and this morning there you were standing on the shoulder waiting for me."

"I get what you're saying," Billy said. "And here's another amazing part of that. My last ride was a couple who picked me up in Spokane and when we got to their exit, they offered to take me home and feed me breakfast. I had no reason to decline, they were really nice folks, and I was just getting ready to say 'Sure' when the next thing I knew, what should come out of my mouth but 'No thanks' before I even knew what was happening.

"They dropped me off, and I walked across to where you saw me. I wondered 'What was I thinking?' Right then, you came along. Can't remember another time I turned down a free, home-cooked meal."

"Well, I'm powerful glad you did. And you're getting a free meal, even if it's not home cooked."

Breakfast arrived, and we bowed heads as I prayed. "Father, thank you for bringing Billy along today. What a fantastic answer to prayer. And thanks for this good food. And help us, Lord. Show us the right way in this crazy job we have to do."

After a couple of bites, I looked up. "What can you tell me about your growing up?"

"Not much to tell." He bit bacon and chewed. "Kind of a hard childhood, to tell you the truth. I knew Dad loved me, but he never said it. Got plenty of beatings, thought it was pretty unfair, and it was. But I can smile about it now. He taught us to work hard, and I'm grateful for that."

"How about your mom?"

"She's a good mom. Their marriage was okay, nothing outstanding." He stirred sugar into a second cup of coffee. "After I graduated and moved out, things got a little better. Dad rented out part of the pasture, slowed down, and things went along pretty smooth."

I told Billy about growing up in Dalhart, helping with the store, spending time on my friends' ranches. "All those years what I really wanted was to be a cowboy and have my own place someday."

"I know what you're talking about. That is mostly the same with me. With one exception."

"What's that?"

"Believe it or not, I thought about a career in acting."

"Really?"

"Hard to believe, I know. But I enjoyed drama in high school. Was fairly good at it. My drama teacher encouraged me to pursue it. But it didn't take long to rule that out. I was meant to run cattle."

I nodded. "I get that. That's the whole reason I went to BC. Not just to get a job but look for a spread. Mind you, I almost died in the process."

"Worked you pretty hard up there, did they?"

"No, not that. I mean sure, we worked hard, but I almost died a violent death. That's what I mean."

"A violent death? Somebody came after you?"

"Not somebody. Something. I barely escaped getting killed by a bear."

"Whoa, partner, I gotta hear about that."

The waitress stepped to the table. "Anything else?"

I said, "No, thanks. Just one check, please." She walked away, and I continued. "The boss sent two of us into the high country to find some lost horses. It was quite a ride. Took us six days to get to the last meadow, up pretty high. The other guy got sick, so I was on my own at that point.

"The ranch owner had warned us to be on the lookout for grizzlies, but I was not prepared for what happened, I can tell you that.

"When I got to the last cabin, I corralled my horses and took a walk to see a canyon. The other cowboy said it was a grand sight, about a half mile walk. Like an idiot, I didn't even think to take my gun. Won't do that again."

Billy sat in rapt attention.

"Anyway, the canyon was amazing. I laid on my belly with my head over the edge for a long time, until the light was fading. When I scooted back and stood up, I heard a grizzly growl in the woods between me and the cabin."

"Oh man. What'd you do?"

315

"Wasn't anything to do but freeze on the spot. No tree in reach and a long drop behind me. Pray and wait to see what happened—that was my only option.

"But I didn't have to wait long. Less than a minute later, a bear exploded out of the woods coming straight at me. He covered two hundred feet in seconds. It was surreal."

"But here you are talking about it. I gotta know what happened."

"Well, it was totally God. Just before that bear got to me, I found a rock and picked it up. He stopped, stood up on his hind feet, roared like the dickens, and got ready to take a swing. I aimed for his nose and gave it all I had, praying all the time, and that rock hit him right on the nose. He dropped on the spot and never moved."

Billy was shaking his head. "That's about the most amazing firsthand account I've ever heard, I can tell you that."

"Well, it changed my life, that's for sure."

"In fact, that's a fairly good indication God's not finished with you, right?"

"I agree. And I'm still working on that dream, but I've got to take care of this crazy homicide charge first."

"So how do you want to start?"

"Research. Need to find facts, starting with the first name of this Johnson guy who set me up. The Coeur d'Alene phone book lists 27 Johnsons, so that's a dead end. But I figure the library should have a newspaper archive, right?"

I figured the Coeur d'Alene library would have a newspaper story from October 27, seven weeks ago. We found the place and parked. But the locked door had a sign.

"Library closed for structural repairs. Scheduled reopening January 2. Our apologies for the inconvenience."

I shook my head and turned to Billy. "Wouldn't you know it?" I tapped a forefinger against my temple, "Think, Brandon, think." But Billy beat me to the punch.

"How about the newspaper office?"

Everybody reads the paper, but nobody knows where it's produced. We asked four people for directions to the *Coeur d'Alene Press* but nobody had an idea. We finally scored when we pulled up to a crosswalk guard in the middle of the street. Billy stepped out and when a gaggle of students was safely across spoke to the old man.

"Oh yes, I know where it is. Delivered papers when I was a boy. Back in the thirties. I wanted a pony and my dad said I would have to earn my own money. Just head over—" He interrupted himself. "Hold on, here's another batch of kiddos."

The old fellow spoke to the students, "Now you boys and girls sit tight right there for just a second." He swiveled back to Billy and related turn-by-turn how to get to the newspaper office a mile east.

"Okay, kids. Let's get across this street."

"I'm sorry, young man, but our policies don't allow me to give you access to the archives."

"What?" Billie and I looked at each other, eyebrows cocked. "Why not?"

"It's policy. I think you'll find most newspapers do the same. The boss isn't here, but it wouldn't make any difference. He's very adamant about it, a real stickler for policy."

I bit my tongue as we walked out in silence. At the curb, I ran my fingers through my hair and stopped just in time to avoid knocking my wig off. I leaned against the front fender of the Chevy while Billy stood, arms folded, staring into the distance.

After a long moment, I spoke. "Library closed, paper office uncooperative, where does that leave us?" I shook my head and rubbed the heels of my hands against my eyes. "There's gotta be a way."

"Who else would know about this?" He looked at me, "Lots of people would know about this story, right? This isn't a big city. It's not like this kind of thing happens all the time."

"True. The problem is it didn't happen nearby. Bishop Lake is eighty miles north of here. Five weeks and eighty miles is going to narrow the field." More silence, more staring into space.

"Hold it. I know another guilty party. Besides the driver."

Billy's eyebrows shot up, his head bent to the side. "What other party?"

"I can't identify the driver, and we're not having any luck on that angle, so maybe we should work on the identity we do know."

"And who would that be?"

"The crooked lawyer who offered to help me. Introduced himself to me on Monday as Mark Morgan, but right after that I saw him on TV. Marc Malone, County Attorney."

Billy looked at the ground, scratched his neck. "Hold on, I don't get something. This happened eighty miles north, and Coeur d'Alene is in the same county?"

"What do you mean?"

"Well, the county attorney would be the prosecutor for crimes in his county, right? Is Bishop Lake in the same county as Coeur d'Alene?"

"Oh, I see what you mean. No, Bishop Lake is in Bonner County. Malone told me the case is here because the population in Bonner County is too small to support a prosecutor's office. I paused. "But who knows whether that was another lie?"

A car of high school girls drove by, one hanging out the front passenger window. "Hey, groovy. Love the Janis Joplin look." The girls whooped and sped off. I rolled my eyes.

"Okay, so how are we going to get any information out of him?" Billy said.

I drew a breath and sighed through my nose. "We've got a couple of options, I reckon. One, I go back to him, tell him I've thought it over and would like to hire him to be my lawyer."

"You think you can trust him with that? If he is the crook you say, why wouldn't he just call the police on the spot and have you locked up. You don't have any witnesses to the conversation, right? It's your word against his. Sounds risky to me."

"Agreed." I tapped a finger against my upper lip. "So that brings us to plan B."

"As in Billy, I take it?"

I laughed. "Well, you're the only one left."

"So, what would that look like? Am I going to just waltz in and make up a story to hire me?"

"Probably not. I may have a better idea. I think we can put your drama skills to work."

CHAPTER 57

COME LET US TAKE COUNSEL TOGETHER

Wolf Creek, Thursday December 3

Julie loved teaching, but some days took the keen edge off that affection. Danny, her challenge student, required more attention and drained more energy than all the rest combined. At thirteen, he was two inches taller and much stronger than she. From his thick shock of unruly hair to his size eleven boots, he intimidated her. Danny had never been taught respect and constantly challenged her authority in the classroom.

Like today. He came in after lunch and stood talking to a friend even after she rang the bell.

"Danny, please take your seat."

"Make me."

"Don't be silly. Please sit down."

He turned back to his companion. "And yesterday I went trapping with my uncle. You should see the coyote we caught." He stretched his hands all the way apart. "My uncle said he was the biggest coyote he'd seen in a long time."

"Good for you, Danny." Julie broke in, refusing to be discounted. "I'm glad you had such a nice time trapping with your uncle. But you don't want to cause trouble for the whole school, do you? Everyone is waiting for you. We can't start till you take your seat." She understood the honor versus shame culture of village life. An appeal to community values usually worked best.

Danny sat, but resisted her all afternoon. Three-thirty could not come soon enough. Six hours of teaching, dealing with Danny, and worrying about Cody had depleted her.

She straightened the room and walked home on the narrow path she had shoveled yesterday through ten inches of fresh snow. The thermometer registered six below Celsius, but she'd fed the stove at lunch time, so the cabin was toasty.

Julie moved around her small space, straightening books on their shelves, wiping the counter, arranging the firewood, checking the cupboard to update her grocery list. She sat at the table and rubbed the back of her neck.

"Father, I'm so worried about Cody. I feel so far away. Please give him grace, Lord. Help him to know you're near. Please protect him. Please help this nightmare to be over soon."

She reached for the phone and flinched when it rang before she touched it. It was Linda.

"Oh, Linda, I was just going to call you." She stood and paced between the foot of the bed and the wall where the phone was hung with a long, coiled cord to the receiver.

"Really. Well, we had the same idea at the same moment. How are you?"

"I'm a wreck. Tough day of school and worrying about Cody. I'm so concerned about him. Just wish I could hear something."

"Well that's understandable, Julie. I mean, I'm sure it's all going to work out, but it's hard to live without any word from him."

"I know. I know. I keep thinking I'll wake up from this bad dream. It's just so unreal."

"Cody's a strong guy. Tough, self-sufficient, resourceful. I have no doubt he's taking all this in stride."

Julie sat on the bed. "Thanks for saying that, Linda. I'm sure you're right."

"Of course I'm right. Even the little bit I've been around him, I've been impressed with his strength of character."

"Yes, that's true."

"And think about the stories he will have. His kids and grandkids will be mesmerized."

"I hope I'm around to see that."

"Anything you can tell me about that?"

"Well, in fact, yes." She related, verbatim, Cody's non-proposal speech from Sunday night.

"Wow. Julie, I love it. That is fantastic, eh? What did you say?"

"I asked him if he was proposing. He said 'No, just clarifying.' Wanted to be sure I knew his intentions before he left."

"Then what happened?"

"He asked if he could kiss me."

"And what did you say?"

"What do you suppose?"

"Yes?"

"Of course."

"What more can you tell me about your relationship? Seems like it's moved pretty quickly."

"Yes, I know what you mean—that surprised me too."

"Are you okay with it?"

"Yes and no." She hesitated a second. "You know I've never gotten serious with anyone before. To tell you the truth, I've never felt this way about anyone. So, I don't know if it's normal or not to ..." She paused, searching for language. "Well, to fall in love. How do you know if it's the real thing?"

"Wish I could help you with that. Never been there myself."

Julie sighed. "I mean, I'll admit I've been a little confused about it, but on balance the good outweighed anything that concerned me. In fact, the only concern I had was how fast it was going. I really enjoy being with Cody—he's not just another guy. And I was ready to take it a step at a time until this craziness started. Now, who knows what to expect?"

Wolf Creek, Saturday December 5

Julie woke with Danny on her mind. "What am I going to do with this boy?" Still lying in bed, she closed her eyes again.

"Father, look at me. I'm a mess. I've tried everything I can think of. Please shed light on my path. Please show me how I can teach these students. I don't want to be a failure. Jesus, help me. I need you."

His behavior notwithstanding, Julie refused to believe the kid was bad. Times like this, she recalled Solzhenitsyn, "The line separating good and evil passes not through states, nor between classes, nor between political parties either, but right through every human heart."

That boy was redeemable. But how? She needed a breakthrough, an idea of how to go forward.

After she lit a fire in the stove, she dressed and headed to the village store for tea. The snow squeaked under her boots as a pack of village dogs ran yipping past her and stopped to crowd around something in the road before darting off again in pursuit of some canine attraction insensible to her.

Interesting how they work together as a pack. Survival, maybe. Strength in numbers.

She reached the store and closed the door quickly, luxuriating for a moment in the robust embrace of wood heat.

"Pretty cold, eh?" Sandy spoke from behind the counter. She was a pleasant lady, a little frazzled, but always smiling. She and her husband, Ken, owned the store and the stage line. Sandy kept the store and the apartment upstairs. Ken drove the "Wolf Creek stage," a four-wheel-drive bus.

"Hi, Sandy. Yes, brr." She pushed her hood back and combed fingers through her hair. "Is it normal to be this cold so early in the winter?"

"Not that unusual," Sandy replied. "Just wait till January. Gets down to forty below."

"I'm not sure I could tell the difference."

"Oh yes, you will." Sandy kept talking while she turned back to the pile of screws she was sorting on the countertop. "I've heard lots of people say that, but not after they've experienced it. You'll feel the difference, trust me."

"Well, at any rate, it will be an adventure for someone from the Lower Mainland." Julie headed for the tea shelf.

"And as long as I have my Twining's Earl Grey I'll survive." She stooped to scrutinize the selection of teas.

"How are things going at school?"

Julie straightened up. "Okay. I guess." She paused. "Well, to tell you the truth, not very good."

"Oh? Having classroom management problems?"

"How did you know?"

"Lucky guess?" She peered into a jar of screws looking for something. "But I spent fifteen years teaching in a village school."

Julie's jaw dropped. "What? You've never told me that."

Sandy winked. "I have now."

"But why not till now?"

"Timing, Julie, it's all about timing."

"I don't know what you mean."

"Before now, you would have found it merely interesting," Sandy said as she scooted screws around on the counter. "But now, I have your attention. You're in a teachable moment."

"Oh, my goodness. I've had a mentor next door all this time and didn't know it."

"You've read *Dare to Discipline* by James Dobson, I assume."

"No. I don't recall that book."

"I'll loan you my copy. You'll benefit from it. But there are some things particular to a village context you won't see in any book."

"Like what?"

"Any small, isolated community like Wolf Creek runs on consensus."

"Okay. Makes sense."

"I'm guessing you've got a problem student. Right?"

"Yes. You nailed it."

"One of the older, bigger boys."

"Right again."

"What have you tried?"

"The usual. Give him as much free rein as I can. Let him tell his stories. Plenty of patience." She backed up to the stove, arms crossed in front of her. "But none of this has won him over, at least not consistently. He'll be fine for a day, and then he starts in again. He seems to relish challenging my authority."

"Not unusual when you put a young female over a big teenaged male. And in this community, you absolutely must avoid pushing him into a corner or shaming him. That's a definite no-no." She used a small scoop to pour the sorted screws into two jars. "You need to get the community involved."

"How do I do that?"

Sandy placed the jars of screws on a shelf and turned back to Julie. "Have you noticed how the tribal leadership deals with discipline problems?"

Julie's furrowed brow signaled the answer.

"You've met the chief and council, right?"

"Sure."

"Well, if I were in your shoes, I'd ask to meet with them and get their advice. You're an outsider, which puts you at a disadvantage in the classroom. Seeking their counsel shows you don't have all the answers and honors their leadership in the community. On top of all that, they know how to deal with unruly students. They can help you."

"Well, that makes a lot of sense." Julie set a box of tea on the counter and reached for her wallet. "I'm going to do just that. Thanks so much, Sandy."

"No problem."

CHAPTER 58

GOOD NEWS FROM A DISTANT LAND

Kamloops, Saturday December 5

Rod, weary and famished, finished a long Saturday of veterinary house calls and headed home where he anticipated celebrating the weekend with a grilled steak and a hockey game.

Bo greeted him as he stepped into his apartment. Rod knelt to caress the dog. "Hey, buddy, how was your day? I'm ready to eat. How about you?" The dog whined and licked his face. Rod let him outside and turned to answer the ringing phone.

"Hi, Rod, this is Betty Brandon."

"Oh, hello, Mrs. Brandon. How are you keeping?"

"We're doing okay. We just heard from Cody and thought you might be interested."

"Oh, good. What can you tell me? When did he call?"

"He didn't call, he wrote two letters, and it looks like we were worried for nothing. He's just taking his time on a leisurely trip down the West Coast."

"What? That doesn't make sense. Were you surprised to read that?"

Gary Brumbelow

"I'll say. He didn't explain anything about the legal problem in Coeur d'Alene. Said he wanted to wait until he could talk face to face. So, it must have turned out okay."

"Hmm. Seems a little strange."

"Well, he actually sent us two letters, one from Seattle mailed on Tuesday and another from Portland mailed on Wednesday. His writing was, well, kind of coy. But he's probably still recovering from stress."

Rod opened the door for Bo. "So, you think everything's okay?"

"Yes, I think so. Here, I'll read one of his letters to you."

Hi, Mom and Dad,

You're probably surprised to receive a letter but under the circumstances, this was the best way to communicate.

I met with a lawyer in Coeur d'Alene. It didn't take very long. As I anticipated, they'd made a mistake, and the prosecutor knows I'm not guilty. I was only in Coeur d'Alene for a couple of days, and now, I'm back on the road.

I'd never seen much of the Pacific Northwest and figured even though it's an indirect route to Texas, I may not get another opportunity to visit places I've heard so much about.

I hope you both are well. I'll drop you a note again and call when I can.

Love, Cody.

"Well, that seems pretty straightforward." Rod stooped and scratched Bo's ears. "What route do you suppose he intends to take? Will he go through California?"

"No telling. He's got an independent streak, as you know."

"Yes, I do know. But maybe you'll get a phone call from him one of these days."

"I'm sure we will. But I wanted to give you this update. How are things with you, Rod?"

"I'm fine. Keeping busy with work. But when you love your work, that's how you want it, I reckon." He felt funny invoking a Texas word, and Betty laughed.

"Sounds like Cody's rubbed off on you."

"You could say that for sure."

"It was very nice to talk to you, Rod."

"Same here. And I'll call Julie and catch her up with the news."

He was looking for her number when the phone rang.

"Rod, it's Diana Schwartz." He groaned inside. Diana's husband had died in a tractor accident last summer, and she was trying to operate without him—with little experience around cattle.

"What's up, Diana?"

"Sorry to bother you at dinner time, but I've got a cow in labor and having trouble. Can't remember how to run this puller."

The steak would need to wait.

Wolf Creek, Monday, December 7

The entire population of Wolf Creek—counting the secondary students who boarded in town, and the young people in college or trade school, and anyone away for medical care, or temporarily living somewhere else—was just over two-hundred souls. Even in winter, bundled up and treading on snow, you could walk right through the

Gary Brumbelow

village and back in less than thirty minutes. Julie did it every day.

But today she had a destination. The chief and council were meeting today and she'd managed to get on their agenda.

The big, log A-frame in the middle of the village served as the band office. The building rested a couple of feet above its surroundings, protection against flooding in the spring runoff. She approached the building not sure what to expect, stamped the snow off her boots, and walked in.

From the empty reception area, she looked into the great room. A fireplace blazed in the center. The Christmas tree, decorated by her students, stood near the large south window with a view of hills topped by thick timber and flanked with deep snow.

Two men and three women occupied stuffed chairs in a half circle around the fire, talking quietly, sipping coffee, and nibbling on smoked salmon strips. They looked up as Julie approached.

The chief, Andy Rosette, motioned toward an empty chair near the tree. "Have a seat. We'll be with you in a minute."

CHAPTER 59

WITH THE CROOKED YOU SHOW YOURSELF ASTUTE

Coeur d'Alene, Monday, December 7

Coeur d'Alene residents prided themselves on their civic engagement. The high school ball games were always packed out, neighbors took care of each other, volunteers swooped down on every bit of litter in the roadways, most folks went to church on Sundays, and the town motto was "A world to gain in Coeur d'Alene."

Everyone put great stock in law and order. On Independence Day, the police community was honored with marching bands, a couple of floats, and speeches. The mayor always ended his address, "God bless America, God bless Idaho, but especially God bless Coeur d'Alene." And the crowd, anxious to get to the hot dogs and homemade ice cream, cheered wildly.

But invoking a deity's blessing isn't equal to living in virtue. Notwithstanding the warm community spirit, evil lurked in high places, including the Kootenai County Courthouse where a 1965 Chevy Impala nosed into the parking lot on a cold December morning. A young man in a gray business suit stepped out of the passenger side and stood holding the door open while he spoke to the driver.

"If this works, it will be a miracle of the holy water, as my uncle used to put it."

"Well, I don't know about the holy water, but we have been praying for a miracle," said the hippie behind the wheel. "And we need one. Think you can remember your lines?"

"Down pat," Billy said. "That's the least of my worries." He regarded the imposing Georgian Revival architecture, its three stories looming above him like Mt. Everest over a lame Sherpa.

He plucked a briefcase from the seat he'd just vacated. "Here goes nothing. Pray, brother, pray." He took a deep breath and walked into a mist of fear, hoping those weekend hours of practicing the big ruse would do their magic.

In the empty lobby, he ran his eyes down the directory until he came to "Marc Malone, County Attorney, 305." He headed for the stairs, then checked himself. A real law student would take the elevator.

Two floors up, the doors opened to a short hallway. At the other end, a smoked glass door announced, "Kootenai County Attorney." Three steps beyond, and he was at the reception desk. A lovely young woman looked up. "Can I help you?"

He swallowed. "Um, is Mr. Malone in?"

"What's your name, please?"

"Oh, sorry. I'm Dean Beckett."

She frowned at her computer screen. "I don't see you on Mr. Malone's calendar. Do you have an appointment?"

Breathe, he told himself. "No, I don't have an appointment. I'm just a huge fan of his and wondered if I might get five minutes to meet him and tell him how much I admire his work."

"Oh?" She tilted her head, eyebrows raised.

"Yes. I've been studying the law, and I've read all his cases. I find his approach to prosecution intriguing. He's been a huge inspiration to me to pursue justice. I drove over from Spokane and was hoping I could catch him at an opportune moment."

She looked down, bit her lip. "Well, of course Mr. Malone's time is precious." She drummed her fingers on the desk. "But he does have a soft spot for students. Why don't you have a seat, and I'll see what he says, Mr. Beckett."

He sat as she glided to a door, knocked, and stepped in. He heard a murmur of voices and the knot in his stomach morphed to mush. *I must be crazy. What if this thing blows up?* His courage flagged, and he was ready to leave when she came back.

"Mr. Malone will see you now. He can give you ten minutes."

"So, what happened? You were in there a long time. Please tell me it went well." I spoke and backed out of the parking space where I had alternated between praying and panicking for forty minutes.

"It was amazing. Hit pay dirt. We're looking for Frank Johnson."

I repeated the name. "Wow, good work, brother. Tell me all about it."

"Well, I told the receptionist I was a huge fan and drove over from Spokane in hopes of meeting him. Said I'd read more of his cases than anyone's and admired his work. Wondered if I could just get five minutes of his time. She decided to ask him, and it worked, just like we rehearsed, in like Flynn."

"What's he like?"

"He was okay. I mean, not rude but not real friendly either. I gushed about his performance in Idaho vs. Carruthers, Idaho vs. Matthews, Idaho vs. Grenfall. Those hours reading in the law library Friday were time well spent. A little flattery opened him up, and he couldn't stop talking about himself."

"So how did you get Frank Johnson's name out of him?"

"That was all of God. I asked him what he was working on now, and he spilled his guts about your case." Rod shook his head. "Well, not exactly spilled his guts, but said enough I knew it was about you."

"But how did you get him to say Frank Johnson?"

"That was totally providential. He couldn't remember your status with reference to immigrating to Canada, so he buzzed his secretary and asked her to bring him the Frank Johnson file."

"Yes. Thank you, Lord."

"Praise the Lord and pass the phone book."

Fifteen minutes later, we parked across the street two doors down from 522 Randle Street. The neighborhood looked about thirty-five years old, lower middle-class, simple homes of similar pattern, mature trees, attached single-car garages facing the alley.

No sign of life at 522 in the middle of the day, and nothing distinguished the house from its companions.

We drove around the corner and entered the alley. Little of the house was visible from the back where a high laurel hedge parted only enough for the narrow driveway.

"No sign of a dog," I observed.

"And the nearest streetlight is half a block away," Billy replied.

"So far, so good."

Every day exposed me to discovery by the law. We needed to act quickly. But we wanted to establish a pattern to Johnson's comings and goings, so we spent forty-eight hours watching.

Monday evening, he left at nine. The next morning, we watched bleary-eyed as he pulled into the alley at six. Tuesday, same schedule. We would make our move Wednesday night.

CHAPTER 60

THE LORD WEIGHS THE HEART

Wolf Creek, Wednesday, December 9

Julie Stewart closed her eyes. She wanted to experience the moment at a kinesthetic level, feel the slow rocking motion that rippled up her spine, heaved her up and down, wanted to draw in the unique aroma of horse flesh, hear the steady plod of hooves against the wet gravel.

She was riding a horse. *If Jessie could see me now.*

Her sister had suggested she level with Cody about her fear of horses, and she had agreed. But with Cody gone, and no way to know when he'd be back, she'd opted to work on her phobia and be ready to ride with him whenever he returned. *Make it soon, Lord. Please make it soon.*

And she had another reason for riding sooner—the young man walking ahead of her right now, leading his horse with his teacher astride.

"This is good, Danny. I'm so glad I asked you to teach me how to ride." He smiled, and Julie wanted to hug him but settled for a silent prayer of thanksgiving. *We're making progress, Lord. I had despaired of ever seeing his behavior change, and now look at him. Thank you.*

The Monday meeting with the chief and council had launched a new beginning with this unruly student. They'd listened to her carefully and brainstormed. The fruit of that session was now in full bloom. The teacher and the school-hating teenager were enjoying a shared experience. They were beginning to understand each other, and that early trajectory encouraged hope.

At her cabin, she dismounted. "Thanks a bunch, Danny." They shook hands. "You've been a big help. Now I'm not afraid to get on a horse. I even enjoyed it."

He grinned. "You're doing great. Never knew anyone who was so afraid of horses." He mounted and turned the horse toward home. Clouds of vapor rose from the beast's nostrils. "I guess I'm enjoying school. A little bit, anyway. I better get going. I've got English homework to do." He flashed another grin and spurred away.

Coeur d'Alene, Wednesday, December 9

At one a.m., we glided back to Johnson's dark, empty house. We had watched him pull out again at ten o'clock, and then we found a truck-stop parking lot and tried to sleep a few hours in the belief that a forced entry would be less risky after midnight. Driving without lights in the quiet back alley, we nosed into the backyard, the Impala almost concealed by the hedge.

"Let's pray," I said. "Lord, it feels funny asking you to help us break into this house. But we need to safely expose this lie and prove my innocence. So please help us, Lord. We're depending on you."

We tugged on gloves and black stocking caps and headed for the back door.

Dalhart, Texas, my hometown, boasted just over five thousand souls. Billy's parents' Montana ranch lay a half hour from the nearest hamlet. Between us we didn't have enough suburban sensibilities to anticipate that "city folks" locked their doors and windows. All of them.

Finding the back door locked, we tried the bedroom window, stole all the way around the structure without discovering any point of entry.

"We're gonna have to break glass," Billy said under his breath. We stood in the shadow of the garage.

"Think about that, Billy. We're whispering, and we're going to break glass? I don't think so." I stepped to the rear entry and ran my fingers along the frame. "Reckon we can force the door open without making much noise?"

I went to the car and came back with the crowbar we'd bought at Star Hardware, downtown Coeur d'Alene. "Let's try this."

I pushed the wedge end of the bar between the backdoor and frame as far as it would go and applied pressure. The wood groaned.

"Wait," Billy said, "this could muffle the noise." He picked up the heavy rubber door mat and gasped. "Oh, my goodness. Would you look at that?"

"What?" I followed Billy's eyes to the concrete where the mat had been. There, shrouded in shadow but clearly visible lay a key.

Ten seconds later, we stood in the dark kitchen. "Thank you, Jesus." Billy pumped his fist and forearm in celebration.

I lit the kitchen table with my penlight. "Now that we're in, what next? I'm way out of my league."

"Me too." Billy pulled off his cap and scratched his head. "What exactly are we looking for?"

"Anything that indicates a motive for murder. Why does a guy decide to kill his wife?"

Billy pursed his lips. "Hmm. Insurance? Maybe he stood to collect a big, fat payout."

"Okay, that's a start. And I think I know where to look." I pointed my light at a small desk in the corner.

"Yes. In fact, that's the place to look for evidence no matter what his motive was."

"Okay," I said, "I'll start with this file drawer. Why don't you poke around the rest of the house. See what you can come up with."

I sat on the desk chair, pulled open the drawer, and blew a low whistle. "Somebody is organized. Look at these typed file labels, color coded, the whole nine yards." But Billy was busy elsewhere and didn't hear.

I thumbed across the file folders to "Insurance," pulled it out and shuffled through "Auto" and "Health" to "Life." "Got it." I extracted the stapled bundle and riffled pages until I came to "Benefits." Frank Johnson was insured for one hundred thousand dollars, Joan for ten thousand. "Enough to cover funeral expenses, I reckon."

I shoved the papers back into the folder and replaced it in the drawer in its original location.

Billy returned from his fishing expedition. "Struck out, Cody. Couldn't find anything that mattered. Clothing, shoes, books, odds and ends on shelves and dressers. And guns."

"Sure enough? What kind of guns?"

"Twelve-gauge pump shotgun. Ought-six-bolt-action. Also, a box of 9mm ammo but no pistol. Must be packing."

I whistled low. We exchanged a long, thoughtful look. "Father, protect us."

Billy nodded. "Oh, and a bunch of camera equipment. Two thirty-five-millimeter SLRs, three lenses, a shoebox of negatives."

"Let's take those negatives. Might come in handy."

"Gotcha."

"What about framed pictures? See anything in a picture that might be a clue? What did she look like? Unhappy marriage? Anything like that?"

"No pictures of a woman. Lots of pictures of this guy." He showed me a six-by-nine framed photo of a man with a fishing pole. "Look familiar?"

I took the picture and squinted. "Yes, this is Frank." A weird discomfort rose in my chest. "Wow, I sure see him in a different light now."

I handed the frame back to Billy. "You know, believe it or not, it did seem like something was funny about that guy. I helped him, and he sort of shooed me away. Like he wanted to get rid of me." I shook my head. "This whole thing is still surreal to me." I pressed my lips together and cocked my head. "If I didn't believe in God's providence, I'd be bitter at how all this has fallen out." I shook my head and looked at Billy. "Know what I mean?"

"Sure. That is, I can't fully identify with it, but I can imagine it must feel weird."

I sighed and returned to the present. "But it's kind of strange there would be no pictures of her, don't you think?" Before Billy could answer, I spoke again. "We should go through the dressers."

I followed Billy to the master bedroom. We paused in the doorway and Billy spoke. "You know those movies where somebody comes home and finds his house ransacked by a villain looking for something?"

"That's not gonna happen here. We need to leave things as we found them."

I stepped to a chest of drawers, while Billy went to the dresser. Penlights in mouths, we opened drawers and mumbled their contents to each other—socks, shirts, pants, sweaters, jeans, sewing materials, crafts.

I was halfway through my examination when Billy accidentally pulled the bottom drawer all the way out. He bent down to guide the drawer back onto the rail and stopped.

"What's this?" He set the drawer on the floor and peered into the cabinet.

I turned toward him. "What?"

"Something is in there. Looks like an envelope taped to the back." He reached in, I heard the sound of ripping tape, and he pulled out a large envelope. "This was taped to the back where it would never be seen without fully removing the drawer."

I stepped over and watched as Billy slit an edge of the envelope with his pocketknife and withdrew the contents, a five-by-seven color photograph. The grain indicated the picture had been enlarged, but it was clear enough. A man and woman closing in on a kiss, eyes closed, lips puckered. The field of view appeared flattened. The picture had been shot with a telephoto lens.

I took all this in, then looked more carefully at the faces. The woman was young, tanned, blonde and beautiful. The man's thick, silver hair suggested he was in his mid-fifties at least. The profile looked vaguely familiar. A moment later Billy and I recognized the face at the same time.

"Marc Malone." We spoke in stunned unison.

"What does it mean?" Billy was first to break the silence.

"I don't know, but it's important. Let's take it, straighten up, and get out of here."

CHAPTER 61

HURT BY THEIR ADULTEROUS HEARTS

Coeur d'Alene, Wednesday, December 9

We were on Thirty-Second Avenue headed for the freeway before either spoke.

"Do you think that's Johnson's wife?" Billy said. "She was having an affair with Malone and Frank found out and killed her?"

"Must be that," I said. "At least it makes sense. Frank must have suspected something and tracked them down and caught them red-handed."

Westbound for Spokane on Interstate 90 at three a.m., we had the road to ourselves except for the occasional semi. We thought much and spoke little while the *ka-thump* of the road kept time.

"But something's strange about this," I said. "Why would Malone believe Johnson's story about me? That doesn't add up."

"I see what you mean. If he knew that Frank knew about the affair, wouldn't he suspect Frank as the killer?"

"Or maybe he didn't know Frank knew. But even if he didn't, why would Malone come after me? I mean, he's a professional prosecutor. He would naturally suspect Johnson."

"Could there be some other reason for Malone to ignore Frank and come after you?"

"Like?"

"I don't know. Maybe their families are friends." Billy scanned the horizon. "Or maybe Frank has a public profile that would make it hard to prosecute him so Malone's just taking the easy way out."

We ka-thumped the last fifteen miles to Spokane, each lost in a tangle of twisted thoughts. Back in my room, we lay down to sleep, Billy on an air mattress on the floor.

"Let's pray about this, Billy."

"Sure."

"Lord, first off, thanks for sending this brother to me. What a gift. Where would I be without his help? Thanks for answering our prayer, for helping us find something useful. None of this could have happened without you. And we still need your intervention. We know this picture is important, but we don't know what it means or what to do with it. Please go before us once again. Please show us the way."

Thursday, December 10

"You make a mean breakfast, bro." Billy smiled and poured another cup of coffee.

"It's more like you're the perfect guest, my friend. Instant oatmeal, camp toast, jam, and coffee. You could call that a mean breakfast only if you're using the dictionary definition of mean."

We laughed, and Billy said, "So, what's the plan?"

I sighed. "This is exactly where I was one week ago. I asked God for direction, headed for Coeur d'Alene, and there you were. I figure since we prayed last night, let's do the same thing and see what happens."

"Ready when you are."

I threw the paper plates in the garbage and rinsed the coffeepot.

"Okay, let's go. Gotta get gas, though."

Two blocks before the freeway, I turned right into a self-service station and convenience store and stopped at the pump. I had just killed the engine when Billy went stiff and hissed, "Cody, look."

A striking young woman walked from the store toward a BMW on the other side of the pump. She twisted a lock of long blonde hair around a forefinger and reached for the door with the other hand. Hers was a beauty to turn men's heads, but the two heads turned toward her in that moment were smacked by something more than mere looks.

She was the woman in the photograph leaning in to kiss Marc Malone.

The visual overload triggered short-term mental paralysis for both of us. She was pulling on to the street before we recovered, Billy first. "Don't let her get away."

I roused myself and started the car. "Right. We'll get gas later." I eased into light traffic two cars back from the Beemer before speaking again.

"Looks like we were wrong about the picture."

"Majorly."

"In other words, it's not Malone and Mrs. Johnson in the photo," Billy said. "It's Malone and an unidentified woman."

The Beemer entered the right turn lane for Interstate 90.

"Looks like we get to go west somewhere," I said. "Hopefully not far, looking at this gas gauge."

"In fact, almost young enough to be his daughter."

"Oh, wow. I wonder if Malone is married."

"Yeah, he's married."

"How do you know?"

"Spotted his wedding ring the other day. Plus, he had family pictures on the credenza in his office."

The Beemer exited the freeway, drove two blocks north and turned west on Main while we followed well behind.

"What's all this add up to?"

"Looks powerful. Like an affair to me. Reckon she's his mistress?"

The Beemer pulled into a downtown parking garage. "She's going to be here a while. Let's circle the block. If this is the only exit, I'm going to drop you off and get gas."

Ten minutes later, I stopped across the street from the parking garage, tank full and motor running. Billy sauntered over from a bench outside a store front and climbed in. "Feels good in here. I was thinking about running around the block to warm up."

"Thanks for keeping an eye out," I said. "Now we can follow her as long as needed. Anyway, it's looking like Frank somehow got hold of a picture taken of Malone and his mistress."

"He probably took it himself. Remember I found camera equipment in his closet."

"So, maybe Frank's using that photo to blackmail Malone."

"Yes." Billy sat up straight, snapped his fingers. "That's got to be it."

"What do you reckon that would look like?"

Billy stroked his chin and squinted. "Well, let's see. Somehow Frank manages to get a picture of the county attorney kissing someone he's not married to. Who knows how that happened? Anyway, he finds a way to meet with Malone, shows him the picture and threatens to go public with it." He paused and raised his forefinger. "But for the right price, he'll bury it. Let's make a deal."

I rubbed my nose. "I think we've got it, bro. Frank figures the cops will see holes in his scheme to frame me. I'm a suspect, but they're going to investigate him too. He needs insurance, some way to get the attention off him and on me."

"That's it." Billy waved a finger at the sky. "That's it. He tells Malone, get me off the hook or I'll tell Coeur d'Alene you're having an affair. Hey, Cody, looks like that guy is writing parking tickets and he's coming this way."

"Oh, right." I jumped out and fed the meter. I got back in and wondered out loud, "How does a county attorney get into office?"

"Pretty sure they're elected. Now that you mention it, I saw campaign flyers on his desk."

"Malone is highly motivated to keep Frank happy. Besides his reputation, his whole career is at stake."

"That's right. Malone must have agreed to let Frank off the hook."

"Which is why he's coming after me like a chicken on a June bug."

"Speaking of chicks." Billy pointed across the street at the Beemer exiting the parking garage and turning left.

I pulled out to follow. "How do you reckon Frank managed to get that photo?"

"Good question, but he must have done his homework."

We managed to avoid suspicion for three hours and by 11:00, we knew all the clothing stores in Spokane. At 11:20, the Beemer pulled into the lot of a corner bar in a seedy industrial district. I went the other way at the intersection, turned around in a driveway, and came back to park across the street beside an unkempt machine shop. The cold wind blew paper trash along the sidewalk.

"Better stay hunkered down," I said. "In this outfit I'm nobody to Malone, but if he shows up, he might recognize you."

Billy scrunched. "Keep me posted."

I watched and waited eighteen minutes before a burgundy Chrysler Fifth Avenue eased into the lot from the far side of the bar. I elbowed Billy, "There he is."

The driver's door opened, fancy dress shoes stepped out, and Marc Malone stood. He threw a furtive glance each way, closed the door with a *thunk* and went in.

We looked at each other in a moment of hushed awe before I spoke, "Well, if that doesn't beat all. I mean, it's one thing to see a picture, but this was live."

"Now what?"

I drummed my fingers on the wheel and looked straight ahead. "I think we need to stay right here. I'm guessing this will be nothing more than a long lunch at most. Not sure why, but I feel like we need to find out where she lives. Seems like that could be helpful. If we wait, we might get a chance to follow her home. Sure would like to identity her."

I turned off the car until the cold was unbearable before starting the engine to run till we were warm. Back and forth for a little over an hour. At 12:50, Malone exited the building, got into his car, and left by the same route he'd used when he arrived.

"He's using back streets," Billy said.

Five minutes later, the woman stepped out. She tilted to the car, a little unsteady on her feet, where she stood and groped in her purse for a moment. She pulled out her keys but didn't notice the white paper that flitted to the ground.

Billy and I exchanged glances. "Looks like we get to do a good deed, pick up litter."

I started the Chevy and said, "Jump out for a minute and don't lose sight of her, Billy. I'll be right back." She nosed to the street, and when she looked the other way to check the traffic, I scooted across the intersection, then pulled into the far side of the lot and stopped long enough to retrieve the paper.

Thirty seconds later, I turned from the lot the same direction she'd gone and waited while Billy crossed the street and jumped in. "Two blocks straight ahead, she's turning right."

I accelerated and handed Billy the paper, a small envelope. "Didn't take time to read it."

Billy flipped the envelope over and smiled. "No rush, Cody. No need to risk a ticket."

"What?"

"Debbie Calhoun, 3522 Moffat Ave, Spokane."

"Thank you, Lord."

"I'm starved."

CHAPTER 62

HE ALONE IS MY ROCK

Spokane, Thursday, December 10

A gas station attendant directed us to the Polar King, famous for juicy burgers and thick shakes. As we walked in, the tantalizing aroma of French fries washed over us. I looked at Billy and said, "I can tell already I'm going to like this place."

Ten minutes later, we were chomping down, talking quietly between bites, Billy first.

"So, we've got evidence of an affair involving the county attorney. We've got the woman's name and address. What do we do with all this?"

"Exactly." I twirled a fry through a glob of ketchup.

"We've been making this up as we go along and that's worked pretty good for us so far."

"Yes." I tapped my temple. "What would Columbo do?"

"I love that show." Billy gave a long pull on his chocolate milkshake. "Think back to the incident. Can you remember seeing anything that could be evidence to incriminate Frank?"

"You mean, some kind of object? Something we might go back into his house to look for?"

"Yes, something like that."

I sighed and leaned back, fingers locked behind my head, and emptied puffed cheeks through pursed lips. "Man, I can't think of anything." I shook my head. "I mean, he was wearing gloves, but that doesn't prove anything. He was limping, and he doesn't limp now. Probably a fake limp, but that doesn't prove anything either."

"No. And even if it did, we can't steal a limp from his house." Billy wiped his mouth and bunched his napkin, tossed it into the empty food basket. "Okay, dead end there. Let's try a different tack."

"Like what?"

"The only other thing we have is the picture. There's no obvious connection to the crime, but it's not nothing. In fact, it's very valuable. In the right hands, it could be dynamite."

"Whose hands?"

"That's what we have to figure out."

We looked past each other for a long moment before I snapped my fingers. "Well, duh. We should've thought of this already. There's an entire profession dedicated to this kind of intrigue."

Billy chuckled and lifted his hands, palms up. "Of course. We need a lawyer."

"In Idaho. Let's go to Coeur d'Alene."

The temps had moved above freezing, the traffic threw dirty water everywhere and the Chevy's windshield washer didn't work. We had to pull over every ten minutes and use snow to clean the glass. We reached Coeur d'Alene shortly before five.

"I figured we'd call a dozen lawyers and pick the one we liked best," I said, "but looks like we'll have to take the first one we find."

"Or we wait till tomorrow."

"I don't want to put this off one more day. The clock is ticking so loud I can't hear anything else. When that car dealer gets back from Canada and files the registration, it's game over for me."

We parked outside a convenience store, and I went to the pay phone. The yellow pages listed eleven attorneys. "Lord, please direct me. I don't know how to do this."

The first call reached a busy signal, the next a recorded greeting. But a real human answered the third call, and I breathed "Thank you, Lord."

"Keith Baker's law office, this is Tiffany. How can we help you?"

Not until that moment did I realize I hadn't thought through what to say. "Well, I have kind of a legal problem." *Good grief, I sound like an idiot.*

But the voice remained calm and kind. "Okay. Do you want to tell me about it?"

I drew a deep breath and sighed. "I'm in trouble with the law for something I didn't do." I paused to focus my scattered brainwaves but before I could continue, she jumped back in.

"Okay. Just stay on the line. I'll see if Mr. Baker is available."

I looked at my watch. Fourteen seconds passed before a male voice spoke. "This is Keith Baker. How can I help you?"

I froze. *What am I doing?* The last time I'd talked to a lawyer I'd been deceived and barely escaped with my freedom. A month ago, I'd entered the Williams Lake police station in innocent trust and got locked up for it. *I can't do this. This is not feeling right.*

"I'm sorry. I made a mistake," I muttered, and hung up.

"What happened?" Billy said as I got back in the car.

"I'm not sure. It just didn't seem right. I felt like I was walking into another trap." I rubbed my neck. "I think I'm gonna to need figure out how to do this without the law."

"Okay. Got any ideas?"

"I'm thinking." I rested my temple on my fingers.

"You know, while you're thinking, I'll just call home. Let the folks know what's happening."

Ten minutes later, Billy was back. "Oh man, I got bad news."

"What's that?"

"My sister was in a car accident. She's in the hospital."

"Oh no. Which sister? How old is she?"

"Sixteen. Just got her driver's and was showing off with a friend in the car."

"How bad is she hurt?"

"Two broken ribs, lacerated arm, punctured lung."

"Doggone it, I hate to hear that. What are you going to do?"

"I've got to go, Cody. I'm real sorry, man. Wanted to stick with you to the end, but—"

"I'm sorry for your sister, Billy. And don't you worry about me. I agree. You're needed at home. I'll be fine. Let's go grab your gear and I'll set you out at the freeway."

CHAPTER 63

YOU WHO HAVE MADE ME SEE MANY TROUBLES

Spokane, Friday, December 11

The clock read 5:07 when I gave up sleeping. I'd napped a little but wasn't going to get more shuteye anytime soon. Billy's sudden departure had rocked me to the core. I knew I should be concerned for Billy and his sister, but I was too anxious about my own troubles to think of others.

"Why, God? Why did you send him in direct answer to prayer just to take him away now? I need him, Lord. I need his help." I shook my head. "I need *your* help."

I sagged to the counter and set a pot of coffee to perk. Within a minute, the soothing aroma filled the room. Three minutes later, I savored the brew. After a second cup, the sand in my blood was mostly gone.

I reached for my Bible. "I know there's a psalm that talks about being alone." Five minutes of shuffling pages brought my eye to Psalm 62.

> My soul finds rest in God alone; my salvation comes
> from him.
> He alone is my rock and my salvation; he is my fortress,
> I will never be shaken.

"Oh God, I want to live in that fortress."

> Find rest, O my soul, in God alone; my hope comes from
> him.
> He alone is my rock and my salvation; he is my fortress,
> I will not be shaken.
> My salvation and my honor depend on God; he is my
> mighty rock, my refuge.

I lay the Bible on the table and went to the window. The early shift was arriving at the truck dock across the street, coworkers walked from the parking lot to the gate greeting each other. I sighed and wondered how I would carry on alone.

But the question was nonsense. I just would, that's all. I had to. I'd survived a painful week in October when I first got into Canada and did it alone—hadn't even called home. No reason I couldn't manage now.

I put bacon on, sat at the table with pencil and paper and wrote at the top, "How can I prove my innocence?" The fat sizzled and spit and flooded the room with meaty redolence.

Thirty minutes later, I was on the road to Coeur d'Alene, another forty found me in a phone booth. I located the number for the ISP and dialed. When the receptionist asked, "How can I help you?" I was ready.

"I need to talk to someone in homicide. I have something they'll want to hear."

Seconds later, a male voice came on. "Sergeant Barlow."

"Yes, Sergeant. You don't know me, but I have something you will want to see."

"Oh yeah? What's that?"

"It's a photo, a very incriminating picture of a public figure."

"And what makes you think I'd be interested? I'm a homicide detective."

"Because it's related to an active investigation."

"You have evidence of a crime?"

"Not direct evidence, but it's material."

"Then you need to bring it in."

"No, not just yet."

"Listen, son, I don't know who you are or what your game is, but withholding evidence is a crime." He paused. "What's going on here? I don't have time to play games."

"I assure you this is no game. I've been accused of a crime I did not commit, and I'm going to prove my innocence. I wanted to have a connection with you guys in case I need help."

"If you've been falsely accused you need to come in and talk. That's why we have a justice system."

"I used to think that, started to do that last week and almost got stung bad, found out I'd been framed and was being lied to. So, I realized I have to do this on my own. Thanks for the offer, but I don't trust the system anymore."

"Sure you know what you're doing?"

"No, but I'm a quick learner. Oh, by the way, I might need to reach you after office hours. How would I do that?"

Barlow rattled off a number.

"Okay, you'll be hearing from me."

"Your name?"

"You can call me Idaman."

Gary Brumbelow

"Miss Stuart? Miss Stuart? Did you hear me?"

Julie shook free from her daydreaming. Matthew, a grade-three student, stood in front of her desk. His lifted eyebrows and gaping mouth suggested he was waiting for an answer. But Julie had no idea of the question.

"I'm sorry, Matthew. I was lost in thought for a moment." She coerced her best fake smile, hoping an eight-year-old wouldn't detect the duplicity. Twelve days without a word from or about Cody had shriveled her attention span. *Come on, Julie. You're a teacher of children, for goodness's sake.* "Would you repeat your question, please?"

"Can I put this on the tree?" The boy lifted his hand above the desk, holding something nasty.

"What is it?"

He broke out in a huge grin. "It's the tail from the muskrat I trapped yesterday. Cool, eh? My very first game to trap." He bounced on his toes and trembled with glee.

She opened her mouth. Stopped. Started again. "If you just trapped it yesterday, it may be a little too fresh. How about you dry it over the weekend and let's see what it looks like on Monday?"

"That's exactly what my mom said." Now Matthew's mouth was wide open. "Okay. I'll bring it back next week." He spun around to return to the tree where other students were stringing tinsel, lights, and more conventional decorations.

Julie sighed. Any small victory was a welcome diversion. Cody had fallen into a black abyss of her imagination, and the worry threatened her ragged heart like gossamer threads in the wind. She could imagine several explanations for why no word from him had reached her, all of them unthinkable.

Was he so focused on being exonerated he had forgotten her?

Had he been jailed in Idaho?

Or incapacitated by an accident? He was given to driving in the dark; had some terrible collision resulted?

Disturbing thoughts plagued her all day till she dragged her weary frame, sorrowing, to her teacherage. She had just stepped inside when her phone rang. Could it be Cody?

"Hello."

"Julie, it's Rod Castle."

Her heart skipped a beat. "Oh, hi, Rod. Are you calling about Cody? Do you have any news?"

"Yes. But I need to start with an apology."

"Really?"

"Yes. I feel so bad. Cody's mom called me last Saturday with news. I intended to call you immediately, but I was interrupted by an emergency, and I just now realized I had never phoned you."

"Oh. Well, I'm glad you remembered. What can you tell me?"

"Cody's mom thinks he's on his way home. They received two letters, one from Seattle and one from Portland, Oregon. She read one of them to me. He did not exactly say, but it sounded like he was on his way home. Sort of the long route, I guess."

An unfamiliar sensation swept through Julie's soul. She pushed against it. "He didn't say anything about the murder? The legal situation in Coeur d'Alene?"

"No. She said he indicated he wanted to wait till they could talk face to face."

A vague apprehension grew. She chatted with Rod long enough to be polite, thanked him for calling, hung up, and worried aloud.

"If he's safe, and headed home, that's good."

"But why don't I feel better about this?"

She feared the answer. But did not want to speak it.

Cody had achieved a huge victory in Idaho. Had started home. And did not think to call and tell her.

She lay awake half the night, tormented by her imagination.

CHAPTER 64

You Will Protect Me from Trouble

Coeur d'Alene, Friday, December 11

Sweat drenched Marc Malone's shirt, dripped from his nose, ran into his eyes. His muscles hurt, and he sucked air. But he kept jogging. Just three more minutes.

He hated exercise but liked looking good. For years, his daily routine at the Cottonwood Athletic Club had kept him fit. These days, it was also therapy for a brain sore from thinking. The election was eleven months away, a rival had emerged from nowhere, and the Johnson case was scheduled for February 18. He had less than two months to work a miracle in the courtroom or his career was trashed, his reputation ruined.

Besides all that, Brandon's Boy Scout background yielded little to build a prosecution on. For the hundredth time, he cursed the web of lust that had snared him and blasted his stupidity. He was loathing every aspect of this disaster when the treadmill timer beeped.

An hour later, back at his desk, he pulled out the page from October. The "Clear Frank Johnson" column had zero entries. He'd tried to persuade the Chamber of Commerce president, a personal friend, to consider Johnson for a board position. That effort failed spectacularly.

"Tarnish Cody Brandon," the other column, had one entry. He'd admitted in their first conversation to angry driving in the past. But Malone's sleuthing had failed to surface it.

The county attorney swiveled toward the window and swore.

Coeur d'Alene, Saturday, December 12

Sixty days after drowning his wife, Frank Johnson sat in his cluttered living room channel surfing and picking at Mexican take out. He'd changed jobs, ditched his bowling buddies, missed two mortgage payments, and gained twenty pounds.

He reached for the last taco but changed his mind, shoved the food carton away and looked at the floor. His chest was smoldering with a fire antacid couldn't touch. It wasn't just indigestion. He'd murdered his own wife. *I'm guilty as hell.*

For the first couple of weeks, he'd had no remorse. His misery was over, no hassling, no fighting, no demanding, no shaming, no whining, *I'm free.* Joan was gone for good, and someone else would take the hit.

And, just to be sure, just in case anything went wrong, he was protected from the lawful penalties for murder, thanks to the misdeeds of a certain county attorney. *Thank you, Mr. Malone.*

But now, weeks later, his assurance evaporated, Frank was desperate for peace. Forty-nine channels failed to hold his interest. He hit the off button and stood at the window shaking his head.

He didn't move when the phone rang. It was probably just that woman from the news channel, and Frank had no stomach for more interviews. She could just talk to the answering machine again, as far as Frank was concerned.

"This is Frank Johnson. Leave me a message."

"Hello, Frank. We've never been introduced, but we've met. About eight weeks ago. Remember the day you broke down at Bishop Lake? Or supposedly broke down? October 13, right? About noon. You'd been driving south and parked and waited for someone to come along and give you a push."

Frank darted to the phone, in his haste kicking three empty beer cans across the carpet. "Who is this?"

"I'm glad you picked up, Mr. Johnson. Wasn't sure I could finish before the tape ran out."

"Who is this?" Fear and anger pushed out his words with force.

"I'm the guy that came along that day beside Bishop Lake. That was me. You were blocking the road. I had to stop. But I would've stopped in any case. What kind of jerk would pass by a stranded driver? I stopped, and you limped over to me. You were limping then, but I noticed you're not limping now. That was part of your ruse."

Frank felt dizzy. Could this be happening? "I don't have to listen to this."

"That's right, you don't. But it will be better for you if you don't hang up. I'm not angry, but if you hang up now, it will be worse for you."

"What's that supposed to mean?"

"You asked me to help you push your car out of the way so traffic could get by. So, I did. I asked if you needed anything else. You said no. Said you knew what the problem was. Your distributor cap was always popping loose. You'd fixed it lots of times. Didn't need any more help.

"But nothing was wrong with your car. As soon as I was out of sight, you pushed it into the lake and drowned your wife."

"You can't prove that."

"You'd memorized my plate number, and then, you sicced the law on me. Made up a lie about me. Said I was in a rage 'cause I'd been following you and couldn't pass. You were trying to tend to your sick wife in the backseat, and when you finally had room to pull over, I got out and slammed and kicked your car and pushed it into the lake."

"You're a liar. And nuts besides."

"We both know who the liar is. The ISP put out a warrant for my arrest. It took a few weeks before that news reached me, but as soon as I heard about the warrant, I came back. Was ready to talk to the police. Figured somebody had made a mistake, and I'd be exonerated.

"That's when I heard your make-believe story. You'd set me up. And then I found out I was being set up again by the county attorney. I realized I couldn't trust the system. Had to do this on my own. So that's what I'm doing."

"You must be crazy. I have no idea what you're talking about." Fear and curiosity glued the phone to his ear.

"Well, for my part, I figure you and I need to talk. What do you say about that? Just the two of us, man to man. I think I'll come by soon.

"Oh yeah, one more thing. Remember the picture you took? The one you're using to blackmail the county attorney? Sort of like an insurance policy to make sure you don't get charged for your wife's murder? I've got that picture. You don't want to talk to the law. If you call the cops, I'll give the picture to Malone. He'd be off the hook, and you'd lose your insurance. And we both know your story will not hold up in court.

"So, let's talk, okay? I can meet you anytime, anyplace. Whaddya you say?"

CHAPTER 65

THE RIGHTEOUS ARE BOLD AS A LION

Coeur d'Alene, Saturday, December 12

Frank spit out an expletive and slammed the phone down. He ran to the bedroom, yanked away the bottom dresser drawer. The envelope was gone.

He swore and paced the floor, slammed a fist against his palm, swore again. He dropped on a chair and held his head. "Gotta think." A deep moan rose from his chest as he shook his head. "What a mess. What now? What am I gonna do?"

His frazzled, alcoholic brain kept returning to one word. *Run. Get out of here.* From somewhere deep, he wanted a change of scenery. He had to move, had to do something.

He'd try to find Brandon. Fix this problem. From a shelf in his closet ,he took his Beretta 9mm and turned out the lights.

From the convenience store three streets down, I just had time to get in place to see Frank's white Datsun turn left out of his alley. I followed at a distance as he drove south, then west on the interstate. The traffic on the freeway was heavy enough to avoid suspicion but light enough to keep Frank in view. I watched and drove and thought aloud about the extreme measure I was about to take.

"Okay, genius, you've got him on the run, now what?" I'd made the call purely on impulse, like flushing quail from cover to get a shot. But, in this case, the bird was armed, and the hunter was not.

"I assume he's carrying. Why wouldn't he? We found the ammo Wednesday night but no gun. Don't know where he's headed, but it's only prudent to assume he's locked and loaded."

Yet I was confident I could outmaneuver Frank. "He's gained a lot of weight, if I'm not mistaken, possibly drinking. He's in a panic, not thinking clearly. His reflexes will be diminished, while I'm at the top of my game."

Two miles beyond the city's edge, Johnson took an exit and turned left over the freeway onto a dark road. I doused my lights and sat until he topped a ridge a half mile up the hill, then turned to follow, thankful for a moon bright enough to make headlights optional.

In a couple of miles, the road came to a lake where Frank parked on the narrow shoulder next to the water, just beyond a dark marina, long since closed. He killed his lights and sat. I eased into the marina parking lot and used my hand brake to avoid rear lights. I slid to my passenger seat and waited for a cloud to cover the moon before slipping out the door and crouching.

"Lord, I may be headed into danger. But I'm trying to do my part, what you've left up to me. I can't trust the law. I need you, Father. Please do your part. Please protect me."

I paused at Frank's rear bumper, strained to catch some audible clue to what he was doing. I heard low, mostly indistinguishable muttering. The word "God" floated out, probably swearing, but I decided to take it as a cue, moved to the rear passenger door and swung it wide. "Okay, Frank, let's talk."

Johnson twirled around in his seat, a piercing scream emanating from his lungs.

"Yeah, it's me, Frank. Lost the beard, but I'm the same guy. And we need to talk, just you and me."

Johnson's face grew tight. "Talk? You want to talk? Here's all I have to say to you." He swore again and drew his right hand from his coat. I saw steel and dropped as the gun fired and the shot went high.

"Hold on, Frank. You'll only make things worse for yourself." I took a quick peek, saw Johnson's red eyes. "I'm not armed. And I know you're hurting, Frank." I moved behind the car.

"You know nothing, you little creep."

"Maybe not, but I can guess. You were stuck in a bad marriage. Felt like you couldn't go on, had to get out of it. Am I right?"

Another wild round shattered the rear window. "You don't know the half of it. I stuck it out longer than most guys would've. It's not like I didn't try. But it was no use, there was no living with that woman."

He was out of the car now, stumbling toward the back, gun pointed. I had counted on his reflexes being impaired and they were, thank God. He spotted me and raised the gun, but I ducked and rolled as the shot went wide, then scrambled to my feet and made for the front of the car. I crouched low. "But why kill her, Frank? Why not divorce?"

"Like I didn't think of that?" Johnson leaned a hand against a rear fender, stopped to catch his breath. "Is that what you believe? She would never—Why am I even talking to you?" He swore, his rage and venom mounting in a rush of obscenities. "So, I killed my wife. What's it to you?"

He turned back along the driver's side and moved to the front, unaware I had doubled around behind him. I stayed low and quiet, taking advantage of his clumsy inebriation to slip up behind him.

I lunged at his waist and chopped at the gun like a linebacker stripping a football from a receiver. The pistol skittered across the road, and we hit the pavement. I landed hard on my ribs, felt a scrunch, saw stars, and lost my grip.

Johnson dove for the gun and almost reached it before I grabbed a boot and twisted it with all my might. Frank screamed in pain and swore.

I got to my feet and stepped toward the gun, but Johnson kicked hard and brought me down again, grabbing my wrist with surprising strength. I tried to pull free, but he held on and clamped down on a finger with his teeth. I almost swooned, might have blacked out but for the alcohol on his breath. I slammed my knee into his groin, his teeth released my finger as he doubled over in pain.

I grabbed his knees again, but he pulled a leg free and booted me, missing my head and hitting my shoulder. Something strong and wild rose from my heart, and I knew I had to win this fight. Remembering the grizzly, I leaned in, swung as hard as I could and landed a blow square on his nose, feeling the cartilage crunch. He yelped, blood flowing down his face, and went limp while I scooted to kick the gun into the ditch.

A siren wailed, blue and red lights pierced the dark. I set the tape recorder on the hood of Frank's car and leaned against the fender, my chest heaving, my weary frame trembling from the exertion of the fight. My injured finger throbbed.

Whatever happened next was up to God. My recent experience with law enforcement did little to reassure me, but nothing remained for me now except to stand still and trust God. *I wait for you, Lord.*

The patrol car stopped, two officers stepped out, guns drawn, yelling, "Hands up." I complied, while Frank lay insensible on the road. "Turn around and place your hands on the car," one cop demanded. He frisked me and ordered me to turn around and stand still.

"What's your name, son?"

"Cody Brandon."

"Show me your driver's license." I retrieved it and handed it off. He scanned it and looked at me. "You're under arrest, Mr. Brandon. Are you aware of the warrant out on you?"

Here we go again, I thought. Yet to my amazement, a perfect calm descended over my heart. "Yes sir, I am. But I—"

"Save your breath. Later." He reached for his handcuffs, "Turn around please." Once again, I complied, but not before I had spotted his name tag: Barlow. "I phoned you yesterday, Sergeant. Called myself Idaman."

He secured the cuffs and turned me around again. He searched my eyes. "So that was you. What's going on?"

"I was set up, lieutenant. This guy framed me. And then a lawyer lied to me. Been trying to prove my innocence. Anyway, you'll find his .45 over there." I nodded toward the ditch.

Barlow's partner, attending to Frank, stood. "He's pretty beat up, but his vitals look okay. EMT is on the way. And guess who he is?" He dangled a wallet. "Frank Johnson."

Barlow's eyebrows leaped. He looked at me, then Frank, then back at me. He stood silent for a long moment, then spoke to his partner, nodding in my direction. "Put him in the car." He pulled a heavy plastic bag from a vest pocket and stepped toward the ditch.

His partner, Officer Willis, walked me to the car and put me inside. I told him where to find the tape recorder, and what it proved. He closed the door. I heard his radio crackle, as he spoke into it for a couple of minutes. Finished, he stepped to the front of the car, where Barlow met him, holding the gun in the bag. They stood and talked. I sat and watched and imagined what I could not hear.

"This beats anything I've seen in a long time," Barlow said.

"What?"

"Think about it. Malone says Johnson is not a suspect in his wife's murder. Has constantly barked at us to find Brandon."

"Okay."

"So, we get a call from Brandon to respond to this scene. The call comes in to my cell phone. I gave that number to Brandon—called himself Idaman—yesterday. Didn't know it was him. He told me on that call he was going to handle this himself. Said he couldn't trust the system." He paused for a second. "If he were out to kill Johnson, would he tell me about it beforehand?"

"Seems unlikely."

"He says this is Johnson's gun. We'll know soon enough."

"The prints won't prove who owns it."

"Of course. We're not proving anything here. Just sorting facts. Trying to piece things together." Barlow paced, stopped, pointed my direction. "Maybe Brandon's innocent."

"Oh. Almost forgot." Willis walked to Frank's car and snatched the tape recorder. "He told me he has Johnson's confession on this tape."

Surprise crossed Barlow's face. "Johnson's confession."

"Should I play it?"

"No. Not yet." He pulled another evidence bag from his pocket. "Secure it for now. We don't want to mess up this investigation."

Willis dropped the recorder into the bag and sealed it.

Barlow spoke again. "You didn't hear me say this, but we may soon say a final goodbye to Mr. Malone. We've suspected his duplicity for a long time, put up with his arrogance and shenanigans way too long. Looks to me like things are increasingly pointing to our dear county attorney. In fact, Brandon told me yesterday he has an incriminating photo of a public figure."

"Malone?"

"I don't know. We'll see shortly. But if Malone's in big trouble ... well, let's just say it wouldn't hurt my feelings."

Barlow got into the front passenger seat and spoke to me in the mirror.

"How did you manage to make the call?"

I shrugged. "I didn't. I saw a shadow moving over there," I gestured toward the marina. "Just had time to give him your number. Wondered if he'd come through."

"Ah. You lucked out. That's old man Cunningham. Not a more reliable or conscientious night watchman in the county." He pointed at my vehicle. "That your car?"

"Yes, sir. I parked there and sneaked over here. Tried to talk man-to-man with Frank but didn't get far. He got trigger happy, you might say."

The ambulance arrived, Willis spoke to the crew chief and got back behind the wheel of the patrol car.

"Johnson finally woke enough to hear he's under arrest for driving under the influence."

"And more than that," Barlow added. "Reckless endangerment at least, and maybe attempted murder. Let's get back to the office. We've got work to do."

CHAPTER 66

My Hope is in You

Coeur d'Alene, Monday, December 14

I stood in line for twenty minutes in the common room of the Kootenai County jail for my turn at the phone. Mom answered on the second ring.

"Hi, Mom."

"Cody. So glad you called. But hold on a minute, Dad's going to the other phone."

I heard Dad pick up the extension. "Hello, Son. How are things? You've kept us guessing as to your whereabouts, so I'm glad you called. Are you getting close to home?"

"No, I'm actually in Coeur d'Alene."

"Oh, really?" Dad said. "We figured from your letter you were touring the West Coast and would head east and possibly even be here by now."

"Yes, sir, that's exactly what I wanted you to think. Please forgive me for the deception, but it was the only way I could think of communicating with you without compromising you if the police called to ask if you'd heard from me."

"They did call," Mom said, "and we told them exactly what we knew, that you had mailed us from Seattle and then Portland, and it looked like you were touring the West Coast. Or headed back down here. We really didn't know."

"Then my scheme worked perfectly. I wanted to communicate something with you but needed to throw them off my tracks. I made a big circle to mail a letter from Seattle one evening and another from Portland that would postmark the next day and then drove back here. Needed to take care of something."

"Well, if that doesn't beat all," Dad said. "Sounds like you've got a story to tell."

"That I do. And I will be home soon. But just one more wrinkle."

"What's that?" Mom asked.

"I'm getting ready to break my own rule, calling for help."

"Well, we're both glad to hear that, son," Dad said. "How can we help?"

"Well, here's the story. As you know, I was convinced a simple mistake would explain all this nonsense about a murder charge. But it wasn't a simple mistake—I was framed. A man drowned his wife. It's a long story, but remember I told you about stopping to help someone push his car off the road?"

"Yes," They spoke in unison.

"As soon as I was out of sight, he pushed the car in the lake with his wife in the backseat. And told the law I had done it. My fingerprints were on the trunk. He framed me, and the police put out a warrant for my arrest. I was charged Saturday with voluntary manslaughter and assault with intent to commit murder."

"I can hardly believe this," Mom said.

"Yeah, really. But I managed to get the evidence that proves my innocence. That story is too long to tell. Anyway,

I just had my arraignment. And I'm free to go soon as I post five-thousand dollars in bail. But I have less than a hundred bucks."

Mom yelped. "Five-thousand dollars? Bail?"

"This is unbelievable." Dad said. "You're in jail again?"

"Yes. Crazy, huh? But as soon as the bail is posted, I'm a free man."

"How much time are you allowed on the phone?"

"Ten more minutes. Anyway, the evidence in my favor is solid. But I will have to appear at the trial in three months. There is a breaking and entering charge, but I'm not too worried about that."

"I don't know how much more news I can take right now," Mom said.

"It's going to be okay, Mom. And along the way, I've learned some important lessons about trusting God."

"I assume we can wire this money to the court?" Dad said.

"Yes. Here's the phone number for the court clerk." I recited the digits.

"When do you expect to start home, son?" Mom said.

"Tomorrow. As soon as the bail is posted, I'll get my car, stop at the pawn shop, and be on my way."

"The pawn shop?" Dad said.

"Another part of the story. Too long to tell over the phone. But I'll be home soon, and we'll have all the time we need." I paused. "In fact, I may be home a lot longer than I wished."

"What do you mean?" Mom regained enough control to speak.

"Well, I've lost my inheritance."

"What?" Two parents spoke in unison.

"Yes, don't you remember? Grandpa said I had to be at the same job a year before turning twenty-four, and now I've lost my ranch job. I had no choice, I was framed and had to leave. Now I don't meet the qualification, and without that inheritance, I can't see any way I'd ever have a down payment to buy a ranch."

After a moment of silence, Dad said, "No, Cody, not twenty-four. Twenty-five."

"What?" I shook my head. "No, Dad, I know it's twenty-four. I still have that card from my graduation, showed it to someone just the other day."

"That may be, son, but it's not the card that counts. It's the legal document. You know how your grandpa was with details. It wouldn't be the first time he got an important date wrong."

I was stunned, but not convinced. I really wanted to believe Dad, but knew better, had looked at the card too many times, operated too long with the understanding that my twenty-fourth birthday, ten months away, was the drop-dead date.

But Dad wasn't done. "Hold on. Let me pull out that file." I heard a drawer open. "I know what I'm talking about, son. You're about to get a readjustment in your planning. You've been thinking the money was lost?"

"Yes, for five weeks, since November ninth, the day I lost my freedom, my first night in the Williams Lake jail. I didn't know for sure I was going to be deported, but when they told me it was likely, I realized everything in my life was about to change.

"I can't describe the feeling, like I was falling into a deep hole. That was the worst moment. Then two weeks of misery in jail, and after that I was consumed trying to clear my name, but the bitter taste never left my mouth.

It's great to be exonerated, but that doesn't bring back my inheritance."

I sighed heavily, "I wish I could believe you were right, Dad, believe me, I really wish that were true."

"Hold on, Son, I've got the file. I need to set the phone down for a second." I heard paper rustle, pictured Dad at his desk, the high plains of Texas receding beyond his window thirty miles west to New Mexico. He picked up the phone and spoke three syllables that lit my heart on fire.

"Twenty-five."

I tried to speak, had no words, could not give voice to the rush of thoughts in my heart. All I could muster was, "Read it again, Dad."

"I'll read the whole paragraph. 'I bequeath to Cody Micah Brandon two hundred fifty thousand dollars, to be transferred upon his twenty-fifth birthday, providing he has satisfactorily completed his university program and provided he has continued employment in the same job for at least one year without interruption.'"

Great, heaving sobs rose from somewhere deep inside me, and I could not stop nor speak. A weight like that of Wolf Creek Mountain, a burden under which I had staggered for weeks, slid off my shoulders. I could breathe. And hope. And dream.

The future lay open before me, even more precious. What had been lost was found again. I was free, my dream intact.

"Oh, Dad. Oh, Dad. Oh, God. Thank you, God."

"I'm so happy for you, Son. Just the good news you needed, huh?"

"I can't tell you how good. I think I just need to process for a while. I'll call again from somewhere down the road."

"We'll look forward to that."

CHAPTER 67

You Will Protect Me from Trouble

Wolf Creek. Monday evening, December 14

In the ten seconds it took Julie to shove a dry pine log into the stove, the room filled with the fragrance of burning wood. She closed the door and went back to the pen and paper at her table.

> Dear Cody,
>
> I don't know if I'll mail this, but even if not, just writing will give me a chance to untangle my thoughts.
>
> You've only been gone two weeks, but it seems much longer. I haven't heard from you in all that time and, until yesterday, hadn't heard anything about you either. I called your mom yesterday and found out you had been in Seattle and Portland and maybe you were on your way home. That news left me with mixed feelings. It was good because it indicated you had been able to clear things up in that crazy business in Coeur d'Alene. But a shadow passed over my heart to know you had started home and had not called me.
>
> I hope that doesn't sound demanding or smothering. After talking to your mom yesterday I spent hours wondering what to do, whether or not to bring it up. If you hadn't said what you did just before you left, I don't

think I would feel this way. But your words imprinted themselves on my heart.

She put down her pen and rubbed her wrist.

"I'm not going to mail this," she spoke aloud. "Not yet, anyway. But I feel a little better having written it."

She sighed and looked out the window. A small black squirrel sat on a low branch of the Ponderosa pine outside her window, nibbling a seed in its paws, bright eyes alert to danger.

"Hey, little guy, you never get to relax, do you?" She drummed her fingers on the table. "Ever vigilant. I guess that's how God made you. And you do it well."

The thermometer just beyond the glass registered minus ten degrees. But the robust wood heat on this side bathed Julie in its cozy warmth. She laid her head against her arms on the table and slept. Soon she walked along a forest path, overhanging trees showering her with golden leaves. The setting seemed strange, but she felt no fear, only perplexity. She couldn't remember her destination, was unable to see more than fifty meters or so as the trail twisted through the woods.

She rounded a bend, and there was Cody, smiling and waiting for her. She ran, stumbled, looked down and recovered. But when she looked up again, he was gone.

This happened three times. She stopped walking, unsure what to do, troubled in heart and mind. A junco chirped nearby, and again, and again. She woke.

The phone was ringing. Not fully awake, she lifted the receiver.

"Hi, Julie, it's me."

She shook her head briskly as if to dislodge the dream. "Cody?" She rubbed her forehead.

"Are you okay? You don't sound like yourself."

She squeezed her eyes shut. "I must have fallen asleep."

"The weary teacher?"

"Something like that." She ran a hand through her hair. She was coming awake, and the dream haunted her. "What about you? Are you okay? Did you get home?"

"I'm not home, but yes, I'm better than okay. And on my way home."

"Yes, I know."

"What do you mean? How could you know that already?"

"I called your mom yesterday. She told me she thought you were on your way home."

A moment of silence passed. "Oh, well, I can explain that."

"She said you had written her from Seattle and Portland, and they guessed you were seeing some of the West Coast before heading for Texas." Her chin quivered as she heaved a sigh. "So where are you now?"

Cody laughed, and tears rose in her eyes, her breath caught in her throat. "Is that funny?"

"I'm sorry, Julie," His kind, solicitous tone warmed her slightly. "I'm not mocking you. I could never do that. That was a laugh of joy. Let me tell you what happened."

He explained the trip to Seattle and Portland, his scheme to send mail home and then, "I'm still in Coeur d'Alene. I just finished this business here today. It got complicated but God intervened. I have to appear in court in the next few months, but they've assured me all the charges against me will be dropped. In the meantime, I'm free to go. My folks wired the bail money, and the Idaho State Police just released me. In the morning, I'll get my stuff I pawned the other day out of hock and then I'm headed to Texas."

Only now was her brain fully functioning. "Oh, Cody, I thought you were halfway home. I wondered why you hadn't called." Her voice cracked. "I'm so glad it's all over, and glad you haven't left yet." Now it was her turn to laugh, and he joined her. "You get what I mean, right?"

"Of course. Listen, Julie, I have ten dollars in quarters. Let's use it up. How have you been?" They talked for twelve minutes, all about his Coeur d'Alene adventure, meeting Billy, about Julie's breakthrough with Danny, the horseback ride, and actually enjoying it.

"Uh-oh, here's my last quarter, and I haven't told you the best news of all. Here it is. I need to say this quickly. but I was going to call Rod."

"Want me to do that for you?"

"That would be great, Julie. Thanks."

"Sure. No problem."

"Tell him I'll call him when I get home."

"Okay, but what's the best news of all?"

"Julie, Julie. Are you sitting down? Here it is—the inheritance is not gone. Praise be to God, it's still intact."

"What? What? How can that be?"

"Grandpa got the date wrong. He told me the deadline was my twenty-fourth birthday. He wrote that on the card. But Dad just read the legal document to me. It's my twenty-fifth birthday. I have plenty of time to reapply for residency. Mr. Holder is holding my job. I can come back, pick up where I left off, and the money is due twenty-two months from now."

Her hand flew to her chest. "Oh, Cody, that's such good news for you, almost too good to be true."

"I know, Julie, don't I know."

Just then the quarter ran out, but she was okay. She looked out the window, tears flowing. Her squirrel friend was gone, but he'd be back. And so would Cody. He was free, he could go home, and he would return to her.

She crumpled the letter and threw it into the stove, smiling through her tears.

CHAPTER 68

HE WENT BACK TO HIS HOME

Spokane, Tuesday, December 15

I put my guitar in the front passenger seat, shoved the saddle in the back and drove away from Peter's Pawn Shop. I didn't like leaving my chain saw, but I barely had enough money to buy gas for the fourteen-hundred-mile trip to Dalhart.

Besides, it was just a machine. I had my crafted Rosewood guitar and my hand-tooled leather saddle. I wouldn't sweat the steel.

A million diamonds danced on the surface of Harrison Slough as I hauled for Texas, away from the nightmare of Coeur d'Alene. Dalhart by Thursday.

The sheer delight of freedom washed over me in waves. Five weeks of festering worry rolled away, the north beckoned, and I figured to follow soon. First, I had to go south, but I'd be back.

My heart was in British Columbia. A mountain ranch waited for me someplace north, someplace wild. And a lovely schoolteacher. How could I resist?

Why would I even try?

Gary Brumbelow

"La Bamba" played on the radio. I laughed and drummed my fingers on the wheel. Life was good.

ABOUT THE AUTHOR

Gary Brumbelow is a husband, dad, grandpa, pastor, and Jesus follower. He writes twentieth-century outdoor adventures that honor Christ and delight readers who believe God is active in our world and good will ultimately triumph. He loves writing but craves physical activity. Cold months find him splitting and burning firewood. Summer is for camping with family in the Cascades or flying his stunt kite at the Oregon coast.

Like most native Texans, Gary was a wannabe cowboy. In his early twenties, he spent a couple of years on a 350,000-acre mountain ranch in British Columbia's interior—an hour from the nearest town. Fifty-below winters, wolves, grizzlies across the river ... all normal. He never recovered. Today, Gary lives in Oregon but writes stories about the magic up north. Readers are invited to catch him at garybrumbelow.com.

NEXT IN THE MOUNTAIN RANCH ADVENTURE SERIES

BOOK TWO—CHAPTER ONE

Dalhart, Texas, March 1988

I woke up coughing. Smoke filled the top half of the room. I rolled out of bed and scrambled into the hall where I heard crackling. In the kitchen, flames rose from a blackened pot on the stove, the adjacent cabinets already afire.

Rummaging through the hall closet, I found the fire extinguisher, pulled the pin, and pointed at the blaze. But when I squeezed the trigger, a puny stream of foam dribbled from the hose and dropped to the floor. "Who knows when this was last serviced?"

I pulled Mom's mop bucket from under the sink and stood, holding my breath, to fill it. Then turned it off. What could a gallon of water achieve against those flames?

Fear rose in my chest. "Lord, I need your help."

I grabbed the wall phone but couldn't get a dial tone. "Gotta get out of here. Go for help." I dropped the receiver and went to the key hook inside the front door. The hook was empty.

"Oh yeah, in my jeans." Coming home last night to a dark, silent house, I didn't hang up the hooks for fear the jangling keys might wake my folks on the other side of the wall. They were planning to leave early this morning to drive to Amarillo.

Mom must have left a stove burner on. Not like her.

"Oh Lord, please protect our house!" My mind flipped between panic and confusion.

I crawled to my room, grabbed jeans, shirt, and boots, and scrambled to the porch to dress, then ran to my truck parked in back. Smoke rolled from the soffit down the entire rear of the house. I fired up the truck and raced down the long drive, gravel spewing. At the road, I saw my gas gauge and stopped.

"I was going to fill up last night," I said to the air. I had intended last night to park at the bulk fuel tank by the barn and refill but decided it could wait till this morning. Now it was this morning, the house was on fire, and the gas tank was on empty. Two miles lay between me and the nearest phone.

"Gotta try. Jesus help me." I peeled onto the pavement and barreled toward town.

I topped out at ninety, my old truck shuddering. A half block from the gas station my motor quit, and I coasted to a stop beside the pump.

The store was empty except for the clerk, a former high school classmate. She played Solitaire, one eye on the Saturday morning cartoons.

"Emily, I need to use your phone. My house is on fire, and my phone didn't work."

The girl's mouth dropped open. She shoved the desk phone at me without speaking.

"I need to see a phone book. I don't know the number."

"Sure." She pulled a small, dog-eared directory from beneath the counter and handed it to me. I read aloud and dialed the seven-digit number.

"Dalhart Fire Station. Are you reporting an emergency?"

"Yes. My house is on fire. On highway 1727 two miles east of town." I rattled off the address.

"Is anyone in the house?"

"No."

"Are other buildings close enough to be in danger?"

"I don't think so. The nearest is our Quonset hut and it's about sixty feet away."

"Okay, we'll have a crew there as soon as possible."

I replaced the receiver. "Thanks, Emily."

"Oh gosh, I hope it's going to be okay." Her face registered true concern.

"Thanks." I started for the door. "Me too."

As I pulled the fuel nozzle from the pump to fill my truck, a siren in the distance assured me help was on the way. But what would they find on their arrival?

The wail grew closer until two fire trucks roared by, blaring horns. I shut off the pump, stepped inside to toss twenty bucks to Emily and ran back. In my truck, hand on the ignition key, I remembered something and sat transfixed.

The letter to Immigration Canada was on the kitchen table.

And not just the letter. My entire file—all the correspondence, names, addresses, phone numbers, every scrap of information I needed to get back into Canada—was in a cardboard box six feet from the stove. Just yesterday I had finished the five-page application, written a cover letter, and sealed the envelope to mail today.

"If that box catches fire ..." I couldn't bring myself to finish the sentence out loud.

After weeks of calling their office and getting shuffled from one desk to another, the application had arrived

Gary Brumbelow

Wednesday. It spelled out the process for reentering the country. I did not remember all the steps, but could not forget the next-to-last sentence: "Failure to respond by April 1 will automatically close your file with no opportunity to reapply for one year."

But I could not spare a year. Six months, maybe, but a year would breach the deadline on my grandparent's inheritance, a small fortune. Losing two-hundred fifty-thousand dollars would shatter my dream of buying a wilderness ranch in Canada. And marrying Julie Stewart.

Worse than that, I had called Immigration Canada so many times they had added another line. "This office cannot respond to any further telephone inquiries. Please file the application and await word from us."

I peeled onto the road and slammed the pedal to the floor. A deep agony of woe rose in my chest. This could not be happening. After all the trouble of last fall—being framed for murder, my truck motor blowing up miles from nowhere, the unavoidable delay causing me to lose a promised job, getting kicked out of Canada, narrowly avoiding an unjust arrest, eleven agonizing days of tracking down a killer, confronting him and almost getting shot. I figured my troubles were behind me, thought I could reapply, return to BC and Julie, and pick up where I left off.

So I thought.

But if the box was destroyed, it was all over. And I wasn't sure I could survive another overwhelming defeat.

As I passed the last house on the edge of town, a plume of smoke in the distance signaled doom. *No, God!* I shouted and slammed the wheel with a fist. *No!* I jammed the pedal so hard my leg cramped. As I drew closer, I saw flames above the roof. Firemen scurried. My chest pounded.

I slid to a stop beside the first fire truck and ran to the back. Every part of the house was blazing—windows, doors, roof, walls. I tore at my hair and ran to a helmeted fireman directing the hose of water.

"There's a box on the kitchen table. I have to have it. I can't lose it. I have to have that box."

"Get back!" he ordered. Another crew member grabbed my arm and pulled. "Come back here!"

"But the box! The box!" I screamed like a man in torture. "I can't lose that box!"

The beefy fireman dragged me away. He pinned my shoulders against the back of the fire truck and put his face within spitting distance of mine.

"Listen to me, son! Listen to me!" He yelled, his face screwed up in anger. "You've got to get a hold of yourself. You're making our job harder. You're in the way! We're trying to salvage what we can, but you're not helping. You stay back here!"

"You don't understand!" I tried but failed to escape his grip. "My future is in that box."

"You're right, I don't understand." He nodded. "But it doesn't matter. You're not listening. Whatever was in the box is gone. It's six hundred degrees in there. Everything in the kitchen is destroyed. We're trying to save the rest of the house. Do you understand?"

I stared at him without seeing. His eyes burned into me until I sagged and sat on the rear bumper. He walked away. I held my head, elbows on knees, my brain a fog of loss and grief.

Gradually the smell of smoke, the heat of the flames, the yelling of firemen restored my senses. I stood and walked to the Quonset where I leaned against the steel. I was two people in one body. One part of me listened to their shouted jargon, tried to handle the horror that my parent's home was collapsing, all their worldly goods fuel for a wicked inferno.

What would this mean for them? They weren't due home till supper time. It would be long over by then. And what would be left? I tried to imagine their reaction, ached for this injury to their world.

The other part of me fixated on my own loss. Just one box of paper reduced to ashes had converted a bright future into a black, bottomless hole.

Made in the USA
Columbia, SC
26 June 2024

37540378R00228